HEROES IN LOVE

David C Dawson

www.BOROUGHSPUBLISHINGGROUP.com

PUBLISHER'S NOTE: This is a work of fiction. Names, characters, places and incidents either are the product of the author's imagination or are used fictitiously. Any resemblance to actual events, locales, business establishments or persons, living or dead, is coincidental. Boroughs Publishing Group does not have any control over and does not assume responsibility for author or third-party websites, blogs or critiques or their content.

HEROES IN LOVE
Copyright © 2020 David C Dawson

ISBN 978-1-951055-46-2

To Luke: a suitable friend

HEROES IN LOVE

Chapter 1

Friday the thirteenth of June dawned hot and humid. Summer in Britain could be unpredictable, and this year was already the hottest on record. London especially was never good with heat. The little air conditioning available on public transport was often inadequate, and where there was none, the grubby windows on buses and trains were often jammed shut. Water companies were quick to introduce rationing, and in Billy's view not enough people in London invested in deodorant in this most un-British weather.

As he reached the tube station at Wood Green, Billy's phone beeped. He stopped to pull it from his pocket and found a message from his bestie and work colleague, Vikki.

"Watch out. Man Cock is trying to dump more clients onto us. I'm at breaking point and I'm sure you are. Have a good day sexy xx"

Despite the familiar sinking feeling in his stomach, Billy smiled at Vikki's text. *Man Cock* was the secret name they had for their manager at Cockfosters Area Social Services in North East London. Billy was not the best of friends with his boss, Caroline Prenders, who had turned passive aggression into an art form, yet insisted on calling her bullying approach to management CCW: care and concern in the workplace.

She abbreviated everything. Which was why Billy and Vikki had shortened her job title to Man Cock ASS. A small act of rebellion that helped Billy and his fellow social workers get through each day.

Poor Vikki. He knew her workload overwhelmed her, and she had threatened to leave the service on increasingly frequent occasions. Billy wanted to do the same, but he had no idea what else he could do. And at the moment, he needed the money badly. Things would be even worse if Vikki left.

He shoved the phone back into his pocket and turned to enter the station only to be stopped by the shrill screech of Whitney Houston singing "I Have Nothing" announcing an incoming call. He retrieved his phone and read the name on the screen. *Prenders.*

Billy had thought it prudent not to label his boss's number *Man Cock* in case she were to ever see the offending words on his phone. He considered ignoring the call. If she asked him, he could tell her he was on the train and had no reception.

Dutifully, he answered, "Hello, Caroline. How are you this morning?"

"Billy," came the purr of Man Cock's voice. "I'm so pleased I caught you. I thought you might already be on the train and I'd missed you."

Billy cursed silently.

"We've got a bit of a crisis with Polly leaving," Caroline continued. "I need to reallocate her clients among the teams. You'll be pleased to know I've passed most of them on to the B-team, as I know they've got capacity. But there are a few we must take. And after all, we are the A-team."

Whenever Caroline Prenders said this, which was often, Billy had visions of Mr T from the movie of the same name. Less a vision, and more a fantasy about the star Bradley Cooper.

"Caroline," he began, "I really don't think I can—"

"Now, Billy," she cut across him. "You're a capable young man. Even though you've not been with us long, I know this to be true. We all need to pull together during this difficult time. You know as well as I do we can't let our clients down. I'm only handing one extra case to you. He's a nice old gentleman in Hackney with some mobility problems, but nothing significant. I'm sure you can squeeze him into your week without too much difficulty."

Billy's grip on his phone tightened as Caroline spoke. Her ability to offend with faint praise was legendary in the department. To call him a capable young man when at twenty-nine he was only two years her junior was guaranteed to irritate him. He took a deep breath.

"My caseload is already over the guidelines set by—"

"Guidelines, Billy," Caroline responded quickly. "They're not carved in stone. Don't let me down on this one. We've got your performance review coming up shortly, haven't we?" He gripped the phone even tighter. "And I was hoping to make some recommendations for your advancement."

He opened his mouth to speak, but Caroline was in full flow.

"I've looked at your diary. You can schedule visits to Mr Stuart after you see your agoraphobic client in Shoreditch on Fridays. Start next week and introduce yourself. The sooner the better for continuity. I'll email you his details so you can read the case notes."

"Caroline. I really think—"

"You've got this afternoon booked as leave, haven't you? I presume it's to see your mother?"

Even coming from Caroline, it was a low blow to talk about the extra time he needed to visit his mother in hospital. Was she trying to make him feel guilty for taking time off?

He said nothing.

"Well, you take as much time as you need to sort things out there," she said. "And in return, I'm so grateful that you're taking on Mr Stuart. I'll see you at the departmental next Wednesday. Bye now."

Billy pulled the phone away from his ear and stared at it. His day had only begun and already he wanted to turn around, go back home, and slam the door on the world.

His phone beeped as another message arrived from Vikki.

"Has Man Cock got hold of you yet? She's a bitch. Don't let her bully you. xx"

Too late, he thought. *Too late.*

***

Billy had promised his mother he would be at the hospital by two that afternoon. Her oncologist was coming to see her then. But a series of disasters throughout the morning delayed him. His train failed to turn up due to a shortage of crews. He was forced to take the bus, which crawled through the traffic and made him late for his case review meeting in south London.

By the time he arrived, the meeting had already started. A man from Westminster education services with a loud voice and bad breath accused Billy's department of flagrant negligence in the case of an eight-year-old boy and his abusive mother. The man's argument turned personal when Billy arrived, and the meeting dragged on with frayed tempers for nearly three hours. It was well past lunchtime before he finally headed for the station, on his way to the Royal Marsden Hospital in Chelsea.

As the train rattled through the tunnels under London, he sat and stared into space. A half-eaten sandwich lay in its wrapper on his lap, and he clutched a plastic bottle of water. A combination of the morning's events, the heat, and anxiety about what he might learn when he got to the hospital robbed him of his appetite.

Had his life really been reduced to this?

He was nearly thirty, doing a job he liked but for a manager he loathed and feared in equal measure. His last boyfriend had gone off with another guy as soon as Billy's mother got sick again nearly a year ago. He struggled to remember the last time he had gone on a date, let alone had sex. These days, his life seesawed between work and caring for his mother. He studied his distorted reflection in the window opposite. Not a bad looker for someone who was rapidly disappearing over the hill into his thirties.

His early twenties had all started so promisingly.

He'd won a scholarship to drama school, and in his final year, at age twenty-two, he was the first to get an agent. Despite the dire warnings of his acting tutor, work turned up on a semi-regular basis for the next five years. He was the first choice when casting directors needed a sensitive-looking young man with curly brown hair and gentle, puppy-dog eyes.

Then, one day, his mother called him and told him she had cancer. After the surgery and chemotherapy, her recovery took nearly a year. During that time, he turned down offers of parts in soap operas and TV commercials to look after her. She had no one else.

Within six months the offers dried up. Another sensitive-looking young actor with curly brown hair and gentle puppy-dog eyes became the preferred choice for casting directors.

Billy was broke and needed a job.

He moved back into his mother's tiny house and considered his options. He had fallen out of love with acting. He wanted nothing more to do with the fickle world of entertainment, even if he had been offered work.

He decided the only other skill he had acquired over that year was as a carer. He applied for a job as a social worker and, to his surprise, was successful. His clients were older people whose company he enjoyed and whose life stories he looked forward to hearing when he visited them. The only downsides were the awful management and low pay.

And then last year the cancer recurred.

Billy's mother faced more surgery and chemo. His plans to move out of her house and reestablish his independence vanished overnight. Now, between the daily grind of work and caring for his sick mother, his social life had come to a dead halt. He had no time for himself, and certainly none for a boyfriend.

Two weeks ago, his mother passed out, and he rushed her to hospital. Her white blood cell count had fallen dangerously low. She had been in hospital ever since.

***

Billy was nearly an hour late when he finally made it down Fulham Road and into the entrance of the Royal Marsden Hospital, where he ran into a black-haired, brown-eyed vision of masculinity. Literally ran into. Publicly crashed into a stunning man wearing a white fitted t-shirt, a linen suit, tan loafers, and stood tall like a catwalk model. Too late, Billy skidded to a halt and into the arms of the handsome stranger.

"I'm so sorry," Billy blurted out.

The vision of masculinity reached forward and grabbed his shoulders to stop him from falling.

"No problem." The man looked directly at Billy and held on to his shoulders for a moment or so longer than was probably necessary.

Billy wanted to crawl away and hide in a corner. He had never considered himself a cool guy. The roles he played in soap operas as a sensitive-looking young man with an apologetic, hesitant manner were in truth no more than an extension of his own personality. He was uncomfortable in large social gatherings and preferred his own company.

But this man with wavy black hair, deep brown eyes, and strong arms was someone he would dearly like to spend more time with. Billy struggled to find a witty phrase, a bright piece of banter to rescue the moment.

"Sure."

Sure? Billy shook his head at the crassness of his response. The man smiled, dropped his arms, and strode off.

Shit.

When Billy arrived at his mother's room on the third floor of the hospital, the oncologist was already at her bedside.

"Dr Jerome," Billy said as he entered the room. "I'm really sorry I'm late. I've had a nightmare day."

"Don't worry, Mr Walsh," the oncologist replied. "And it's Mr Jerome. We get to drop the doctor title once when we get to my level. But please, call me Arvind."

"I'm sorry, um, Arvind."

Billy looked across to his mother, who was tucked up like a fragile china doll in the crisp linens of the hospital bed. Plastic tubes connected her to complicated-looking machinery. An oxygen mask was strapped to her gaunt, emaciated face, and her thin, bony hands rested delicately on top of the sheets. Her eyes had not opened since he entered the room.

"Please, take a seat." Arvind gestured to the chair. "Your mother's resting, and I need to talk to you."

Billy's chest tightened, and he forced himself to breathe deeply as he sat on the small plastic chair next to the bed. He leaned across and kissed his mother on her cheek. She made no response. Billy took her fragile hand in his and gently massaged the protruding joints of her long fingers.

The oncologist's face betrayed no hint of expression as he spoke, calmly, in a low voice. "I'm afraid your mother hasn't much time left," he began. "When the time comes, we'll give her morphine to ensure she has no pain. That means she'll sleep a great deal. We'll continue to provide the nutrients she needs. But that's all we can do now. I'm sorry." Arvind Jerome's mouth creased into a faint smile, and he raised an eyebrow. "Do you have any questions?"

Billy couldn't think of anything to say. The speed of his mother's decline had taken his breath away. He felt winded, as if punched in the stomach. He looked from the doctor to his mother. Her breathing was steady and even. She remained in the same position she lay in when he first arrived.

Arvind Jerome cleared his throat. "Relatives often ask how long," he said. "And my answer is that it's impossible to say. But what I can assure you, Mr Walsh, is that we'll do everything we can to ensure your mother is in no distress."

Billy looked back at him. "But how long is it likely to be?" he asked. "Months? Weeks?" he stopped. A million thoughts clouded his brain, including the empty house. A house that, finally, would be devoid of the constant presence of this maddening, bossy, constantly demanding woman. What should he do? What should he plan? The change in the situation was too sudden. He needed time to catch up.

Once more Arvind Jerome's face displayed a controlled, professional smile. "We can't say. But prepare yourself for sooner rather than later. Is there someone who can help you plan? Your brother or sister? Your wife?"

Billy shook his head. "It's only me."

Chapter 2

When Arvind Jerome left the room a few minutes later, the door eased shut behind him, and the noise and bustle from the corridor beyond slowly receded. Billy was left with the low hum of the machinery beside the bed and the even rhythm of his mother's breathing. He massaged her delicate fingers with his right hand while he reached with his left to wipe away a thin trickle of saliva that formed at the corner of her mouth.

"Is that you?"

Her voice was timid and hesitant, as if responding to a late-night anonymous phone call. Her lids flickered open, and she stared with glazed eyes at the ceiling.

"Are you home, sweetheart?"

Billy leaned forward and kissed his mother on the cheek. His mouth stayed close to her ear as he responded, "I'm here. Don't worry. Go back to sleep if you want."

His mother closed her eyes, and her head slowly turned sideways to rest in the cup of his hand.

"You're so late, Geoffrey," she murmured into his palm. "I thought you'd be back hours ago."

Tears pricked the corner of Billy's eyes at his father's name. Geoffrey Walsh had walked out on them over fifteen years ago. He kissed his mother on the forehead, eased his hand away from her face, and sat back in his chair.

"It's not Dad," he said half to himself. "It's me."

His mother's eyes opened again, and she turned her head to look at him. "I know that, Billy," she said. "Why on earth would you say it was Dad?"

He smiled at hearing the return of that down-to-earth, matter-of-fact tone of voice he was used to.

"Had a nice sleep?" he asked.

"No," said his mother flatly. "This bed's 'orribly uncomfortable. And I had a terrible dream about that nurse who keeps calling me Sarah instead of Mrs Walsh. I don't like overfamiliarity."

"Do you want some water?" he asked.

"No, dear," his mother replied. "I want to see the doctor. When's 'e comin'?"

"I'm afraid you missed him. He left a few minutes ago. You were asleep."

"Then why didn't you wake me?" Her tone was reproachful. "I want to know when I can go 'ome. Did he say?"

He shook his head. "You need to rest. Why don't you close your eyes and think nice thoughts? Maybe you won't have any more bad dreams."

She sighed and turned her head away. "Nice thoughts," she repeated. "Don't be so bloody silly. I've got cancer. 'ow can I possibly 'ave nice thoughts?" She slid her hand away from his massage. "Come back tomorrow."

He sat for a few more minutes, watching the bedclothes rise and fall as his mother's breathing resumed a steady rhythm.

"Sleep well," he said. "I'll be here in the afternoon."

***

Billy stood on the half landing of the second-floor staircase and stared out the window overlooking the hospital's small garden. He felt as if he were frozen in the headlights of an oncoming truck, not knowing what to do next. The oncologist had confirmed fears Billy had held for a while, but dared not think about too deeply. Another parent was about to be stolen from him, this time through cancer. His mother had become both mother and father to him when Geoffrey Walsh walked out. Billy was in his early teens when his father left. His mother was there for Billy when he had struggled with his muddle of teenage hormones and anger at his father's desertion. Billy had been vile to those around him for a long time after his father had left.

Now he would have to deal with the loss of his second parent by himself: the penalty for being an only child, and soon to be an orphan in the world. He thought briefly about what he might do once his mother died. He could sell the little family home in Wood Green they had inherited from his grandparents, and go traveling. Or he could return to acting. Try to renew his contacts. Find an agent who might take him on. Quickly, he dismissed the idea. It felt cynical, and somehow disrespectful to even consider making plans when his mother lay sleeping in a bed on the floor above still very much alive.

When his mother had confused him for his father a few moments ago, he attributed the slip to the drugs. Maybe he would lose her mentally before he would lose her physically. He pictured days of sitting by her bedside, watching her sliding away from him.

How long?

He closed his eyes and tried to take deep breaths. As he inhaled his body spasmed from the emotional afternoon. He leaned his forehead on the window, and his shoulders heaved as a wave of sobbing engulfed him. He felt so alone.

"Hey. You okay?"

The voice was familiar. Billy pulled back from the window, opened his eyes, and turned to see the black wavy hair and brown eyes of the man he had collided with in the hospital entrance under an hour ago. Clumsily, he tried to wipe his eyes with the back of his hand and merely succeeded in smearing his hand with a gob of snot from his nose. His humiliation was complete.

Then the man's oh-so-kissable lips moved, and he said, "Come on. You need a coffee."

The cafeteria was on the ground floor of the hospital, close to the entrance. It was noisy and packed with people, and there was a long line at the counter.

Billy's Good Samaritan introduced himself as Daniel. He invited Billy to find a table, while he queued up to buy them hot drinks.

As Billy waited, he reviewed the rollercoaster day. True, most of it had been downhill. Steeply. But this last turn lifted his spirits. He looked across the crowded cafeteria at Daniel standing in line. His back was to Billy as Daniel ordered coffees from the bored-looking assistant on the other side of the counter. He stood tall and confident. His dark blue linen suit gave him the look of a Hollywood actor in sharp contrast to the shabbily dressed people on either side of him. His haircut was obviously expensive, and he was well groomed.

Billy looked down at the sleeve of his shirt. The remains of his egg sandwich from earlier was smeared across it. He licked his fingers and rubbed the stain, in the hope of making the stain disappear.

"Here you are. I got some chocolate chip cookies as well. I love them, and I thought you might need the sugar."

Daniel placed a large plastic tray on the table. He handed Billy a chipped mug of cappuccino, and sat opposite. Billy slid his arm into his lap to hide the egg-stained sleeve. "You okay now?"

Billy nodded. "Yeah. It's been a really shit day, and I guess it all finally got to me. Work went tits up this morning. Then I met my mother's oncologist this afternoon, and—" He stopped. Not wanting to repeat what he had learned.

"I'm sorry," Daniel said. "I can only imagine how you're feeling right now. I've lived a pretty charmed life in the last few years. It's been a while since I experienced someone being ill like that. I guess I'm not going to be much use to you. But I saw you standing there looking so miserable…" Daniel stopped and stared at Billy for a moment. "Have we met before?"

Billy sighed. The two men had collided in the hospital entrance earlier, yet Daniel already had no recollection of him.

"I mean, apart from when you nearly sent me flying out there." Daniel indicated the hallway behind him and smiled. "I guessed you were late for something."

Billy studied Daniel's face. "I don't think we've met," he answered.

"Hang on a minute," Daniel said. "Weren't you in that hospital drama a couple of years ago? Are you an actor?"

Billy's self-esteem flooded back. "Well, as a matter of fact, yes," he said with an attempt at modesty. "I was in *Blue Lights*. Although I only had a minor role—"

"Yes, but you were in it quite a bit at one point. What happened? Have you moved on to better things?"

Billy picked up one of the mugs of coffee from the tray and set it down in front of him. He thought how best to answer Daniel's question without demolishing his chances with him.

"Actually, I'm not acting anymore," he said finally. "Things became complicated when my mother got sick, so I've stopped for a while."

"Oh, I'm sorry." Daniel reached across and laid his hand on Billy's. His face crinkled into a smile. "I'm sure you'll return to it when you're ready."

Billy laughed nervously and glanced down at Daniel's hand. The egg stain was clearly visible on the sleeve of his shirt. He slipped his hand away from Daniel's and hid his arm under the table again. "What do you do? Do you work in the hospital?"

Daniel chuckled and shook his head. "There's not much chance of that. I faint at the first sign of blood." He picked up a chocolate chip cookie. "I'm a music director for theatrical stuff. And I'm also a freelance singing coach." He bit into the cookie.

"Oh, wow." Billy felt inadequate. First he crashed into Daniel in the hospital entrance hall. Then he allowed himself to be caught weeping on the staircase. Now he found out Daniel was a music director, probably for some big show in the West End. Billy wanted to crawl into a corner and pull an imaginary shroud over his head.

"Hey, look." Daniel had a way of brightening a moment with an infectious enthusiasm and an open, smiling face. "I've got tickets for a show that's transferred to the Soho Theatre in Dean Street. It's tomorrow night. A friend of mine's directing it, and she got me some comps. I've got no one to go with and—" Daniel stopped, his mouth in mid-sentence. "Oh shit, there I go again. I guess I'm a bit—"

Billy smiled. "I'd love to come if you're offering. Now that Mum's in hospital I'm kicking my heels a bit at weekends."

"That's better." Daniel laid his hand on Billy's shoulder. "You're a whole lot better when you smile." A worried look crossed Daniel's face. "I warn you it's going to be a bit of a weird show. Donna doesn't do conventional. It's like a musical. And then—" He stopped again. "Other stuff."

Billy shrugged.

"It's okay, I love musicals."

***

As Billy watched Daniel leave the cafeteria, a grin spread across his face from ear to ear. He felt sixteen years old again. It was the same feeling he had the day Stephen Watkinson snogged him round the back of the abandoned warehouse after school. That had been Billy's first kiss with a man. Well, a teenager. But Stephen was mature for his age. And it was a great snog.

Of course Billy had yet to kiss Daniel. Or was he jumping to conclusions? He had probably not said enough to be interesting. That was usually his downfall. He had only talked about his mother and his job and—damn. He had hardly been witty. Then he considered, he knew precious little about Daniel, aside from the fact he was some big musical director in the West End. And he had displayed bad manners by failing to ask Daniel who he was visiting in hospital.

Even so, he had invited Billy to a show tomorrow evening. A date.

How quickly his day had turned around with this random meeting. From that miserable call with Man Cock, giving him yet another client, through to the news he had been dreading about his mother. Even after all that, life now seemed a bit more bearable.

A strange impulse came over him. Perhaps it was because he felt like a teenager again, or simply because he was still in the hospital. He was unsure why, but the feeling was strong.

He would go and tell his mother.

***

"Are you awake?"

Billy leaned over the bed and looked closely at his mother's peaceful face. Her eyes were closed, her breathing steady, and she failed to stir when he spoke.

"I won't stay long," he began, "but I came back to say I'm going on a date tomorrow. I hope you're pleased. It's been a long time. Well, you know that. And I'm sure it won't lead to anything. But..." He trailed off and looked again at the sleeping figure.

Why was he bothering? It was a stupid idea. For a moment it had made him feel better. Now he felt faintly ridiculous. He stood and headed for the door, then stopped when he heard a now-familiar voice behind him.

"You won't forget your condoms, will you?"

Chapter 3

Soho was packed that Saturday evening. Crowds of men spilled out onto the road from the pubs and cafes that lined Old Compton Street. The summer heat continued even at six thirty in the evening. As Billy navigated his way through the sea of revelers, he was distracted by the number of shirtless men standing outside the Duke of Wellington pub at the end of the street. It was quite a sight, one that Billy had missed, and he stopped to admire them for a few minutes. He had not been down to Soho for nearly six months, partly to avoid his ex, who worked in a bar there, and partly to save money and repay some of his debts.

He headed towards the junction with Dean Street. The route took him past the Admiral Duncan pub where Jason, his ex, worked. The place was packed, and there was a crowd of drinkers standing outside. Doubtless Jason was inside working away at the bar. It had been one of the advantages of their relationship. The odd free drink here and there. Now the venue brought nothing but bad memories. He quickened his pace as he drew near, even though it was unlikely Jason would be outside.

"Hey, Billy."

He looked around to see who had shouted his name but could not see a face he recognized. He turned back to head on to Dean Street.

That was when he felt a hand on his shoulder. "Hey, Billy. Stop a moment," Jason's voice commanded.

"Long time no see. How're you doing mate?" The tall Australian wrapped his arms around Billy and embraced him in a stifling bear hug. Billy tensed his shoulders and tried to pull away. After a moment, Jason released his grasp and took a step back. "Hey, what's up? You know, I have washed this week."

Billy shook his head. "Look," he began. "I haven't seen you for over a year—"

"One year, three months, two weeks and three days. You didn't return my calls, messages—"

"I can't stop now. I'm going to be late, and I've got nothing to say."

"Do you want to have a drink some time?"

"I don't think so." Billy felt his eye begin to twitch. "It's a long time ago. After everything that happened, let's leave it as history."

"Hey, don't be like that, mate. You owe me, you know?"

Billy shook his head to stop it twitching. He turned and started to walk away.

"Billy? Mate?"

Billy kept walking and left Jason behind him as quickly as he could. He turned onto Dean Street and strode up the road towards the Soho Theatre. His skin felt like an army of ants had crawled across it, and he rubbed his forearms hard. Of all the people he had to meet. And this evening of all evenings, on his first date since he and Jason had split up. He stopped and leaned against a lamppost to steady himself.

"You all right, mate?" a man with an Australian accent asked.

Billy turned quickly to check that Jason had not followed him. The voice came from a waiter smoking a cigarette. He leaned against a wall by the kitchen entrance of a burger restaurant.

"You want a glass of water or something?"

Billy shook his head. "I'm okay. Really. I think it's the heat."

The waiter nodded. "Hotter than a hairy armpit," he replied. "Take it easy, mate." Billy smiled at the earthiness of the simile. It was one of the qualities he had liked about Jason.

Billy continued farther up the street a few hundred yards. He had happy memories of the Soho Theatre. It was the site of his first off-West End appearance, even before he went to drama school. He and a group of friends won a best newcomers award at the Edinburgh Fringe Festival that year. After Edinburgh, the Soho Theatre took their show for a two-week run. They sold out nearly every night, and the reviews were glowing. He paused at the entrance. Billy felt a nostalgic buzz of excitement. Did he miss it? Had he made the wrong decision quitting work as an actor and retraining as a carer?

"Billy. Over here."

Daniel's shout shook him from his musings. He was standing by the window, a glass of wine in his hand. He wore the same linen suit and tan loafers Billy saw him in at the hospital the day before. As Billy approached, Daniel held out his arm to shake hands.

"Good to see you again." The handshake was firm, reassuring. Daniel continued to hold his hand and drew him closer. "Have you seen your mum today?"

Billy nodded. "She was sleeping, so I sat with her for a while and read. I found the reviews for this show online. It looks great."

"It's a good job you said that," Daniel replied. He released Billy's hand and put his arm around the waist of a slim woman with black dreadlocked hair standing by his side.

"This is Gaylene Ramsay. She's the director."

"Hey, it's good to meet you," Billy said enthusiastically. "You must be really pleased. They're saying great things about your show." He held out his hand, but Gaylene ignored it and leaned in to kiss him on either cheek.

"Hello, Billy," she said. "Or should I say, Doctor Hastings I presume?" and she raised a defined, black eyebrow.

Billy smiled with embarrassment.

"That's a long time ago now, and—"

"Oh no," she said. "Like Daniel, I was a big fan of *Blue Lights*." Her mouth broke into a sunlit smile. "And that's not the only thing I remember of yours. *The Wreckless Revue*?"

Billy's eyes widened in astonishment. "You can't have seen that show? Here?"

Daniel laughed. "Sounds like you've got a fan, Billy. Let me get you a drink."

"I'll have a white wine, same as you," Billy replied.

"Sure." Daniel turned to Gaylene.

"No thanks, darling." She shook her head. "I need to get front of house. I'm helping out on lights." Gaylene turned back to Billy. "Good to finally meet you. Enjoy the show." She kissed both men on either cheek and headed towards a door at the back of the bar.

"Gaylene doesn't miss much," said Daniel. "*The Wreckless Revue*? What was that?"

"I'll tell you about it another time," Billy replied. "Come on, I'll help you with the drinks."

***

"Sensational, sweetheart."

Daniel put his arms around Gaylene's slim waist and hugged her. He and Billy had waited patiently at the end of the show for the cast to emerge from backstage. The auditorium was full, and the audience rose as one at the finale to reward the performance with a five-minute standing ovation.

Billy had enjoyed the show. It was an immersive musical called *Lives Alone*. It told the story of four children in 1920s America who were orphaned in different ways. The music was not the sound of mainstream West End or Broadway, but Billy loved how it told the story through tunes based on folk songs and bluegrass music.

Gaylene smiled serenely and absorbed Daniel's praise like a pampered cat. "I'm so glad you liked it. I was sure you'd think it a bit weird, even by my standards."

Daniel glanced at Billy. "How could I ever say that about something as original as the wonderful production we've just seen? It really should transfer."

Gaylene laughed. "You must be kidding," she replied. "I haven't got a prayer. This is too adventurous for West End producers. As far as they're concerned, it's Disney, Agatha Christie, or more bloody Abba."

"No, I'm serious," Daniel insisted. "This is a great show, and it deserves a bigger audience."

"Then, Daniel darling, find me the producer with the balls to do it." Gaylene sighed. "I'm destined to be strictly off-West End with the projects I choose. And maybe I'm happier that way. Less pressure to be accessible or conventional." She turned to Billy. "What did you think, Doctor Hastings of *Blue Lights* fame?" she asked, her eyebrow arched once more. "Did Daniel warn you it would be weird? It's what he usually says."

Billy avoided betraying Daniel's prediction about the show. "I loved it," he said. "I had no idea such barbaric social engineering happened in twentieth-century America. It's a really original idea for a musical. And where did you get the young actors from? They were brilliant."

Gaylene smiled broadly. "Aren't they fantastic? We spent months auditioning." She glanced from Billy to Daniel. "So where are you two headed now?"

"I thought we'd go for some sushi," Daniel said. "Would you like to join us?"

"Oh no." Gaylene laughed. "I'm quite certain I'd be in the way. Have fun, boys." She turned to greet an earnest-looking young man waiting to take his photograph with her.

Daniel looked at Billy. "That was a gross presumption on my part," he said. "I'm sorry. You okay with sushi? There's that great place in Brewer Street. Do you know it?"

Billy nodded. "Bento in Brewer," he said. "I love it. Good food. Cheap and cheerful. My idea of heaven. I was worried you'd suggest somewhere extravagant like Soho House."

Daniel's eyes opened wide with amazement. "On my income?" he asked.

"But I thought you were a West End musical director?"

Daniel laughed. "I hope I haven't misled you," he said. "I'm a bit lowlier than that. Come on. Let's go get some sushi. I'm starving."

***

Billy knew Bento in Brewer well. It was a regular haunt when he worked as an actor. There was a sound studio around the corner where he would go to record voice-overs for adverts. The restaurant was small, and the owner refused to take bookings. As Billy expected, Bento in Brewer was almost full when they arrived. But luck was on their side. A couple by the window were getting ready to leave.

"Perfect timing," Daniel said as he settled into his seat. "And we get a great spot for people watching."

Billy looked out the window warily. "I usually avoid the window seat." He leaned his elbow on the table and rested his hand against the side of his head to shield his face from passersby in the street. "I used to get stared at."

Daniel smiled. "Didn't you like all that fame when you were on TV?"

Billy shook his head vigorously. "Not at all. Stupid I know. But that's the bit of acting I really hate. I love the craft and working with other actors. I much prefer being on stage. But somehow I got drawn into television work." He sighed. "Maybe I let my agent run my life too much. Anyway, that's all in the past now."

Daniel laughed. "But you're still young. You could go back to it if you wanted. What's stopping you?"

Billy shrugged. "Money. Mother." He sighed. "Me." He picked up the menu and turned it so they both could read it. "That's enough about me," Billy said. "Let's get some food. What exactly did you mean when you said you hoped you hadn't misled me about being a music director? Aren't you really?"

Daniel nodded. "I am a music director. I work with a company called *Therapy on Stage*. We work with kids of all abilities and use music and drama as therapy."

Billy looked up from the menu. "I've heard of them. Didn't they do that big show at the Royal Albert Hall last year?"

"That's us. *Uniquely Different* was the show. Six hundred kids from around the country. I tell you it was hell to bring together."

"But an amazing show," Billy enthused. "You even had the Royal family there. Didn't it win a special award at the Oliviers?"

"Closest I got to being a West End music director." Daniel laughed. "I love the work I do with *Therapy on Stage*, but it's never going to make me rich and famous, I'm afraid." He tilted his head on one side and looked at Billy. "Disappointed?"

"Are you kidding?" Billy replied. "When I met you at the hospital—"

"Crashed into me at the hospital," Daniel corrected.

"Mm, thanks for the reminder of my clumsiness." Billy felt his cheeks burn with embarrassment. He pointed to Daniel's jacket. "But you were wearing that smart suit and you looked so—"

"Smooth? Sophisticated? Suave?" Daniel prompted, his mouth curled up into a winsome smile. "I love all those words." He placed the palms of his hands on the front of his jacket. "The truth is, this is the only suit I possess. I was at the hospital yesterday to pitch for work on behalf of *Therapy on Stage*. We already do work with kids with chronic illnesses at Great Ormond Street hospital. We thought the Royal Marsden might like to do something similar."

"And were you successful?"

Before Daniel had a chance to answer, there was a loud bang on the window beside them. They both turned to see what happened.

Jason happened.

Chapter 4

"What the hell?" Daniel tried to stand, but his chair wedged against the one behind and he fell back into his seat. He turned to Billy. "Do you know that guy?"

Billy looked in horror at Jason's face on the other side of the glass, smiling and pointing at Daniel. Jason raised his left hand in a fist at Billy and slammed the palm of his right hand into the crook of his elbow. They could hear Jason's muffled voice through the window.

"Now I see why you ran away from me like that," he shouted. "Got a busy evening planned, heh?"

Daniel turned to Billy. "He seems to know you."

Billy clasped his hands behind his head and looked up at the ceiling. "Not anymore." He shook his head, looked across at Daniel, and dropped his arms down to rest on the table. "I'm so sorry. This is why I don't like window seats. Perhaps it's best if I go and speak to him."

"No need." Daniel tilted his head towards the window. "He's gone."

Billy turned back to the window to see Jason saunter off into the Saturday evening crowd. Relieved, he wondered if he should give Daniel an explanation. But then, Jason was in the past. A messy past, but at least it was over. Billy decided that a first date was not the best time to go into details.

"Look, I'm really sorry about all that."

Daniel waved his hand dismissively. "No need for any apology." He rested his hand on Billy's arm. "As long as you're okay?"

Billy smiled. "I'm good. It's…a long story."

"Misser Waaalsh."

The words came as a shout from the back of the restaurant. A short Japanese man headed towards them. He was elegantly dressed in a tuxedo, white shirt, and black bowtie. He squeezed his way past the diners crammed into the small space, and finally arrived at their table.

The Japanese man held out his hands to greet Billy. His eyes twinkled behind thick-framed glasses. "Misser Waaalsh. We no see you for long time. You sick?"

Billy pushed his chair back with difficulty in the small space, and stood up awkwardly. He turned to shake the man's hand. "Akio, it's so good to see you. No, I'm not sick. I've been busy."

Billy gestured to Daniel. "Let me introduce you to—"

Akio released Billy's grasp and placed his hands on Daniel's shoulders. "Is no need. I know Misser Richaards. He big friend of Bento in Brewer. He always bring nice people here."

Billy smiled and squeezed back into his seat.

"You ready to order, my good friends?" Akio asked. "Or you need few minutes?"

Billy shook his head. "I'll have what I always have. The mixed chirashi sushi." He turned to Daniel. "It's kind of a tradition, you see."

"Me too," replied Daniel. "That's easy then. What do you want to drink?"

"I'll have green tea and a glass of water." Billy smiled. "It's another tradition."

Daniel turned back to Akio. "Two mixed chirashi, a pot of green tea, and a jug of tap water please."

Akio bowed to the two men, took their menus, and went back to the kitchen, shouting the order as he went.

"I'm surprised I haven't seen you in here before," Daniel said. "Looks like you were quite a regular."

"You probably wouldn't have spotted me, even if I was," Billy replied. "I used to wear a beanie hat and glasses. But I don't eat out much anymore since Mum got sick. There's not been a lot of time. Or reason, to be honest."

"But you need to get out," Daniel protested. "You mustn't lock yourself away. It's not healthy."

Billy shrugged. "I know, I know. But I'm knackered most of the time. My clients are pretty demanding—"

"Clients?" asked Daniel. "What sort of clients? You know, I don't actually know what you do. I know you're an actor—"

"Was an actor," Billy corrected.

"Once an actor, always an actor." Daniel was undeterred.

"Maybe." Billy felt faintly embarrassed telling Daniel he had given up his acting career for a full-time job as a social worker. It seemed such a climb down. But when the money had dried up, he had no choice.

"I work with elderly people in the community. Assessing their needs, making sure they get the right services. It's hard work, especially with all the cuts the government keeps heaping on us. But I find it rewarding. Most of my clients are really lovely, and they're so grateful when I sort things out for them."

A waitress arrived with their tea. Billy picked up the teapot.

"Shall I be Mother?"

Daniel laughed. "That's exactly what my mum used to say. She came from Manchester and had all sorts of odd superstitions and stories. She said if two people poured from the same teapot then they'd have a quarrel."

"Yup. Mum says the same." Billy handed a cup of green tea to Daniel. "And she's always telling me off for crossing on the stairs—" His voice tailed off as he remembered his mother's familiar sayings and superstitions. Whether it was about spilling salt, putting new shoes on the table, or making sure knives never crossed, she never tired of warning him.

He pictured her lying in the hospital bed. What superstitious thoughts ran through her mind now? He drew breath sharply, as the emotion of the moment threatened to overwhelm him.

"Are you okay?" Daniel rested his hand on Billy's forearm and gave it a comforting squeeze. Billy looked down at the hand and back at Daniel. He laid his own hand on top of Daniel's and interlaced their fingers.

"Thanks," he said.

"Water?" The waitress had returned and stood over them. Daniel slid his hand away from Billy's.

"Yes, please," he answered.

The waitress filled two glasses from a pitcher and placed it on the table. Billy cleared his throat.

"Is your mum still alive?"

Daniel shook his head. "She died when I was seventeen. She had cancer as well. My dad was furious." He stared out the window for a moment, as if reliving the memory. "It was bizarre. He acted like she'd done it to him deliberately. He stayed around for a few years. Now he's living in Thailand or Vietnam or somewhere like that. I don't really hear from him, apart from the occasional birthday phone call."

"I'm sorry," Billy said.

"Don't be. It was the best thing that could happen. And maybe it helped me grow up a bit."

"Do you have any brothers or sisters?"

"No. Only me. You?"

Billy shook his head. "Same. It's just me." He raised his cup to his lips and took a sip of tea. Daniel watched him for a moment.

"What about your dad?"

Billy put down his teacup and shrugged. "He buggered off years ago. No idea where he is. Best thing really. He hated me."

"Really?"

"I was fourteen," Billy explained. "I got in the way it seemed. When I look back on it now, I think he was really jealous of me and Mum. She and I got on really well—" He realized he was already talking about his mother in the past tense. "Get on really well. We like the same TV shows, and the same music. Mum got me into a Saturday morning drama club and she loved to come and watch me. Dad hated it. He said it would turn me into a poof." Billy laughed as he recalled his dad's dismissive comment. "He was right about that." He chuckled.

"'They fuck you up, your mum and dad,'" Daniel said.

"Yup," Billy agreed. "Philip Larkin got it right with that poem. Well. Fifty percent right in my case."

"Hundred percent in mine," Daniel said.

"Really?" asked Billy. "Both of them? What was so wrong?"

Before Daniel could answer, the waitress arrived at their table.

"Mixed chirashi sushi?"

The two men cleared a space on the crowded tabletop, and the waitress set their plates down in front of them.

"Cheers." Daniel held up his glass of water.

"What are you doing?" Billy asked. "Don't you know it's bad luck to toast with only water in your glass?"

Daniel laughed. "Fuck that." He raised his glass again. "Here's to good fortune."

"Cheers." Billy clinked his against Daniel's and put it back down on the table. "So what was so wrong with your parents?".

"Pentecostal church." Daniel picked up his chopsticks. "They were heavily into it. Both of them. Need I say more?"

"Oh shit, really?" Billy mixed wasabi and soy sauce on his plate. "Did they know you were gay?"

"Oh yes. And they tried to fix me." Daniel picked up a piece of salmon with rice, dipped it in soy sauce, and transferred it to his mouth. "I love this place," he said with his mouth full. "The food's always so fresh." He swallowed and took a drink of water. "It was a complete screw-up," Daniel continued. "I fell in love with one of the elders at the church. Well, more an infatuation, I suppose. He was a brilliant musician and that's how I got my love for music. He was closeted and swore me to secrecy. But his wife found out about us and there was this huge scandal. And right in the middle of it Mum got sick. Dad said her illness was my fault because I'd invoked the wrath of God by closing my heart to the Holy Spirit. He sent me away to this retreat thing to cure me."

Daniel enclosed the word *cure* in invisible quotation marks with his chopsticks. "While I was away, Mum died. So he blamed me for her death as well. And I blamed him for sending me away while she was ill. We hardly spoke after that. I managed to get a scholarship to college and escaped that stifling little world when I was eighteen."

"How did you get over it?" Billy asked.

"You think I'm over it?" Daniel laughed. "Well, maybe I am. A bit. I went really wild at college. The sex was great, and I found I was pretty good at writing music."

"Though you say it yourself," Billy said wryly.

"Oh, come on," Daniel protested. "In this business, if you don't big yourself up, there's a whole bunch of people who'll stomp all over you to get the work instead."

Billy shrugged. "You're probably right," he said. "I've never been good at that side of things."

"It didn't seem to stop you getting work when you were acting."

"Oh, that was my agent. I was really lucky. He put me forward for parts and I seemed to get them."

Daniel sat back in his seat, narrowed his eyes, and looked across the table at Billy.

"Don't you think the reason for that may have been—just the tiniest bit—because you're a good actor?"

Billy shrugged, feeling pleased and awkward at the same time. He never knew how to react to praise. His mother had always impressed on him the value of humility and the danger of self-importance.

"Why don't we go for a walk by the river after this?" Daniel asked. "We can have a drink on the South Bank."

***

The Saturday evening crowd in Soho showed no sign of thinning when they emerged from the restaurant an hour later. Billy hurried after Daniel, who strode down the street towards Piccadilly Circus. As they reached the corner of Great Windmill Street, Daniel stopped suddenly and turned. Billy notice too late and crashed into him. Daniel wrapped his arms around Billy's waist.

"You're beginning to make a habit of this, Mr Walsh." Daniel smiled, and gazed directly at Billy. "I might begin to enjoy it." He leaned forward and kissed Billy on the lips. Billy tensed at first. He never felt relaxed kissing in public, even in an area as tolerant as Soho. But he closed his eyes and enjoyed the warm tenderness of Daniel's kiss.

He placed his arms around Daniel's shoulders and drew him closer. The kiss lasted several minutes and Billy felt the palms of Daniel's hands slide down his back to press firmly on Billy's backside. As his body pressed hard against Daniel's, Billy felt his erection stiffen.

"Get a room, you two," a man shouted from across the street.

Slowly, Daniel relaxed his hold on Billy. The two men remained in embrace and stared at each other.

"What do you think?" Daniel asked. "Do you want to get a room?"

Billy nodded. It had been a long time since he felt this good with a man. "My house is empty," he replied. "But it's a long way to Wood Green."

"Come to mine," said Daniel. "I'm across the river in Battersea. We can walk down to Embankment and get the river bus. It's beautiful at night."

Billy dropped his arms and held Daniel's hand. "We can have that drink on the South Bank another time," he said and smiled.

Daniel's phone rang. "Oh shit." He pulled the phone out of his pocket and looked at the screen. "Hello?" Gently, he released Billy's hand from his and turned away to speak. "No, no, it's no problem at all, darling. I'm with a friend. We were going to—" Daniel paused to listen. He glanced at Billy and the corners of his mouth turned upward in a brief smile. "Of course I can, sweetheart," he continued. "Does it have to be tonight?" He paused again to listen. "Yes, of course," he said at last. "I'll be there as soon as I can. Probably twenty-five minutes. I'll be as quick as I can, my darling." He put the phone in his pocket, sighed, and turned to Billy. "I'm sorry," he said.

Chapter 5

The rain started late on Thursday night, and continued without let up. By Friday morning enough water had collected to form transient lakes on many of London's dusty streets, as the drains failed to cope with the deluge. The hottest English summer on record looked destined to turn into the wettest one. At the same time, the temperature had dropped by over ten degrees, and the wind had picked up. The Friday morning mix of tourists and workers shivered as they struggled against the onslaught of the driving rain.

Billy did his best to keep dry under the bus shelter on Euston Road as he waited for a 205 to take him to Old Street. It was eleven in the morning, and he was on his way to see the new client Man Cock had assigned to him the previous Friday.

But his mind was on other matters.

Apart from a few brief text messages during the week, he had heard nothing more from Daniel since his abrupt departure on the Saturday night. Billy had grown used to expecting little from first dates, even second dates. A third date in gay terms was bordering on commitment. But he had hoped for more from Daniel. In the restaurant it seemed like they were really getting on. And then that kiss in Brewer Street.

"Look out, Billy."

A hand in the crowd pulled him back from the roadside as a black cab drove at speed past the bus stop, straight through a large puddle. Those around him who failed to move in time shouted at the receding taxi. They shook the water from their puddle sodden clothes. Billy turned to see who his rescuer was.

"Hey," Daniel greeted. "That was close. Sorry to grab you like that, but it's better than a soaking."

"What are you doing here?" Billy picked up his rucksack from the puddle where it fell when Daniel grabbed him. "Shit, it's soaked."

Daniel looked down at the bag. "Well, at least it wasn't you," he said. "Look, I'm really sorry about last Saturday night. I know it was incredibly rude of me to run off like that. Are you around later?"

Billy turned as he heard the sound of an approaching bus. It was the 205. He shook as much water from his rucksack as he could and debated his answer. "I'm due at the hospital by six thirty this evening."

"How about after that?"

The bus stopped and the doors opened. Billy joined the line of rain-soaked people as they waited to get on board. "I'll be heading home to get something to eat. It's going to be a long day."

Daniel's face broke into a broad grin. "I'll buy you dinner," he said. "It's my atonement for behaving so badly at the end of Saturday night."

Billy fumbled in his pocket for his wallet and stepped into the bus. "I'll have to get back from the hospital," he said over his shoulder.

"Don't worry. I'll meet you there. In the lobby," Daniel shouted back.

The doors slammed shut, and the bus lurched forward. As he stumbled past the crowd of passengers standing in the narrow aisle, he looked out the window to see Daniel smile and wave as the bus sped up.

Billy squeezed past a group of people crowded around the staircase and climbed to the upper deck. There was a seat at the front next to a young woman wearing headphones with the music turned up loud. Grudgingly, she cleared a shopping bag from the seat next to her to let Billy sit.

The front seat on the top deck was pure nostalgia. It reminded him of when he was a young boy, and his mother took him on shopping trips. He sat alongside her in the front seat, looking down on the traffic from the top deck pretending to be the driver as the bus crawled along.

Carefully, he opened the wet rucksack and took out his laptop, which miraculously was dry. He needed to reread the notes about his new client. He remembered the man's name was Charles Stuart and that he had mobility difficulties, but the rest of the information had gone out of his head after the encounter with Daniel.

Billy thought back to Saturday evening, and the bizarre phone call Daniel had received before he disappeared. Who was it from? Why was it suddenly so urgent for Daniel to rush off like that?

And he had heard him use the word *darling* several times during the call.

On the one hand, Daniel worked in the entertainment business, which was full of people who were prone to say "darling" and "sweetheart" to colleagues. But Daniel didn't seem to be that sort of a theatrical lovey. Which was part of his attraction. As far as Billy could make out, Daniel was much more straightforward. So who was the call from?

Maybe it was another lover. After all, he and Daniel had yet to get on to a discussion of previous relationships, apart from the embarrassing incident with Jason. And Daniel hid any curiosity he might have had about that. Much of the time they either talked about their respective dysfunctional families, or Daniel's theatrical therapy work with disabled children and refugees. It was a subject that fascinated Billy, and Daniel was more than willing to talk about it.

Perhaps Daniel was already attached, and Billy was simply an extended one-night stand.

The laptop screen finally flashed to life and Billy found the notes about Mr Stuart. At seventy-eight, the man was a retired heating engineer. He lived alone in a single room apartment on the seventh floor of a housing cooperative. He was American, and had lived in England since the 1960s. He had been in the US Air Force, stationed at one of the many bases that existed in the UK back then, defending Western Europe from the Soviet threat during the Cold War.

Good. He should have some interesting stories to tell.

***

"Who the hell are you?" the voice growled from a dented intercom speaker beside the entrance door to Churchill Buildings in Bullingdon Place.

Billy took a deep breath, shook away the rain that dripped into his eyes, and tried again. "My name's Billy Walsh, Mr Stuart. I'm your new social care planner from the council."

"What the hell happened to Angela?"

"She's no longer with us, Mr Stuart."

"Shit, another one gone. What the hell's wrong with them all?"

"It's pouring with rain out here. Do you think you could let me in please?"

"How do I know you're from the council? How do I know you're not going to come up here and mug me?"

Billy took another deep breath and wished he had worn better shoes that morning. His socks were soaking wet and squelched uncomfortably as he shifted nervously from one foot to the other.

"Mr Stuart. Your front door key is in a special safe outside your flat. Only Angela and I have the code for that safe. Remember? It's the security system we operate."

There was a pause while his client apparently digested this information. Finally, the lock on the entrance door to Churchill Buildings buzzed. Billy pushed the door open quickly, before Mr Stuart had second thoughts.

As Billy crossed the threshold he heard the crackle of a voice growl from the loudspeaker once more. "Seventh floor. The elevator's out so you'll have to walk." As the door eased shut behind him, Billy heard the intercom again. "I've got the police on standby, so don't try anything when you get up here."

***

Billy stood in front of the key safe of flat 712 Churchill Buildings and tapped in the code Angela had left for him in the client contact file. The small box snapped open. Billy retrieved the key from inside and closed the safe. He opened the battered front door and stepped inside. The door slammed shut behind him, leaving him in a small entrance hallway that was unlit. Billy paused to let his eyes grow accustomed to the gloom.

"Who's that?" a voice with an American accent growled from the end of the hallway.

"It's only me, Mr Stuart," Billy called. Cautiously, he felt his way down the narrow corridor towards a door set slightly ajar in front of him. As he approached, the door swung open to reveal an elderly man in a wheelchair. Billy smiled brightly and quickened his step.

Billy held out his hand in greeting. "Hello, Mr Stuart," he said. "I'm Billy Walsh, your new social care planner. How are you today?"

The man in the wheelchair eyed him suspiciously for a moment. Slowly he lifted his right arm and grasped Billy's hand in his. The handshake was surprisingly strong, given the effort his client seemed to use to raise the arm.

"I've been better, young man," Charles Stuart replied. "Call me Chuck. Everyone does." He looked Billy up and down. "You look like a drowned rat in a rain tub. You wanna towel or somethin'? They put 'em in the cupboard in my bedroom somewhere."

Billy shook his head. "I'll be fine, Mr Stuart. Chuck. I'll go and put my coat and shoes back in the hall. I don't want to drop any more water in here."

Chuck shrugged. "It's all the same to me."

Billy turned to go back to the front door.

"But on your way back," Chuck called, "you can go by the kitchen and fix us some coffee. I haven't had any since Mohammed came this morning."

Billy walked back to the front door. He set down his rucksack, took off his thin waterproof and hung it on a coat hook by the door. He bent down and unfastened his soaking wet trainers.

"Mohammed's your morning carer, isn't he?" Billy shouted as he struggled with the laces on his shoes. "How's that working out?"

No reply. Billy removed his shoes and wet socks. He left the shoes by the front door, put his rucksack over one shoulder and walked back down the corridor to a tiny kitchen on the left. He crossed to the sink and squeezed out as much of the water from his socks as he could.

"What did you say?"

Billy turned to see Chuck was sat in his wheelchair right behind him.

"You're gonna get trench foot if you're not careful, young man. Go get yourself a towel from my bedroom and let me fix the coffee," Chuck commanded. "You don't know how to use the darned machine anyhow."

Obediently, Billy squeezed past the wheelchair and crossed the hallway to Chuck's bedroom. Gloomy daylight filtered through the net curtain at the window. It barely illuminated the room, which was sparsely furnished and scrupulously tidy. A single, hospital-style bed stuck out into the room, and opposite the bed stood an imposing, dark-wood wardrobe. On the far wall beneath the window was a chest of drawers.

On the wall immediately to the right was a low wooden bookcase. There were a few books on the shelves together with three or four silver trophies with faded ribbons tied around them. The top was cluttered with about a dozen photographs in simple metal frames. Billy reached out and picked up one near to him. The photo was black and white, and showed a young man in military uniform, being presented with a medal. There was a large plane in the background. Billy set the picture frame back down next to the others. They all showed either military airplanes or flying officers standing in front of airplanes. In several, the stars and stripes flag was clearly visible.

"Did you find the towel?" Chuck shouted from the kitchen.

Billy crossed to the wardrobe and opened its two heavy wooden doors. On the left hung a neat row of shirts and jackets. On the right were five shelves of carefully folded clothes. Billy scanned the shelves for towels, but could see none. He squatted down to hunt in the bottom of the wardrobe. There he found a small pile of bed linen wrapped in plastic bags, and alongside the linen a stack of towels, tidily folded. He took one from the top of the pile, stood and closed the wardrobe doors. He unfolded the towel and began to dry his wet hair.

"I see you did."

Billy turned to see Chuck in the bedroom doorway. A tray was balanced across the arms of his wheelchair. On it were two mugs, a sugar bowl, and a small jug.

"You can carry this for me," said Chuck. "I'm not that safe a driver in this darn thing."

Billy threw the towel over his shoulder and picked up the tray. He followed Chuck as the wheelchair moved slowly down the corridor.

"I'll wash the towel and bring it back next time," said Billy.

"No need for that," Chuck said over his shoulder. "I can't imagine it's dirty after two minutes. But if you like, throw it in the laundry bin. They collect it every other week."

Chuck positioned his wheelchair alongside a small white-topped dining table in the sitting room. He locked off the brakes and tapped the tabletop.

"Put it here."

Billy placed the tray on the table and slipped the rucksack off his shoulder onto the floor. He opened the bag and pulled out his laptop.

"Angela's left me comprehensive notes, Chuck, so I don't need to bother you with unnecessary questions."

"It makes conversation," the American replied. He reached for his coffee. "A fella gets lonely here, day after day. Don't hold back on the chat."

"Okay, then. Let's chat." Billy closed the lid of his laptop. "We can do this stuff in a minute. I read you came over in the U.S. Air Force. And I saw the photos in your bedroom. Do you want to talk about that?"

"No," said Chuck. "That was a long time ago." He picked up his mug with difficulty. "We can talk about the damned political situation in America if you like. I read all about it online. I'm not one of your senile old people, you know. I gotta brain."

Billy cleared his throat nervously. "Where were you from in America originally, Chuck?"

"You wouldn't know it." Chuck took a drink of his coffee. "Place called Riverside," he continued. "East of Los Angeles. Pa was a cook on the airbase there."

"Do you have any—" Billy was interrupted by his phone ringing. "I'm sorry, Chuck," he began. "I forgot to—"

"Answer it," Chuck replied. "I'm in no hurry."

Billy pulled the phone out of his pocket and looked at the screen. It was Daniel. "It's not an important call."

"Answer it," Chuck ordered. "Don't stop on my account."

Billy held the phone to his ear, and half turned away from Chuck. "I'm with a client now," he whispered.

"I'm so sorry," Daniel said. "I wanted to say that a friend of mine's opened a place called The Stage Café down in Fulham. He's offered me a discount. Let's go there tonight."

"Sure," Billy said. "Look. I've really got to go."

"I'll wait for you in the lobby at the hospital. Take as long as you like. The café will be quiet on a Monday so we don't have to book. And look," Daniel cleared his throat. "I really am so sorry about

Saturday. Rushing off like that. I'd had a great time. I don't want you to think that—"

"I had a great time too," Billy said quickly. He glanced round to see Chuck watching him closely. "Look, I've got to go," he repeated. "But I'll see you tonight. And thanks." He put the phone back in his pocket. "I'm so sorry about that."

"Gotta girl?" Chuck asked.

"No." Billy smiled.

"It's a guy."

Billy looked at Chuck to see his reaction. He liked to test out his clients for possible homophobia early on.

"Whatever." Chuck sniffed and shrugged. "Now." He fixed Billy with a steely stare. "Tell me when they're gonna fix my bath hoist."

Chapter 6

Billy came to the end of a chapter in *Howard's End*. He had been inspired to read E. M. Forster's novel after he went to the Young Vic to see *The Inheritance*, a two-part play that reset the novel amongst a group of gay men in New York. His reading progress was slow, partly because he found it difficult to concentrate with all that was going on in his life, and partly because he was dyslexic. As an actor, learning a part had been hell. Friends often helped by recording his lines, so he could listen to them on his phone, rather than laboriously decipher the blurred squiggles on the page.

He looked across at his mother. She had been asleep when he arrived twenty minutes ago. He put down his book on the narrow cupboard next to her bed, and stood to lean over her sleeping form. Her breathing was even. She seemed comfortable and at peace. He kissed her forehead and looked closely at her lined face.

Billy so longed to talk to her. To hear her voice. That abrupt, direct way of speaking she had: a thin veil that masked her natural warmth towards him. He had never asked his mother why she was so hard on him. She had been that way as long as he could remember. Only when he shed tears, such as the time his hamster Harry died, or when his first love Adrian dumped him, did she soften and reveal her affectionate side. Her abruptness made these moments all the more precious. Moments he treasured.

He resumed his seat on the hard, plastic chair next to her bed.

When he had fallen in love with Adrian, Billy had come out to his mother.

"He's too pretty and he knows it," she had said. "He'll break your heart."

And she was right. Adrian was the most beautiful man he had ever seen. They met in Billy's first year at college. Adrian was three years older than him. He was tall with broad shoulders, and thick black wavy hair, which fell across his eyes provocatively. They were together for seven months. Their relationship was passionate and fiery. Only after it ended did Billy acknowledge that perhaps he had been more in love with Adrian than Adrian with him. Quite possibly Adrian was not in love with him at all, despite professing his undying devotion on frequent occasions.

Then one day Adrian had announced he wanted to end it.

"I need some space," was the only explanation he offered.

A week later Billy saw him with another guy from Billy's year.

Clearly, he had needed more than space.

"I told you he'd break your heart," his mother said. "And you know what? This won't be the last time. You know why? 'Cause you love too much and too deep. You're like me. You can't do anythin' half-arsed. It's all or nothin' for you, ain't it?"

That was when tears had welled up in Billy's eyes, and his mother wrapped her arms around him. She ran her fingers through his hair, as she had when he was a small boy, and gently smoothed it down again.

"I'll always be here to pick up the pieces, love," she had said. "Go out and find another man. This is the start of your big adventure."

Sitting by the bed, Billy reached out and placed his hand on his mother's arm as it lay on top of the bedclothes. He gently massaged her pale, freckled skin.

"Only you won't be here much longer, Mum," he said out loud. "What am I going to do then?"

His mother stirred. Billy rested his hand on her lower arm and watched to see if her eyelids might flicker open. Her breathing continued its steady rhythm, and her eyes remained closed.

Billy withdrew his hand and picked up his book from the cupboard by the bed.

"Who knows eh, Mum?" he said. "Am I about to break my heart again?"

Twenty minutes later Billy left his mother's side and headed to the entrance lobby of the hospital. There were people milling around everywhere and he nearly missed Daniel as Billy made for the main doors.

"Hey, Billy."

The voice came from behind him. He turned to see Daniel's tall frame leaning against a pillar, his arms folded in front of him. Gone was the linen suit. In its place he wore ripped jeans and a black T-shirt. Billy waited while Daniel ambled through the crowd towards him. The two men stood opposite each other.

There was a pause.

It seemed neither man knew how to greet the other. Daniel made the first move. He leaned forward and kissed Billy lightly on the cheek. "I'm sorry," he said in Billy's ear.

Billy smiled. Partly at the apology and partly at a young male nurse who walked past smiling at that moment. Billy returned the kiss on Daniel's cheek. "Hey, that's fine," he said. "Let's forget about it and get something to eat. I'm starving."

Daniel led the way out of the hospital entrance. They turned left along the Fulham Road. "How is she?" Daniel asked as they walked.

Billy shrugged. "Asleep," he replied. "I sat and read my book."

"What are you reading?"

"*Howard's End*," Billy replied.

"Oh really?" Daniel asked. "I read that again after I saw *The Inheritance* at the Young Vic last year. You know E. M. Forster is a key character in the play. I'd forgotten what a good read the book is."

"I saw *The Inheritance* too," Billy said. "That's why I'm reading *Howard's End*. When did you see the play?"

"On my birthday. 21st April."

"Same day as the Queen," Billy replied.

Daniel laughed. "I know. It's so appropriate. Two queens on the same day." They stopped at the junction with Old Church Street. "Nearly there," Daniel said, as they waited for the traffic to clear. "It's down here on the left."

***

The décor of The Stage Café was flamboyant and camp. It looked like the baroque interior of an opera house. There were gold cherubs and scrolled flourishes everywhere. Billy and Daniel's table was in a mock opera box and overlooked the main floor of the restaurant. Billy felt exposed. Fortunately it was a Monday and there were only a handful of diners in the restaurant.

The food was exquisite, personally served by a plump and talkative Italian called Valentino, who was Daniel's friend that owned the restaurant. Billy started with roasted scallops and Daniel chose white asparagus. To follow, Billy had a black truffle risotto and Daniel a slow-cooked sea trout in a citrus sauce. Valentino reappeared at the table at frequent intervals to top up their glasses with prosecco.

"But it's complimentary," he protested, when Billy refused to have any more. "I'm testing it for my brother's vineyard in Veneto. I insist." Valentino refilled Billy's glass, replaced the bottle in an ice bucket and descended the small staircase from their opera box. Billy pushed the glass to one side and picked up his water.

"If I have any more prosecco, I'm going to fall onto someone's table down there." He looked over the edge of their box. "We're a bit visible up here, aren't we?"

Daniel laughed. "Perhaps this wasn't the right place to come for a quiet meal," he said. "And now I remember your aversion to being on show when you eat. I'm sorry."

"No, no." Billy shook his head. "The food's great. And Valentino's tried so hard."

"Maybe a bit too hard," Daniel suggested. "I should have guessed it would be like this. I got to know him when I first moved to London. He and his boyfriend lived next door to me, and Valentino used to invite me over. Great food, but he always served it theatrically. Once he made me vamp through The Kings of Leon's 'Sex on Fire' at their piano while he wheeled in a *tarte flambée*. Nearly burned the house down."

"So you're not a Londoner, then?"

"Well, sort of," Daniel said. "I'm from the suburbs in the far northwest. A place called Pinner. Heard of it?"

Billy shook his head.

"And why should you?" Daniel shrugged. "It's full of nice suburban people in nice houses, doing ordinary, nice jobs, and raising nice families."

"Nice." Billy smiled.

"Hideous." Daniel shuddered. "Very middle class. Very middle England. Very…nice. But beneath that veneer of respectability, people gossiped about you like there was no tomorrow. And judged you. Mercilessly. I couldn't wait to get out. Fortunately, I got a scholarship to the Royal College of Music and my parents didn't see me for dust. My grandfather lived in London, and I moved in with him. The little town of Pinner did have one claim to fame, though."

"What's that?" asked Billy.

"It's where Elton John was born, although his name was originally Reginald Dwight. He used to play in a pub. *The Piano Player from Pinner,* they used to call him."

"So you had big shoes to fill."

"See what you did there." Daniel laughed. "Elton escaped from Pinner, too. Made a bit more money than me."

"Is that what you want? Money?"

Daniel reached for his prosecco glass. He paused, the glass held in mid-air. Slowly, he set it back down on the table. "No I don't," he replied finally. "But I'm not sure I really know what I want. I'm steadily working through the things I don't. I don't want to go back to suburban Pinner. Definitely not the Pentecostal church."

"Do you want to direct a big West End show?"

Daniel shook his head vigorously. "God no," he replied. "I did. Once. But then I started working with the kids who come to *Therapy on Stage* and discovered how I could bring real happiness to people. You should see the way they transform. And what we do changes the lives of their parents and guardians too."

Daniel put down his glass and began to wave his arms around excitedly, as though he was conducting the orchestra. "We had this girl with autism last year. Her mother told us she had no high expectations for her daughter. Then, at the end of term, the girl went on stage and did this little dance number in front of an audience of parents. Her mum was in tears."

Billy admired Daniel's passion. His enthusiasm. He wished he could feel the same about his work.

"What do you want?" Daniel's question made Billy feel awkward. He knew it was coming, but he had no ready response.

He shrugged. "I can't think beyond Mum at the moment," he said. "It's difficult to make plans. I'm working through each day as it comes."

Daniel reached forward and rested his hand on Billy's forearm. "Sure," he said. "I can't imagine how you're coping at the moment. Who do you talk to about it?'

"No one," Billy said. "It's one of the down sides of being an only child. No siblings to share the burden."

"You can talk to me if you like," Daniel offered. "I'm a pretty good listener."

He looked steadily at Billy across the table. His eyes were so beguiling. As Billy held their gaze, he remembered his mother, lying asleep in her bed back at the hospital. He remembered his one-sided conversation with her: *"Am I about to break my heart again?"*

"Penny for your thoughts." Daniel's words cut through his daydream. Billy shook his head, picked up the prosecco glass, and took a drink.

"Let's go somewhere else," Daniel said. "And talk some more. I've had enough of being on show up here. Do you want a coffee? We can go back to mine if you want."

Billy raised an eyebrow and glanced down to look at the time on his phone. "On a school night?" he asked. "I've got to be in sunny Stockwell first thing in the morning."

"All the more reason for coming back to mine, then," said Daniel. "It's three stops on the Tube from my place. It's the other end of the line from Wood Green. It'll take you forever."

Billy hesitated. The thought of going back to the empty house in Wood Green late tonight, plus Daniel's eyes staring back at him, were enough to sway his decision.

"Sure," he said. "Let's go."

Chapter 7

Daniel was unprepared for the warm night air that hit them when they stepped out of the restaurant. The heavy rain from earlier in the day had cleared. Even though it was long after sunset the summer heat had returned to the city.

"Bizarre weather we're having," Daniel said. "It's like being in the tropics." He turned to Billy. "Are you okay if we walk? There's the bus, but it's going to be rammed full of people at this time of night. And in this weather it'll be steaming hot. Anyway, Battersea Power Station looks glorious from the Albert Bridge." Without waiting for an answer, Daniel set off down the King's Road at a brisk pace. Billy hurried after him.

"I haven't seen Battersea Power Station for such a long time," Billy said as the two men strode along the road. "Have they finished converting it into apartments yet?"

"Apartments, leisure facilities, entertainment complexes, everything the corporate executive's heart could desire," replied Daniel.

"I can already smell the soapy scented aftershave."

"I preferred the place when it was derelict." Daniel sighed. "There was a sort of steampunk charm about Battersea Power Station. Now it's more like a glossy tourist attraction. Still. It's a beautiful one."

The change in the weather had brought people back onto London's streets. The King's Road was full of well-dressed couples, and groups meandering along. Daniel and Billy chatted and occasionally paused to window shop.

Daniel took hold of Billy's arm and the two men stopped by the window of a boutique selling retro clothing. Faceless mannequins modeled fashion from another era. "Did you know this was one of the first clothing stores on the King's Road during the swinging sixties?" Daniel asked. "They claim it's where the Beatles bought the jackets that were the inspiration for their Sergeant Pepper uniforms. My friend Maggie told me that. She's a designer. She's lived in London since the sixties." He pointed at the displays of clothes in psychedelic hues and shiny fabrics. "Look at the prices. Maggie says she used to be able to buy a dress here for a couple of pounds. Now they charge five hundred pounds for that hideous-looking jacket."

He turned to Billy. "I wish I'd been around then," he said. "Don't you? It was all so new. Daring, and different. Anything that dares to be different these days is either stamped on immediately, or some manufacturer picks it up and churns it out for the mass market."

Billy turned his back on the display and leaned against the shop window. He folded his arms and looked at Daniel. "That's a bit of a gloomy view on everything, isn't it?" he asked. "I don't think things are like that at all. You can wear what you want. Much more than you could then. What's stopping you?"

As if to prove his point, two men walked past hand in hand. One wore a leather kilt and a black singlet. The other wore a pair of shiny red shorts with rainbow braces. They slowed when they saw Billy watching them, and both waved. Billy nodded and smiled. Daniel turned to see what Billy was looking at. The man in the kilt paused and curtsied. Daniel bowed in return. He turned back to Billy.

"Probably going to a fancy dress party," he whispered.

Billy raised an eyebrow. "Maybe you envy the fact that they can carry it off," he replied.

Daniel looked down at his own clothes. "And what's wrong with my fashionably ripped jeans and discount store black T-shirt?" he asked.

"The answer's right there in the word you used," Billy observed. "'Fashionably.' If you want to dare to be different, then don't be fashionable." He was surprised by how comfortable he felt challenging Daniel's assertive viewpoint. Maybe it was all the glasses of wine he had with their meal. Whatever, he had become bold once more.

Billy pointed down to the military-style combat fatigues he wore. "I've been wearing these kinds of trousers for as long as I can remember," he said. "Comfortable. Practical, with lots of pockets, and they're easy to get at the army surplus stores. I haven't been fashionable for years."

Daniel leaned forward and kissed Billy on the lips. The move took Billy by surprise. He closed his eyes as Daniel's lips touched his. They were warm, and sensuously moist. Daniel continued to hold Billy's face close after the kiss, and he could feel Daniel's warm breath. It felt good. He opened his eyes as Daniel pulled away.

"Not adhering slavishly to fashion is one of your many endearing features," Daniel said. "You're absolutely right. It was a dumb thing, not a gloomy thing to say. My problem is I feel like I'm struggling to be original with my work. There's so much talent around. How can I compete?"

Billy's renewed confidence continued to embolden him. He wrapped his arm around Daniel's waist and pulled him close. Daniel turned his head.

And they kissed.

Long and slow.

There was a wolf whistle from somewhere on the street, but the two men ignored the sound. In that moment, all that existed in the world was the intimacy between them. Billy could feel Daniel's stubble rub against his, and he turned his head on an angle to heighten the sensation. Daniel placed his hand on Billy's backside and exerted pressure. Billy felt his erection harden as it pressed against Daniel's groin.

When their lips separated, Daniel dropped his hand, and Billy let out a deep sigh. He opened his eyes to see the two men who had walked past in their distinctive outfits had returned. They stood watching, with broad grins on their faces. Billy grinned and waved. Daniel looked around.

"Move along there," he said to the two men loudly. There was a mock frown on his face. "Nothing to see here."

The two spectators smiled, kissed each other, and headed off down the street.

"Thank you," Billy said. "It's been a while."

"For me too."

"Really?" said Billy. "I would have thought a tall, handsome music director like you…"

Daniel laughed. "You've really got the wrong impression of me, haven't you? You seem to think I'm some kind of dapper man about town, slavishly following the chic new look of the season."

Billy took a step back and looked Daniel up and down. "I get it," he said. "When you said you wanted to dare to be different, you really weren't talking about clothing, were you? It's something else." Billy studied Daniel's face. It crossed his mind this confident urbane music director might actually be vulnerable. "What is it?" Billy asked. "Is it your creative spark? Are you losing your mojo?"

Daniel reached for Billy's hand and grasped it tight. "Come on," he said. "It's time we stopped performing a floorshow for the innocent passersby on the King's Road. Let's go and get that coffee. I can explain better when I've got a keyboard in front of me."

As they prepared to cross the River Thames at Albert Bridge, Daniel stopped and pointed out the four giant chimneys of Battersea Power Station. As he had promised, it looked glorious. Its dramatic industrial architecture reflected a rainbow of floodlights, their hues changed slowly against the night sky. Billy had forgotten how beautiful the River Thames looked at nighttime. Day after day he spent much of his time with his head down, hurrying from one deadline to another. This moment to pause and absorb the beauty of the evening made him feel light-headed.

The Victorian wrought iron on Albert Bridge was festooned with white lights. They twinkled as the breeze wafted them back and forth. Downstream Billy could see the towers of Chelsea Bridge and the graceful arc of the chains supporting its roadway. Over in Battersea Park he could see the outline of the Peace Pagoda. Its silhouette stood tall against the trees in the park.

"You're lucky living close to this." Billy sighed. "All we've got in Wood Green is an ugly shopping mall and a notoriety for stabbings in the park."

Daniel dropped his hand down to Billy's chest and gently massaged it. "Poor, poor Billy," he said. "You seem to forget the new artist developments they've built in Wood Green. I've composed music for friends' shows around there a few times now. Not to mention the refurbished Alexandra Palace up on the hill. I'm hoping to perform in a show there next year." He shook his head. "First me. Now you."

"What do you mean?" asked Billy.

Daniel put his arm around Billy's waist and they began to cross the bridge. "Well, I was a bit half empty earlier, when I said all that rubbish about daring to be different. And now you're moaning about where you live. The fact is, I've met somebody who's not bad-looking, and can hold a conversation—"

"Do I know him?"

"Clearly not if you ask dumb questions like that," Daniel replied. He gave Billy's waist a squeeze. "Come on. You obviously need coffee."

***

Daniel's house was one of many small Victorian houses in a long, tree-lined street alongside Battersea Park. The weathered wooden entrance door creaked as Daniel pushed it open to reveal a darkened hall. He flicked a switch, and the hallway was transformed into what looked like the side gallery of a music museum.

Bizarre musical instruments hung from the ceiling. Music manuscript pages festooned the walls at jaunty angles, and everything was lit dramatically by carefully hidden lighting. Billy stood in the doorway and admired this work of art. Although the entrance hall was simple and high ceilinged, someone's careful and imaginative design had made it beautiful. The modest front door through which they entered had not prepared him for this at all.

Daniel turned to look at the expression on Billy's face.

"You like?" he asked. "My friend Maggie did it for me a couple of years ago. Wait until you see the rest of the place."

Billy stepped into the house and closed the front door behind him. He followed Daniel down the hallway to a sweeping arch on the left. Daniel flicked another switch, and spotlights illuminated a baby grand piano in the middle of what looked like the perfect re-creation of a Victorian drawing room. Above the marble fireplace was a magnificent gold-framed mirror. In the bay window of the room was a ruby red chaise longue, its seat dressed with satin cushions. An aspidistra in a large, porcelain bowl sat on top of a tall, mahogany plant stand.

"I feel distinctly underdressed," said Billy. "Can you wait while I go back for my smoking jacket and silver cigarette holder?"

Daniel laughed.

"She's done a great job, hasn't she? Very resourceful is our Maggie. All for less than four hundred quid."

Billy's jaw dropped open. "Surely not including the piano?"

Daniel nodded. "Oh yes, even the piano. Maggie found out some recording studio had gone bust and she jumped in quick to see what she could get. She's the world's greatest collector."

Daniel crossed to the piano and sat at the keyboard. He started to play, and the room was filled with a Chopin etude. After a few bars he paused and switched to a ballad. Billy felt sure he knew its haunting, lyrical tune but could not recall its name. He unhitched his rucksack and put it on the floor, then walked across the room to lean on the piano to watch Daniel play.

"That's beautiful," Billy said. "I'm sure I've heard it before. It's from a musical, isn't it?"

Daniel nodded. "One of my guilty pleasures. Composed by the Sherman Brothers in nineteen sixty-eight after their success with *Mary Poppins*. One of the greatest British musicals of all times." He looked up at Billy as he played. "Given you a clue?"

Billy shook his head. Daniel paused once more and looked down at the keyboard. Then the main theme from *Chitty Chitty Bang Bang* filled the room. Billy laughed.

"Okay, I know that show," he said. "But I don't know the song you played before. Is it from *Chitty*?"

"Yes, it is." Daniel shook his head in mock disappointment. "You don't know your musicals, do you? I sense a compatibility problem on the horizon." Daniel resumed playing the ballad once more. "It's 'Lovely, Lonely Man,'" He continued for a few more bars, and then stopped and looked up at Billy. "I don't know why. It came into my head, and somehow seemed appropriate."

He stood and walked around the piano, placed his hands on Billy's shoulders, and leant his head forward until their foreheads touched. Daniel's eyes stared intently for a moment. Then his face crinkled into a smile.

"That's a lie," he said. "I know exactly why I played it. Come on. Let's go and make some coffee."

Chapter 8

Daniel's kitchen was filled with a jumble of antiquated cooking gadgets accumulated from different eras in the history of domesticity. An ancient, blackened stove stood in the chimney alcove. Next to it, an oversize American retro blender perched precariously on a mottled red Formica work surface, alongside a vintage 1930s toaster. A Victorian clothes dryer hung from the high ceiling above an antique pine table. The walls were covered with framed pictures, mostly collections of actors smiling from bygone West End productions. Every surface seemed cluttered with either elaborate culinary equipment or music manuscripts.

Billy looked around him in awe. The house was narrow but extended a long way back. There seemed to be so much space. "Can I ask a cheeky question?"

"You mean, how can I afford this?" replied Daniel. "I know. I'm lucky. My grandfather left it to me. This was where I ran to when I left my parents and came to London. Grandpa Bob was the world to me. He was my mum's father, and the dad I never had."

"It must be worth a fortune now."

"Three-bedroom terrace house in desirable Battersea?" Daniel turned to the worktop and opened a cupboard in front of him. "I suppose it is. But it means more to me that this was Grandpa Bob's home. Lots of the things I have here were his." He turned back to Billy. "I said coffee, but would you prefer tea?" Daniel crossed to the stove, picked up a large whistling kettle, and carried it to the sink.

"Have you got mint tea?" Billy asked.

"Ooh, there's fancy." Daniel filled the kettle. "Give me a second and I'll gather some leaves from the garden. Peppermint or spearmint?"

"Now it's my turn to say 'ooh, there's fancy,'" Billy said. "I've got no idea, but probably peppermint."

Daniel set the kettle down on the stove and lit the gas. He picked up a pair of scissors from the dresser, crossed to the backdoor, and undid two heavy bolts. "Come and have a look at the outside space Maggie created for me," he said. "It's inspired by Edward Scissorhands. Very Tim Burtonesque."

Daniel swung open the door. He reached through the open doorway and flicked a switch. Billy could see a hazy glow of twinkling lights beckon him into the mysterious space beyond the threshold. He crossed the kitchen and stood at Daniel's side.

"I'll turn off the house lights." Daniel switched off the kitchen light, and Billy waited for his eyes to adjust to the sudden darkness. The scene before him slowly revealed itself. Leading away from the kitchen door, he saw an avenue of sculpted shrubs, each festooned with tiny lanterns. The pathway seemed to be endless, disappearing into the far distance. On either side of the doorway were two Victorian lampposts. A flickering yellow light illuminated huge glass globes on top of the wrought-iron posts.

Billy stepped across the threshold into the garden. The ground felt soft beneath his feet. He squatted down and gently brushed the palm of his hand over its mossy surface. His nostrils were filled with the scent of chamomile. Billy looked back over his shoulder. Daniel stood smiling in the doorway.

"This is how I keep sane in this city of madness."

Billy stood and walked farther into the garden. After a few yards he came across a break in the avenue of shrubs. It revealed a small, half-walled patio lit by two more wrought-iron lanterns. They spilled yellow flickering light onto two chairs and a neat, glass-topped table. Suspended on the walls around the patio were earthenware pots in which grew many different types of herbs.

Daniel appeared at Billy's side with the scissors in his hand. "I've come to get you your tea."

Billy felt as if he had been transported into a film set. The distant rumble of London's nighttime traffic was masked by recorded birdsong. His senses were overwhelmed by the magic of Daniel's west London wonderland.

"It's beautiful," Billy said. "It's so…tranquil. Surely this must have cost a fortune to build?"

Daniel shook his head. "I told you before, Maggie's resourceful. It's all smoke and mirrors. Well, mostly mirrors. She works as a designer on film sets. That's when she can get the work. When the production team is finished with the props, she spirits them away to this little project. It's a work in progress."

Daniel bent down to the chamomile lawn. "I'm afraid it's mostly fake, but it's quite realistic, like the hedge topiary. She weaves real plants in amongst the artificial. And it's pretty well impossible to work out what's real and what's not. She's a genius."

He walked across to the wall of herbs and harvested a handful of mint leaves. Billy continued down the avenue of shrubs. He quickly discovered why Daniel had used the phrase "smoke and mirrors": the apparent infinite length of the garden was created by an enormous mirror twenty yards in front of him. As he walked towards it, he could see his own reflection as he approached.

"I haven't switched on the mist," Daniel said. "The pump needs some fixing. If I did, the romance here would've been overpowering."

Billy turned as Daniel stopped behind him. He held a handful of mint leaves to Billy's nose, and Billy inhaled deeply.

"Peppermint," said Daniel. "I hope I made the right choice." He lowered his arm, hooked it around Billy's waist, and pulled him closer. He leaned forward and kissed Billy slowly on the mouth. Daniel's lips parted as he said quietly, "Shit." He dropped his arm, reached into his front pocket, and pulled out the scissors. "I wasn't planning on giving myself a circumcision tonight."

Daniel let the scissors and the handful of mint fall to the ground. He wrapped his arms around Billy and pulled him close. Suddenly they were kissing wildly, passionately. Daniel placed his hand on the back of Billy's neck, holding the two men close as their tongues hungrily explored each other's mouths. He wrapped his arm tight around Billy's waist, and slipped his hand down Billy's back to push their groins closer together.

Billy had never felt such immediate connection with a man before. Daniel was both passionate and tender. So many men he had met simply behaved like sexual animals. Encounters with them would start promisingly, but soon they would slip into clichéd actions copied from a badly made porn movie.

But Daniel was different. One moment he was kissing Billy with a passionate urgency, and his raw aggression filled Billy with a sense of sexual danger. The next moment Daniel was gently sliding his tongue across Billy's stubble, or tenderly kissing him on his forehead, on his eyes, or his nose.

Finally, Daniel slipped his hands onto Billy's shoulders, and the two men stood with their foreheads touching. Their eyes locked on each other in an unblinking gaze.

"Do you still want that mint tea?"

"Maybe I'll have a coffee after all," said Billy. "I'd like to stay awake tonight."

***

In contrast to the eclectic assembly of period design and unusual furniture in the rest of the house, Daniel's bedroom was a shrine to minimalism. The bare floorboards were sparsely covered by two raw cotton mats, which lay either side of a king-size bed. The bed was the only substantial piece of furniture in the room. There were no cupboards. No wardrobe. Suspended on the wall behind the bed was a Chinese lacquer screen. Lamps concealed behind it cast a warm glow over the walls. Billy stood in the doorway and looked around at the simplicity of the space. Daniel was already in the bedroom, standing at the foot of the bed.

"I didn't let Maggie near this room," he said, as though he felt the need to give an explanation. "It's my sanctuary from the world. I needed to keep it simple. To keep it still."

Billy was surprised by Daniel's sudden change in manner. He seemed hesitant, almost nervous.

"Are you sure about this?" Daniel asked. "It's been a while for both of us. And I know, well, some guys don't like to rush into things on the first date—"

"Second date," Billy interrupted. "And yes. It's been a while for both of us. Isn't that all the more reason?" He crossed the threshold and stood opposite Daniel at the end of the bed, took hold of his right hand, and intertwined their fingers.

"In the last few months," Billy began, "I've learned we have precious few moments of happiness in this world. Since Mum got sick, I've come to understand how much time I've wasted in the past."

He kissed Daniel on the lips.

When their mouths separated, Billy rested his forehead against Daniel's and looked into his eyes. "What's the point of some elaborate Victorian courtship? This feels…feels right." Billy's hand brushed against the front of Daniel's jeans and he smiled. "Seems like someone else feels it's right as well."

Daniel gently rolled his forehead against Billy's. His eyes twinkled. "Why, Mr Walsh, I do declare," Daniel spoke in a faux Southern US accent. "I feel it only right for me to show you a li'l gen'manly hes'tancy. And now you seek to take advantage of me."

Billy tipped his head back and let out an explosive laugh. "Me? Take advantage of you?" He looked behind him. "You brought me upstairs to the bedroom. And that's a really good name for it. You haven't got another stick of furniture in it. Only one bloody great—"

He was cut short as Daniel pushed him firmly. Billy's feet slipped and he fell back onto the bed. Daniel landed beside him. "Well, what else do you need in a bedroom?" Daniel asked, and leapt astride Billy. He grabbed Billy's wrists and pinned them firmly against the pillows on either side of his head. "This bedroom's strictly for the two esses," he continued. "Sleep and sex. And I'm certainly not sleepy."

Billy was caught off guard by Daniel's strength and agility. The last man he had wrestled with regularly was Jason. But that had ultimately turned nasty. Jason was tall and strong, and he had insisted on taking a dominant role. Billy preferred his sex partners to be versatile.

Daniel held on to Billy's wrists firmly. His biceps flexed as he lowered his upper body until their mouths were mere inches apart. "I hope you're not going to lie there all passive on me," he whispered. His warm breath brushed provocatively against Billy's lips. "I need you to know I look for equality in all aspects of my life. And that includes sex."

Billy succumbed to the temptation of Daniel's lips, and lifted his head from the pillow to kiss them. Daniel teasingly pulled his head back a few inches. His eyebrow lifted, and his mouth formed a crooked smile.

"Come on, Billy," he whispered. "You can do better than that."

Billy arched his back so that his crotch pressed hard against Daniel's cock. He wrapped his legs firmly around Daniel's calves.

His muscles tensed, and he pushed his arms firmly against the weight of Daniel's body bearing down on him.

Daniel's hands slipped, and Billy seized the moment to pull his arms free. He placed his hands against the back of Daniel's head and pulled him close. Their lips connected. Billy opened his mouth to embrace Daniel's. He felt the wet warmth of Daniel's tongue enter his mouth.

And it began to explore.

Hungrily.

Its stimulation hardened Billy's cock further, and he twisted to rub himself against the bulge in Daniel's chinos.

Daniel reached down to Billy's waist and slipped his fingers under the waistline of his jeans. Daniel's warm hands massaged firmly across the base of Billy's back, then they moved down inside his briefs, and Daniel's fingernails grazed the surface of Billy's backside. His fingertips pressed down hard, massaged towards the top of Billy's thighs and the base of his cock.

A wave of euphoria swept through Billy's body. He felt light-headed. It had been a long time since he had experienced physical passion as intense as this. Daniel's body was electric against him.

And alive with sensuality.

Billy pulled his hands away from the back of Daniel's head, and he reached down to pull at the base of his T-shirt. Daniel obligingly sat back and lifted his arms. Rapidly, Billy slipped the T-shirt up and over his head.

He rested his hands on Daniel's chest, and allowed them to rise and fall steadily with Daniel's breathing. Gently, he slid the palms of his hands over the smooth skin of Daniel's pectoral muscles. His thumbs stroked the short hairs covering the hollow in the middle of his chest. Billy splayed out his fingers to caress Daniel's skin, and stroked across his nipples.

Daniel caught his breath and closed his eyes.

"You like that?" Billy breathed.

Daniel nodded, his eyes still closed.

Billy's fingers stroked back and forth across Daniel's nipples, and they grew firm. He grasped them between his fingers and thumbs—and squeezed.

Daniel's breath caught, more sharply this time, and he exhaled slowly in a controlled gasp. He reached for the front of Billy's combats, undid the fly, and tugged them down with his briefs. He placed his hands either side of Billy's cock, created a ring with his thumb and forefinger around the top of Billy's ball sac, and cupped it in the palm of his hand. He moistened the fingertips of his other hand, and placed them on the tumescent tip of Billy's penis.

Billy felt a surge of pleasure rush from the top of his cock outward through his whole body. His back arched and his cock pressed harder against Daniel's massaging fingertips, intensifying the ecstasy of the moment. He looked across the ridge of his chest to see Daniel had already slipped off his jeans and briefs. Precum glistened on the tip of his cock, which extended, ramrod hard, towards him.

Daniel followed the line of Billy's gaze, and looked back with the twitch of a smile on his face. He released Billy's cock from his grasp, dismounted, and knelt on the bed at Billy's side. "I'm going to show you the benefit of being sucked off by a professional singer," Daniel said. "Voice coaching relaxes the soft palate. It means I can take you deeper. We'll both hit some high notes."

Billy's cock flexed in response to the offer. Daniel chuckled and leaned in close to whisper in Billy's ear. "And you're going to take me at the same time."

Before Billy could respond, Daniel sat up and grasped Billy's thighs. He swung his leg over to mount Billy, facing towards his feet.

Sixty-nine was a sexual position Billy had only tried twice before with a former lover. Daniel's cock hung temptingly above his mouth. He extended his tongue and licked the tip, evoking a groan of satisfaction from Daniel.

Then it was Billy's turn to feel pleasure. Daniel lowered his head into Billy's groin and took the full length of his cock in his mouth. Billy felt the back of Daniel's throat make contact. His mouth fell open in a gasp as Daniel's soft palate began to expertly massage the tip.

Meanwhile, Daniel gently lowered his hips, and his penis entered Billy's mouth. He tensed. While he could feel Daniel take him deep in his throat, Billy was uncertain he could reciprocate the expertise of Daniel's technique.

Daniel seemed to sense Billy's anxiety. Gently, he raised and lowered his hips in a regular rhythm, yet never allowing his cock to penetrate too deep into Billy's throat.

It gave Billy confidence, and he used his tongue to stimulate and explore the length of Daniel's rigid penis. The sensation as it rode the inside of Billy's mouth evoked an increasing pleasure. At the same time, his own cock felt fit to burst as Daniel massaged it in the depth of his throat.

Billy lost all concept of time.

His body was overwhelmed by pure pleasure brought on by the simultaneous stimulation. The intensity brought Billy close to climax. He twitched his head to one side to release Daniel's cock from his mouth.

"I'm going to cum," he moaned breathlessly.

Daniel twisted his head to look round at Billy. He swept long dark strands of hair away from his eyes, and wiped his mouth on the back of his hand.

"Good," he said with a grin. "So am I. Let's get there together."

He turned back to Billy's cock and took it deep into his mouth.

Billy gasped as if he had been plunged into ice water. With a renewed confidence, he allowed Daniel's cock to descend deep into his throat. He reached his hands forward to massage Daniel's nipples.

Within a few minutes he heard Daniel groan, and a moment later the warm taste of Daniel's cum flooded his mouth. The intensity of the moment overwhelmed him, and his hips jerked upward in a spasm of ecstasy as he ejaculated into Daniel's mouth.

Daniel rolled off Billy onto the bed, and swiveled around to lie alongside him. He gently ran a hand over the contour of Billy's body, which flexed with the subsiding spasms of sexual satisfaction. He intertwined the fingers of his other hand in Billy's hair, and gently combed it through.

"You beautiful man," Daniel said softly. "Next time, let's make it last longer."

He kissed Billy on the lips.

"I hope you'll stay the night."

Chapter 9

Daniel blinked open his eyes. His body shook and he gasped.

The nightmare had been about his work. A few years ago, the same panic dream would regularly wake him up in the early hours. In it, he was about to play the piano at a major event on the open-air stage in Regent's Park. He opened his rucksack to find it empty. All his music was back at home. And the show was due to start in five minutes. Frantically he tried to remember the repertoire he was about to play. He could see the chorus of two hundred children on the raked levels of the stage. But his memory was blank. He had no idea what they were about to perform.

The audience fell silent in expectation. All the children turned and waited for him to start the concert. Daniel's heartbeat quickened, and his breathing became shallow. His lips were dry, and he gasped for air.

Which was when he woke up.

Why had the panic dream returned?

He looked across to Billy's sleeping form stretched out on top of the bedclothes. His naked body faced away from Daniel. Sleep-tousled hair splayed across the pillow.

Daniel sighed with relief. And gratitude.

All was right with the world. Here lay the most wonderful man. A man who had reignited the elusive spark of his passion for fulfilling sex: a man who was much more than a two-dimensional profile in one of those superficial apps. The same apps he had deleted from his phone with much ceremony nearly a year ago.

What a change had happened in his life, in less than week. There was every chance he would see this man again. And it was clear there was much more to Billy than a night of good sex.

So why had he panicked?

Daniel rolled over and nestled his body against Billy's. He laid his hand on his thigh and gently ran his fingers through the fine curls of hair that covered it. Billy stirred briefly before his breathing resumed its regular, slow rhythm. Daniel leaned in to Billy's neck. He inhaled the musky smell and sighed contentedly.

He had missed having close contact with a man.

Which was not to say there had been no encounters with men in the last couple of years. But none of them came close to the intimacy he felt tonight.

Such closeness.

Such oneness.

It was as if he and Billy had been shaped from the same piece of clay. They fitted together so perfectly. So snugly.

Could Billy fit into Daniel's life so easily?

On the face of it, his life was already full. With work, good friends, and good times.

And the occasional one-night shag.

In the last year his career had progressed at a brisk pace. And he was convinced it was thanks to the absence of emotional commitment: the absence of a needy partner. It gave him the headspace he needed to focus on composing.

Which was his first love.

The only commitment was Anthony.

If he were to carry on seeing Billy, he would need to tell him about Anthony. He had been tempted to do so the other night when Anthony rang. It was bad timing. Maybe he would tell Billy soon. He had to make a decision anyway. The situation could not carry on much longer.

So now what?

He looked at the sweeping curve of Billy's beautiful eyelashes, occasionally flickering as his body twitched to the storyline of a dream.

Daniel knew they would meet again. They must meet again. Daniel felt like the moth to Billy's flame. He was drawn to this beautiful, fascinating man in a way he had not been since his first love at the age of sixteen.

But what would he do if New York was to happen? There were so many events about to explode in Daniel's work life. Exciting opportunities he had only dreamed about in the past twelve years. Opportunities he had worked so hard for. Unattainable dreams he was now, finally, about to grasp.

And now this.

He would have to tell Billy about the possibility of New York at some point, but not yet.

Not tonight.

He would find a time.

Daniel snuggled closer to Billy's body, and he stirred. He turned his head slightly, and his eyelids flickered. The beautiful eyelashes flashed, and the kissable lips parted. "You okay?"

Daniel hugged him. "Oh yes," he whispered. "Perfect. Go back to sleep."

***

Billy lay in the darkness. The warmth of Daniel's arm wrapped around him was comforting. He felt secure. What a relief to be woken from his dream, which was a confusion of work and endless visits to the hospital. In it, he opened the door of his mother's room to find his boss Caroline at her bedside.

"Why weren't you here, Billy?" Caroline asked. Her eyes were cold and unblinking. "Your mother's been calling for you, but you weren't here. She's upset, you know. It's a good job I was here. Don't you care?"

Caroline turned back to look at his mother. "She's sleeping now. Don't disturb her. You'll only worry her more."

Billy tried to walk to the bed. But his feet were frozen.

Immobile.

He could not lift them from the floor. He stretched out his arms, but the bed was beyond his reach.

Caroline stood, and walked towards him.

"What are you doing, Billy?" She took hold of his arms and forced them down by his sides.

"You're too late." Caroline shook her head. "Always late. Never on time. Never where you should be."

Billy's body shuddered as he recalled the fear he felt in the dream.

"Hey." Daniel's breath was warm on his neck. "You okay?"

Billy inhaled deeply, and slowly released the air from his lungs. "Just a bad dream," he replied.

Daniel's arm squeezed comfortingly around his chest. "You too, huh?"

Billy stretched his legs, and slid the heels of his feet down Daniel's muscular calves. He felt Daniel's cock twitch against the top of his thigh.

"Hello," Billy whispered. "Someone else is awake."

Daniel chuckled. "He never sleeps, I'm afraid. Especially when pressed up against a sexy man at five in the morning."

Billy opened his eyes and looked across to the window. The dawn light had begun to penetrate the slats of the Venetian blind. "What was your bad dream about?"

Daniel slipped his arm from Billy and rolled onto his back. "It was nothing," Daniel said. "Too much work. Too many deadlines that all come hunting in the dead of night." He turned his head to Billy. "What was your dream?"

Billy lay on his back and slid the palm of his hand slowly through the curls of hair on Daniel's chest.

"My mother. Always about my mother." He closed his eyes as he felt tears begin to form. It seemed the wrong emotion to feel when only a few hours ago he had made love with this wonderful man. His shoulders shook as a wave of melancholy hit him.

"Hey." Daniel rolled towards him. He ran his fingers through Billy's hair and gently untangled the knots of curls. "It's okay. Let it go if you want."

Billy turned, rested his head on Daniel's shoulder, and sighed as he exhaled. "I'm sorry."

Daniel slipped his hand down to Billy's shoulder and gently massaged. "As if," he said. "I can't begin to imagine what you're going through. Don't put any more pressure on yourself. You're doing all you can for her."

Billy flexed his shoulder appreciatively against Daniel's firm massage. "It's not as though I lack experience in working with older people," Billy said. "They're my working life. I've got this fascinating, but infuriating new client. He was a pilot in the U.S. Air Force when he was younger."

Daniel released Billy's shoulder and sat up. "Come on," he said. "Roll over onto your front. I'll give your shoulders a proper massage."

Billy did as Daniel asked. He rested his cheek on the pillow, and stretched out his arms either side of his head. Daniel sat astride his back and began to massage his shoulders firmly. Billy could feel Daniel's cock rub against the small of his back as he leaned into the massage. He felt his own cock twitch in automatic response.

"Why is this client infuriating?" asked Daniel.

Billy sighed. Partly in response to the calming effect of Daniel's hands, and partly as he recalled Chuck's grumpy acceptance of Billy's presence in his apartment the day before.

"He's clearly unhappy. He's lonely. So he takes it out on me. I met him for the first time yesterday, and he was kind of testing me I suppose."

"How do you mean?"

"The care system's so broken. Clients never have the same social worker for long enough. Clients like continuity, so they get suspicious when a new one of us comes along. I knew Chuck was testing me out."

"Chuck?" repeated Daniel. "Great American name. Sounds like a character from a movie. Do you think you passed his tests?"

Billy sighed again. "Maybe. He was pretty cross when I arrived. But by the time I left—" Billy winced as Daniel's hands found a knot of muscles.

"Sorry," Daniel said. "You're tight there. I'll be gentle with it." The pressure from his hands eased on Billy's shoulder. "He was a pilot, you say?"

"Yes." Billy sighed. The massage felt so good, and he was feeling drowsy. "In the U.S. Air Force. He could be a really interesting guy to talk to. If I only had the time."

"When will you see him again?"

"I'm not due to go again until next Friday. Even then, I've only got half an hour with him. It's barely time to drink a cup of tea."

"Can't you go more often?"

Billy tried to shake his head as it nestled in the pillow. "I've got other clients. It's difficult to fit in extra visits."

"Oh shit." Daniel took his hands away from Billy's shoulders. Billy felt the bed shake as Daniel jumped down onto the floor. He lifted his head from the pillow and turned to see what had happened.

"What's the matter?"

Daniel stood by the door of the bedroom. "I'm sorry," he said. "I completely forgot. I'm doing a residential this weekend."

"What does that mean?"

"It means I'm supposed to be in Oxford at nine, getting ready to run a music workshop for fifty kids with learning disabilities. It's a two-day thing."

Billy sat up, stretched his arms above his head, and felt the stiffness in them had eased. Daniel's body was backlit by a shaft of sunlight coming through a window in the hallway outside. The light threw the muscles of his tall, muscular frame into sharp relief. His cock remained semi-erect.

"What time is it now?"

"Six thirty," Daniel replied. "I'm screwed if I don't get the eight o'clock train from Paddington." He walked back to stand at the foot of the bed. Billy noticed his cock rested neatly, and invitingly, on top of the bedclothes. He shuffled down the bed to sit with his legs either side of Daniel's torso, and rested his hands on Daniel's chest. He watched as Daniel's cock gave a responsive flick.

"I'm going to have to kick you out, sexy man," Daniel said. "What are you doing next week?"

"Working," replied Billy. "But I'm around in the evenings." He yawned. It was too early for a Saturday morning.

"I've got youth drama groups on Monday and Tuesday evening," Daniel said. He took hold of Billy's arms, hooked them over his shoulders, and cupped his hands behind Billy's head. "What about Wednesday during the day?"

Billy closed his eyes, and rolled his head against Daniel's hands. The impromptu massage felt good. "I'm on a course all day. Presentation skills," he mumbled.

Daniel's hands stopped their therapy, and he let out a roar of laughter. "You? An actor? Needs to be taught presentation skills?"

Billy opened his eyes. "Former actor," he corrected. He was momentarily stung by Daniel's reaction.

"Former actor? Come on. Who are you kidding?" Daniel leaned forward and whispered in Billy's ear. "And what can they possibly hope to teach Doctor Hastings of *Blue Lights* about presentation skills?"

He grasped Billy's wrists and thrust him back onto the bed. "Come on, Doctor Hastings," he said. "Let's try some role play ahead of your presentation skills training. How about a little light restraint?"

"I thought you had a train to catch?" Billy released himself from Daniel's grasp, and pushed him back firmly. "You don't want to miss it."

Daniel took a step back. He looked down at Billy's cock, which now stood firmly erect. "My, my, Mr Walsh." Daniel placed the palms of his hands on his cheeks in mock horror. "Now that is a presentation."

Chapter 10

Billy hurried along City Road in Shoreditch towards the Cosmos Hotel. It was nearly nine on another bright, sunny morning, and he was late for his training course. He turned the corner into a side street. A hundred yards down on the left, he saw the faded neon sign for the hotel. Shoreditch had a reputation as being the hip, fashionable part of London. This stature had clearly not rubbed off on the Cosmos Hotel.

The hotel's revolving door moved slowly and grudgingly as Billy pushed hard against its cracked wooden handle. It creaked and groaned before it finally deposited him into the gloom of a scruffy lobby. The windows were hung with grubby net curtains, and several spotlights set into the ceiling were missing. A large flipchart pad was propped up on a stand next to the check-in desk. It displayed the notice "PRESENTATION SKILLS – FIRST FLOOR" in badly scrawled capital letters.

A battered beige carpet covered the floor of the lobby. Billy avoided several ridges and tears in the carpet as he crossed to the staircase. After being with Daniel, Billy had felt fitter than he had for a long time, and he ran up the stairs two at a time. Another handwritten sign at the top of the staircase pointed him towards a room at the end of the corridor.

Half a dozen people gathered around a table at the far end of the room. There were four men and two women. It was like a scene from a funeral gathering. Everyone had a cup of coffee. A few made awkward conversation. The rest stood around listening and nodding.

This is going to be fun, Billy thought.

The men were dressed in suits. The women wore chic black dresses. Billy was the only one in jeans and a T-shirt. He took a deep breath and strode towards the group. He dropped his bag at his feet, picked up a plastic cup, and filled it with coffee from a stained, white plastic jug.

"Are you one of the trainers?" The man asking the question was probably in his mid-twenties. His blue serge suit seemed to be a size too big, and there was a brown stain on his white shirt. As Billy turned towards him, the man's right eye twitched. He looked down at his coffee cup nervously.

"I mean," the man in the blue serge suit continued. "Sorry. I thought…as you—"

Billy shook his head. "Not me," he replied. "I'm only here for the free coffee." He smiled, hoping to put the man at ease. But the eye twitched even more.

"Well, they're late then," the man said. He looked accusingly at Billy. "And I got here especially early."

Billy smiled again and turned away. It was at times like these that he was relieved not to work in an office. Trapped in the same drab, fluorescent-lit space day after day with people like this. It was his idea of hell.

"Ladies and gentlemen. Can I have your attention please?" A woman dressed in a hotel uniform had appeared by the door.

"I regret to tell you that your instructor has called to say she's been taken ill. Today's course is cancelled."

"Outrageous." The man in the blue serge suit was full of self-righteous indignation.

Billy turned back to the man who was now annoying him. "Well, if the poor lady's ill—" Billy began.

"That's not the point. I've come a long way today. And I came early."

Billy put his coffee cup on the table. The man's small-minded intolerance was too much. "If you keep coming early," Billy began, "I suggest you see a doctor. I understand that premature ejaculation is eminently treatable."

He looked around. Two women tried to look shocked, and the men smirked. He winked at them. "But then, it's not a problem I've ever had."

Before the man had time to even think of a response, Billy picked up his bag and walked away.

***

Billy paused outside the coffee shop in the hotel lobby. Its plastic décor, its bright, flickering fluorescent lighting, and the surly-looking member of staff who stared back through the dirty window helped him make a quick decision. No way, he thought.

This time, he avoided the reluctant revolving door to return to the street. A junior member of the hotel staff obligingly held open a side door for him. "We hope you enjoyed your stay," she said brightly with a strong, East European accent.

"Thank you," Billy said. And added with feeling, "You've made my day."

The young woman smiled broadly, and Billy winked back at her. *I wonder how long before you find a better place to work*, he thought to himself.

Billy paused outside the hotel and looked down the busy street. There was a small café with tables outside in the sunshine. Perfect. Even though the traffic was noisy, it was the nearest place he could see to get a coffee, enjoy the sun, and decide what to do for the rest of the day.

Of course he should really go back to work. There was always paperwork to do. Endless admin. He took a seat at a small table outside the café and waited patiently to catch the waiter's eye. Billy had no intention of going back to the office.

He remembered what Daniel had said last Saturday morning. If he was still free today, why should Billy waste his time in the office? Finally, he felt his old sense of rebellion returning. Seize the opportunity while it was there. And later, he would go visit his mother. He pulled out his phone and made a call.

"Hey. Everything okay?" Daniel's voice was good to hear.

"Great," said Billy. "My workshop's cancelled."

"You mean, you'll never know how to make a good presentation?" Daniel's voice was full of mock horror. "What on earth will you do now?"

Billy smiled. "I'm thinking of getting a life," he said. "And it starts with skipping work for the rest of the day. I remembered you said you weren't working today, so I thought we could meet up."

Daniel sighed. "People are off sick so they scheduled me for two performances with the Youth Theatre: one in about half an hour, and another this afternoon. I've just arrived at the venue in Chelsea.

We've got two special needs groups coming for a summer school today. It's full on."

"I could come and watch," Billy said brightly.

"I'm afraid not," replied Daniel. "It's parents only. Much as I'd like to invite you, we've got to respect the privacy of the kids. I'll be through around five. By the time we've cleared up I could leave before six. Do you want to meet then?"

"I'll probably be at the hospital," said Billy. "How about some time after seven?"

"Great," Daniel replied.

Billy heard the shouts and screams of children in the background.

"Shit," Daniel said. "Gotta go. The kids have arrived and it's about to be pandemonium here. See you later."

A waiter arrived with a double macchiato and a *pain au chocolat*. Billy leaned back in his seat, stretched out his long legs, and basked in the direct heat of the sunshine. Perhaps he would sit for an hour and watch the world go by. He rarely visited this part of London. Now he had the time he could take a tour of the area. After all, it was full of history. Around the corner from where he sat were the bells of Shoreditch church, made famous by the nursery rhyme "Oranges and Lemons." Billy remembered his drama teacher telling him about the first ever playhouse in England. It was in Shoreditch, and several of Shakespeare's plays were performed on the stage there.

These days, Shoreditch was more famous as a magnet for internet businesses and fashionable start-up companies. The people walking past confirmed that. They were smartly dressed, oozed affluence, and talked earnestly into their mobile phones. It struck Billy as ironic that a few streets away from these gentrified cafés and restaurants stood rows of social housing.

Of course. Billy's new client Chuck Stuart was only ten minutes' walk from here. He would go say hello and have that long chat he promised himself.

***

"Waddya want?" the familiar growl emerged from the intercom on the wall outside Churchill House.

All of Billy's enthusiasm evaporated. "I was passing, Chuck, and I thought I'd drop in for a chat, if that's okay?"

"You came last Friday. Anyway, I'm busy."

Billy leaned his forehead against the wall above the battered intercom and sighed. It was a bad idea. Perhaps he should go enjoy the sunshine. "Don't worry if it's not convenient, Chuck. I'm due to come back—"

The door buzzed loudly and eased open. "Come on up if you want," Chuck said. "Must be a first. Never had one of you lot up here two days in a row." As the door closed behind him, Billy heard Chuck's voice once more. "Elevator's still out. You'll have to walk."

Billy stepped into the gloomy hallway of flat 712 Churchill Buildings.

"You can make me some coffee now you're here," Chuck shouted from down the hall. "You know where everything is."

"Hi, Chuck," Billy called back. "Thanks for letting me come up."

Billy took off his trainers and walked down the corridor to the small living room. Chuck was hunched in his wheelchair a few feet from the television. He was watching a black-and-white documentary about airplanes.

"How are you, Chuck?"

Slowly, Chuck looked up from the television. He blinked his watery eyes several times behind heavy rimmed glasses. "Been better." He sniffed and turned back to the television. "But then, you knew that already."

Billy went back to the kitchen. This was going to be hard work. The visit was really a mistake. He should have waited to come back on the scheduled day. Billy slipped his bag from his shoulders and put it on the floor. He filled the electric kettle and set it down on the countertop to boil.

The kitchen was dingy and shabby. The cupboard doors were scuffed and grubby. The sink was full of unwashed dishes. The waste bin overflowed, and the two available countertops were covered with discarded food wrappings. Stale food congealed on dirty plates.

It was a depressing, cramped space. Billy wondered how Chuck could manage in his wheelchair. No wonder the man was grumpy. Day after day confined to this gloomy flat on the seventh floor of Churchill Buildings, and alone for much of the day. It was sad to see a man who had once been so active reduced to this. A pilot in the U.S. Air Force. Surely Chuck's military pension would pay for more than this?

Billy washed two mugs and searched unsuccessfully for a jar of instant coffee. Only then did he remember Chuck's complicated coffee machine. It was hidden behind a collection of battered cereal packs at the end of the countertop. He stared at the machine for a moment. Years ago he worked as a barista in Soho while waiting for his next acting job to come up. He was fully trained on coffee making, even if he was not that good.

But this machine was old. It should have been in a museum. Gloomily, he resigned himself to incurring Chuck's scorn when he called for his assistance.

"What you boil the kettle for? You're not making tea, are you?" Billy turned to see Chuck in the kitchen doorway.

"I forgot about your coffee machine," said Billy. "I was making—"

"Instant coffee?" Chuck's voice raised an octave. Billy might as well have said boiled acorns.

"Get out the way, young man," Chuck said. He propelled his wheelchair into the narrow space. Billy flattened himself against the wall to avoid being run over.

"Shit. Mohammed sure leaves this kitchen in a helluva mess," Chuck complained. "Come on. I'll teach ya how to make decent American coffee. Go stand over there."

Billy obediently edged past Chuck's wheelchair. He pushed the cereal packs to one side and stood in front of the large metal coffee machine.

"If you're going to keep dropping in unannounced, young man, you'd better start making yourself useful. I've not drunk that instant coffee shit for years. And I'm sure as hell not goin' to start now. Right. Grab that handle out front and swing it left."

Billy took hold of a large black handle on the front of the coffeemaker and pushed it to the left. It was stuck.

"Come on, boy," said Chuck impatiently. "Put those guns of yours to some good use for a change. It's not just about posing in front of the mirror at the gym, you know."

Billy squared up to the machine and grasped the handle once more. With an effort, he jerked it to the left. The handle dropped, and revealed the coffee filter full of used coffee grounds.

"How on earth do you manage to fix it on so tight?" Billy asked as he carried the filter to the sink.

"And don't throw it down the drain, dammit," Chuck said impatiently. "Damn thing's blocked as it is. Put it in the trash."

Billy looked at the overflowing bin. Chuck followed his gaze.

"Okay, okay," he grumbled. "Use that old baked bean can on the top of that shit. You can clear it away later."

Billy fished the discarded tin can from the bin and carefully tapped the used coffee grounds into it.

"And my muscles aren't weak and feeble," Chuck continued. "If that's what you're implying." He flexed his arms in a strong man pose. "Legs might be shit, but I still work out the rest of my body when I can. I'll arm wrestle you under the table any day, boy."

Even masked by Chuck's shapeless, baggy sweatshirt, Billy could see the man's biceps were impressive.

"I was middleweight boxing champion in the force, four years in a row. That was back in the day." He sighed. "By the third year they'd renamed the competition 'The Chuck Challenge.' I was one helluva boxer." He gestured to another machine alongside the coffeemaker. "That's the grinder. Should be enough in it. When you've filled the filter, tamp it down to get a decent brew. But don't pack it too tight."

Billy's time as a barista came flooding back to him. He held the filter under the coffee chute and switched on the grinder. "Was that when you were here in England?" he shouted above the noise.

"Yeah, that's right," Chuck shouted back. "I was at Alconbury. Over near Cambridge."

Billy switched off the grinder and tamped down the coffee grounds. "Cambridge is nice." He fixed the filter back under the coffee machine. "One of the actors I trained with is from Cambridge. I've been to stay a couple of times. Beautiful city. Why did you move to London? Did you get bored with the countryside around there? It's quite flat."

Chuck did not answer. Billy looked round to see the wheelchair was gone. Chuck must have gone back to the television. Billy's coffee-making confidence grew and a few minutes later he proudly carried two cups of coffee down the corridor. As he passed Chuck's open bedroom door, he saw the wheels of the wheelchair. He stopped in the doorway.

"You okay?"

Chuck held a framed photograph in his hand. It was in black and white, and showed three airmen dressed in heavy air force overcoats. He shoved the picture towards Billy. "Here," he said. "Take a look."

Billy set the cups of coffee on the bookcase and took the photograph from Chuck. "Which one's you?"

"I'm the good-lookin' one in the middle," Chuck replied. "That's Jeff Zuckerman on the left, and Pete Brady on the right. Winter of sixty-three. Damn it was cold. They used to have a helluva job keeping the ice off the planes."

"How long were you there?"

"RAF Alconbury? Five years."

"But I thought you said you were in the U.S. Air Force, not the RAF?"

"I was," Chuck said impatiently. "But here in the UK we were based at RAF airfields around the country. Churchill leant them to us Americans at the end of the Second World War. Pretty well begged us to stay and keep on defending you guys. He was terrified old Uncle Joe Stalin would come rampaging across Europe, and take Britain as well." Chuck sighed. "They were great years. Even though serious shit was goin' on in the world in them days. The Russkies had built the Berlin Wall in sixty-one. Then we got the Cuban missile crisis in sixty-two. A few years later those damn Russians invaded Czechoslovakia. You thought the bomb would drop any day."

"Sounds scary," Billy said. He looked closely at the photograph of Chuck. He was a handsome man in his youth. "How old were you here?"

"In sixty-three? I'd a been twen'y-three. I came over in August of sixty-two. Two days after my birthday on the first. Jeez. I remember it like yesterday. The boys did a hog roast out in the sun at March for my birthday. Then, two days later, we were in the pourin' rain on the east coast of England."

"March?" asked Billy.

"March Airfield in Riverside. East of Los Angeles. That's where I was based before I came to England. It's where Pa was based durin' the war."

"Your dad was a pilot as well?"

Chuck shook his head. "He was in caterin'. Damn fine cook was Pa. Worked in a big, swanky hotel in LA before they drafted him. He loved it so much at March he never left the base at the end of the war. Brought my mom an' me an' my two brothers to go live with him, an' we grew up in military accommodation. Right there in Riverside."

Billy handed the photograph back to Chuck. "It must have been hard to be sent to England and leave all that behind you. Especially if you were with your family, right there on the base."

Chuck grabbed the wheels of his chair and headed back to the front room. "It was time I split from the family. Especially Pa." Chuck wheeled himself over to a narrow table in the front room. He picked up the TV remote control and switched off the television.

Billy followed him into the room with the coffee cups. He set one down beside Chuck and sat in a high winged armchair opposite. "What happened with your dad? Didn't you miss America?" he asked.

Chuck took a sip from his coffee. "Damn fine coffee, young man," he said. "Couldn't have done it better myself." Billy felt a warm glow at the unexpected praise. Chuck put his cup back on the table. "I miss Alconbury more," Chuck continued. "Those were great days. I got some real good flyin' experience. An' I made some real good friends. Happy days."

"Why did you leave?" Billy asked.

Chuck picked up his coffee cup and took another sip. "That's enough about me, young man," he said. "Tell me about your life."

Chapter 11

Daniel listened as Billy recounted the story of his visit to Chuck. "So he wouldn't tell you any more?"

A little after seven that evening, the two men walked down the road away from the Royal Marsden Hospital. Daniel had gone to meet Billy after a disastrous day at work. It was good to see him again. He slipped his hand into Billy's, and they intertwined their fingers.

Everything had gone wrong for Daniel when he arrived at the musical summer school that day. His keyboard had broken down, one of his support staff was off sick, and nearly forty teenagers turned up for the session, rather than the twenty-five he was promised. It was a relief to meet Billy at the hospital and hear about his day rather than recount his own tale of woe.

"Chuck talked some more about his family in America, but nothing about what happened after the Air Force."

"Perhaps he got sent to Vietnam," Daniel suggested.

Billy shook his head. "I asked him that, and he said no. They covered Europe from that base. But here's the weird thing. I read through the notes Angela gave me for the handover. Chuck only moved to London two years ago. He left the Air Force over fifty years ago, but he continued to live in Cambridge. His notes say he became a heating engineer. It seems strange that he should suddenly move."

"Perhaps his wife died, and he didn't want to stay there," Daniel suggested.

Billy shook his head. "He wasn't married."

"Perhaps he's got friends in London he wants to be near. He's in his seventies now, isn't he?"

"He's about to be seventy-nine," Billy answered. "First of August. Leo the Lion."

"That explains his roar, then. First of August? That's next week, isn't it? Are you doing anything special for his birthday?"

Billy shrugged. "I hadn't thought about it. I've only taken him on as a client recently. I should really sort something out for him. It might cheer him up a bit."

They arrived at the junction where the road turned onto Albert Bridge. The two men stopped to look west at the sun as it sank low in the sky. A lone oarsman, out late on the river, propelled his boat across the water at a rapid pace. Its wake caused orange ripples of light to dance outwards in all directions. A small group of ducks bobbed up and down on the water as waves lapped the riverbank. A dog on the towpath barked excitedly and pulled hard against its owner's lead.

Daniel leaned against the iron railing. He draped his arms over the top and rested his chin on them. Billy stood behind, and wrapped his arms around Daniel's waist.

"This is why I love London," Daniel said. He could feel the stress of the day ebbing away from him. "Less than a mile down the river behind us is madness. Political, economic, and social madness. Ten million people desperately scrambling to make a living." He turned his head to look at Billy. "And here? A tranquil scene straight out of a Turner painting. 'The River at Close of Day'. I could write the music to go with it right now." He turned to kiss Billy on the cheek. "We haven't talked about what we're going to do tonight. Any thoughts?"

Billy smiled and shook his head. "Happy to chill with you," he replied. "I'll stop boring on about Chuck now."

"No, no." Daniel stood away from the railing and turned to face Billy. "I love the way you're so interested in your clients." He rested his hands on Billy's shoulders. "It must be rewarding."

"It's only been rewarding today because I wasn't properly working. I was supposed to be doing that ridiculous presentation skills workshop, remember?" Billy sighed. "What am I going to do? Most days, my work drives me mad. There's endless admin and forms to fill in. My boss is a nightmare and a bully. And I don't have nearly enough time with the clients to make a real difference to their lives. It's one long failure."

"Hey." Daniel leaned his forehead against Billy's. He so wanted to help this beautiful man who had crashed into his life. A man whose unhappiness seemed to ooze from every pore. How had someone with Billy's charm and good looks managed to get himself into such a state?

Daniel answered his own question. *Life.*

As a teenager, Billy had supported his mother when his father walked out. Later, he put his acting career to one side when his mum got sick. He was a good man. A caring man. And his instinct to care had led him to social work. But life, and particularly the dog-eat-dog culture of western society, could be unforgiving to those who cared. Carers were in danger of forever being the ones who came second. And Billy was a creative person who seemed to have lost a sense of his own worth. He needed reminding. Daniel decided this was his new mission—along with everything else in his life.

He leaned in and kissed Billy slowly on the lips. "Don't ever say you're a failure," he said quietly. "If nothing else, you're fucking hot in bed."

Billy laughed.

"That's better," Daniel said. "Your mouth goes all lopsided when you laugh. It's really cute."

Billy lifted his head and looked sideways at Daniel. His eyebrow arched and the slope of his mouth became more pronounced.

"That's a compliment?"

"You know it is," Daniel replied. "So you can stop pulling that puppy dog act with me. I looked you up online this morning. Before the hell that was my day started—"

"Oh shit. Another stalker," Billy said. The lopsided smile turned into a broad grin.

"I quote from Top Television Online," Daniel continued, undeterred. "'As Doctor Hastings in *Blue Lights*, his puppy dog smile endeared him to millions each week'."

"I was a lot younger then—"

"And you're so old now?" Daniel paused before his next question. "How old are you anyway?"

Billy looked indignant. "You should never ask a lady her age—"

"Thirty-eight?"

"Fuck off," Billy said with mock indignation. He grabbed Daniel's waist and began to tickle him. "I'm not even thirty yet."

Daniel was absurdly ticklish. It was something he had never grown out of. He tried to reach Billy's waist to retaliate, but failed and collapsed on the ground in a fit of giggles.

"Stop. Stop," he begged.

Billy obligingly stopped the torture. He held out his hands to help Daniel to his feet. Daniel seized the opportunity to pull Billy's legs from under him. As Billy collapsed to the ground, Daniel began to tickle him in retribution.

"All right, all right. I give in," Billy shouted. "Actually, I'm over forty and past it. Anything you want. But please. Stop."

Daniel released his grasp. The two men lay on the ground, panting.

"So you're twenty-nine and you already think you're past it?" Daniel asked. "What must you think of me? I'm thirty-three next birthday. Over the hill?"

"Excuse me, gentlemen. Are you planning on lying there for the evening? This is a public thoroughfare."

Daniel looked up to see a woman police officer standing over them. He scrambled to his feet and held out his hand to help Billy.

"I'm sorry, officer," he said, dusting down his chinos. "My friend's opening in a new play in the West End soon. He was demonstrating one of the scenes to me. We sort of got carried away."

The police officer stared hard at Billy, who in turn looked at Daniel in bewilderment.

"Actor, are you?" the police officer asked. "Weren't you in that *Blue Lights* thing a few years ago?"

Billy nodded.

She held out her hand. "Pleased to meet you."

Billy shook her hand.

"Shame they killed you off," she continued. "I used to like watching that." The police officer released Billy's hand and straightened her cap.

"And next time you two have a tickling competition," she added, "I suggest you do it out of the public gaze."

Daniel looked up to see a group of half a dozen people had assembled nearby.

"Otherwise I might be forced to book you for disturbing the peace." She winked at them both and walked away.

The group of onlookers continued to stare. Daniel looked across to Billy. "You're the actor," he said in a half whisper. "What do we do for our audience now?"

In response, Billy reached out his arm, pulled Daniel close, and indulged in a long, slow kiss with him.

Two women in the group cheered, and there was a ripple of applause.

Daniel opened one eye to see people smiling and clapping. He pulled away from Billy and grinned. Then they turned, and bowed to their audience.

"Thank you, ladies and gentlemen," Billy said. "We won't be here all week. But if you want to throw money now, you're more than welcome."

All except one of the onlookers started to walk away. A white-haired woman with a walking stick shuffled towards them.

"You were so wonderful in *Blue Lights*, young man," she said. "I thought it was you. But my eyesight isn't so good these days." She turned to Daniel. "Are you his boyfriend?"

Daniel shook his head. "We're just good friends."

"Pity," replied the woman. "You make a lovely couple." And she wandered away.

Billy turned to Daniel, placed his hand on his heart, tossed his head back, and fluttered his eyelashes. "My darling," he said, a mock swoon in his voice. "'Tis Venus. The goddess of love. Sent to us in disguise."

"Heavy disguise," Daniel said with mock seriousness. "Can your actor's ego get massaged any more? Two people within the space of a few minutes remember you from a television show you were in a lifetime ago."

"Do I hear jealousy?" Billy ran his fingers through Daniel's hair. "I'll have you know it's still only four years since I played the dashing Doctor Hastings. Clearly I made an impact on my...significant fan base."

Daniel took hold of Billy's hands and placed them on his own shoulders. He wrapped his arms around Billy's waist and pulled him close. "Which is why it's not too late for you to get back into acting. Is it?"

Billy said nothing.

"Is it?"

"I told you the other night. I don't want to go back to that television fame nonsense."

"You seemed to relish it a moment ago."

Billy smiled and gently massaged Daniel's shoulders. "That was a bit of fun, I admit. But having that constant exposure every day gets…well… hard work. There was a time I couldn't take the bus because I got hassled by people. And *Blue Lights* wasn't exactly cutting edge drama."

"Hang on. Wait one minute." Daniel turned his head as Billy continued to massage his shoulders. It felt good. But he was uncomfortable with the elitist tone Billy seemed to be taking. "Just because it's a television soap doesn't mean it's irrelevant. You could say the same about the music work I do. You could say 'it's just something stupid for kids.'"

"I never said that," Billy protested.

"No, I know. But don't dismiss your own work in that way either." Daniel gestured towards a straggle of the onlookers who had been watching them. They were now some distance away. "Those people enjoyed what you did. Millions of viewers enjoyed it. You brightened their lives. That's important. Don't get so high and mighty in your acting ambitions. You can't always be doing Tennessee Williams."

"Hey, that's unfair." Billy stopped massaging Daniel's shoulders. "How come you're having a dig at me all of a sudden?"

Daniel felt Billy's body tense, and he knew he had said the wrong thing. His intention was to encourage Billy, not anger him. "I'm sorry," he said. "I'm really not having a dig. I just think—" He stopped, as he struggled to choose the right words. "I think you're a really talented guy who's having a shit time right now, and who's letting all that shit discourage him from doing what he really wants to do."

Billy resumed massaging Daniel's shoulders. "And what *do* I want to do?" Billy asked, repeating Daniel's question. He shrugged. "That's the big problem."

"Well, you don't want to keep doing what you're doing at the moment." Daniel leaned forward and kissed Billy. It felt good. The moment of tension between them had passed. Once again, Daniel had put his foot in his mouth. It always happened. He knew he had too many opinions. Sometimes he should keep his mouth shut.

But not at this moment.

Billy's tongue rubbed against his lips, and Daniel opened his mouth to reciprocate. Billy was a passionate kisser. His lips felt warm and full. His tongue stimulated the inside of Daniel's mouth in a way he had never experienced before. Not since that time years ago, at the picnic on Hampstead Heath.

Of course. Daniel had an idea. "Why don't we go on a picnic?"

"What? Now?"

"No, not now. Take your American client, what's his name?"

"Chuck."

"Yes. Take Chuck out for his birthday. The weather's set to be hot for at least the next three weeks. It will get him out of his depressing flat. Maybe it will cheer him up."

Billy's jaw had dropped open, and there was a puzzled expression on his face. "But he's on the seventh floor of that awful building," he said slowly. "And he's in a wheelchair."

"Maggie will lend me her car. It's a bit clapped out, but there's bags of room in it. She might even come along, and then you can meet her."

Daniel began to picture the day in his head. Maggie's big old Volvo crammed with the four of them. Chuck's wheelchair and a big wicker picnic hamper in the back. They could go to Hampstead Heath. Or they could drive out to the countryside. Then Daniel had another big idea.

"We could take him to Cambridge for the day. You say he misses it. I'm free this weekend if you are. Let's take him back there. He'd love it."

"No." Billy put his head on one side. "You've not met Chuck, have you? Because I can tell you now he'll hate the idea."

Daniel felt deflated. It must have shown on his face, because Billy leaned forward and kissed him again. "I'm sorry," he said. "You've made a really generous offer, and I've squashed it flat like a fly swat. You're such a nice guy. It's really kind of you, and I think it's a great idea. But I can't imagine Chuck saying yes. I'd love to go to Cambridge again. I've got an old acting friend who lives out there at weekends. It would be good to see him. He's really cool to hang out with."

Daniel felt triumphant. "There you go," he said. "Maybe this acting friend will encourage you to get your mojo back. Do some creative work again. Talk to Chuck and try to persuade him. If you think it's a great idea, maybe he will too."

Billy smiled. "I'll ask him when I next see him," he said. "I need to try and pitch it right."

Chapter 12

"I've said already. No way."

Chuck picked up the TV remote and switched on the television. The bouncy theme tune of a daytime detective series filled the room. Billy winced at the familiar sound. Early in his career he was cast in one of the episodes. He had played a corpse.

"Chuck."

No response.

"Chuck. Can we talk about it a bit more?"

No response.

"Okay. Well, I'm going to call the bath hoist people for you. Could you turn the TV down a bit, please?"

"You can take the phone in the other room, can't you?"

"They'll need you to answer some questions. You know more about what's wrong with it than I do."

"It's stopped working. What could be simpler?"

Billy sighed. Perhaps he would buy Chuck a birthday card and leave it at that.

They had been in the kitchen making coffee when Billy raised the subject of a trip to Cambridge for Chuck's birthday. As soon as Billy said the word Cambridge, Chuck slammed his coffee mug on the worktop and wheeled himself into the living room.

Billy found the number for the bath hoist company, and waited for them to answer. He waved at Chuck and pointed to his phone. Chuck grunted, lifted the remote control, and the music on the television dropped in volume.

"Hi," said Billy into his phone. "I'm calling on behalf of Chuck Stuart. I'm his carer."

Chuck harrumphed. He raised the remote control once more, switched off the television, and looked at Billy as if to say *satisfied now?*

"His bath hoist has gone wrong."

Billy nodded a thank you to Chuck as he listened to the voice on the other end of the phone.

"It's seven-one-two, Churchill Buildings, Bullingdon Place, London, EC two."

Chuck tipped his cupped hand at Billy to ask if he wanted a drink. Billy gave him a thumbs-up. Chuck began to wheel himself into the kitchen.

"Sure. I'll hold."

A tinny version of Handel's Water Music began to play in Billy's ear. He switched the phone to its loudspeaker.

"Do you want me to come and help?" asked Billy.

"Suit yourself," called Chuck from the hallway.

Billy stood and followed Chuck into the kitchen.

"Just how were you proposing to get me to Cambridge anyway?" Chuck asked. He held the metal coffee filter in his hand. "Magic carpet? It's a helluva way."

"Daniel offered to borrow a car from his friend and drive us there," Billy replied. He leaned against the kitchen worktop, placed his phone on it, and folded his arms in front of him. "It was a generous offer on his part. He didn't have to."

"And who's Daniel?" Chuck asked. Before Billy could reply, Chuck switched on the coffee grinder. The kitchen was filled with the machine's screech. After a few moments, Chuck switched it off and tamped down the coffee in the filter.

"Oh, I remember," he said. "He's your fancy man, isn't he?" He fitted the coffee filter back under the machine and gave it a hard twist to the right to lock it in place.

"Does that bother you?" Billy asked.

"Why the hell should it?" Chuck responded. "None of my damn business. And you're right. It is generous of…waddya say his name was?"

"Daniel," Billy said. The tinny version of Handel's Water Music still squawked from his phone.

"Does he know I'm a miserable old son of a bitch in a wheelchair?"

Billy smiled. "I told him it was your birthday next week. The first thing he asked me was what I was going to do to help you celebrate. We don't have to go to Cambridge for a picnic. We could go to some other place in the country. But I've got some old friends near Cambridge who I haven't seen for a while."

"Why the hell would they want to spend their time at my birthday party?"

At least Chuck was talking about the possibility of going out. He had moved on from a flat refusal.

"To be honest, I hadn't really thought it through. But after the way you'd talked about Cambridge the other day, and how you said you'd had such a good time there, I wanted you to have a good time for your birthday. Daniel suggested a picnic. It's a beautiful summer. And you're stuck inside here all day—"

"All right, all right."

Chuck wiped the front of the coffee machine with a cloth. He seemed to wipe the cloth over the same spot again and again. As if lost in thought.

"It's no big deal. If you don't want to go, we'll say no more about it."

"No big deal. Easy for you to say." Chuck switched on the coffee machine. "I'll think about it."

Billy felt a small moment of triumph. It was strange how Chuck had initially reacted so strongly against the idea. And he was curious to know why Chuck had lost his nostalgia for Cambridge. But at least the picnic was no longer completely rejected.

For the moment.

Billy decided to let the idea sink in, and not attempt to persuade Chuck any more. The two men waited as the coffee filtered into two cups below. The gurgling of the machine was accompanied by Handel's Water Music rattling the tiny speaker of Billy's phone. Neither of them said anything.

The music was cut short by a woman's voice on the telephone. "Hello? Mr Stuart?"

Chuck jolted, and his wheelchair shot back against the cabinet behind him. "Jeez, lady," Chuck shouted. "You scared the shit outta me."

***

By the time Billy reached the hospital that evening it was after six. He hurried up the stairs two at a time to the third floor. When he peered through the small glass porthole in the door of his mother's room, he could see her sitting up in bed. He watched as she dipped a piece of bread into a bowl of soup and lifted it to her mouth. She chewed slowly and methodically, almost as though it was painful.

"It's the Divine Sarah," Billy announced as he pushed open the door and entered the room. It had become his pet name for her when he first discovered it was the nickname of the legendary Sarah Bernhardt. His mother looked up from her plate and made a playful pout at him.

"*'Your words are my food'*," she began.

"*'Your breath my wine'*," Billy continued. He crossed to the bed. "*'You are everything to me'*."

He leaned over to his mother and kissed her on her forehead.

"Divine Sarah. Such beautiful words."

Billy sat on the edge of the bed. He took care not to disturb his mother's supper tray.

"It's lovely to see you sitting up and eating again. How are you feeling today?"

"Mustn't grumble," she replied brightly. "I got quite hungry this afternoon, so I've been eatin' like a pig. They're ever so good to me in here. Do anythin' for me. They've been bringin' me extra food. I won't be able to fit into this nightdress soon."

It was an ironic statement. Sarah Walsh's arms were half the size they had been when she was well. Her skin was almost translucent, with the outline of the bones clearly visible beneath. Her cheeks were sunken, and the flesh on her neck hung crinkled and folded. But her eyes were bright, and they retained the shadow of radiant beauty Billy once remembered.

"Do you want to move this out of the way?" she asked, indicating the supper tray.

"No, no," Billy replied. "Finish it first. You need to build up your strength again."

His mother wrinkled her nose. "It's gone a bit cold, to be honest. They do their best. But it probably had to travel a long way from the kitchens. Put it over there."

Billy lifted the tray and placed it on the floor by the door. He returned to the bed and sat down again. "Don't let the nurse catch you doin' that," his mother admonished. There was a twinkle in her eye. "Visitors aren't supposed to sit on the beds."

Billy held his hand to his mouth and feigned shock. "Is it terribly naughty?" he asked.

"Oh yes. Terribly," his mother replied. She laid a hand on his knee. "But don't you move. I want you 'ere. And I'll defend you to the last if they come in an' complain."

Billy leaned forward and kissed his mother on the cheek. Her skin felt cold beneath his lips.

"So what 'ave you been up to today?" she asked.

"Working." Billy sighed. "I've got a new client and he's proving to be a bit difficult. He seems awfully angry every time I go to see him."

"People who are angry usually have somethin' to be angry about," his mother declared. "And it's often somethin' pretty silly. But they won't admit it to themselves. So they never sort it out. And as they get older, they get less and less likely to sort it out." She gave Billy's thigh a gentle squeeze. "Don't ever stay angry, son," she said. "It's a pointless waste of time. I could have stayed angry with your dad, even though 'e left years ago. But why bother?" She lifted her hand and caressed Billy's cheek. "'e was a stupid man. Look what he missed out on. A beautiful son. A successful son. His loss, not ours."

"You must have been angry when he left?"

Sarah's grip on Billy's thigh tightened. She was surprisingly strong for such a frail woman. "I was 'oppin' mad. I could've killed him." She leaned in conspiratorially. "I nearly did once. I'd just got out of 'ospital after the op. You remember?"

Billy nodded. He had started at the big school down the road a few months before. He remembered having to stay at a school friend's for two nights while his mother was in hospital.

"How do you mean 'you nearly killed him'?"

"I'd 'ad me women's op. Doctors discharged me and told me to rest at 'ome. So I couldn't work for two weeks. An' I wasn't bein' paid. I didn't know where the next meal was comin' from. Anyway. In the middle of all this, 'e turns up on the doorstep unannounced. I was actually pleased to see 'im. I pleaded with 'im to stay. Begged 'im. You was out at school. Do you know what 'e said?"

She pulled on Billy's thigh to lever her face closer to his. "'e said 'e 'adn't married me to be a nursemaid to a scrounging malingerer. Imagine? I said, 'You get out and never come back'."

"You never told me that."

Sarah released her grasp and lay back with a sigh onto her pillow. "I didn't want to make you feel bad about your dad. You was only eleven."

Billy was shocked. He remembered coming home from school one day to find her lying on the couch in tears. She had told him it was because of the pain from her operation. And he had believed her. All those years when he was a teenager and dutifully visited his father for a day each week, had he known, he never would have gone.

He slipped his arm under his mother's shoulders and drew her close to hug her gently. She felt frail, as if she might snap like a twig. Her shoulders twitched, and he heard gentle sobbing beneath him. He ran his fingers through her thinning hair. The same way she would stroke his hair when he was a child.

Her voice was part muffled against his chest. "I'm sorry, son. I tried to do what I thought was best for you."

Billy comforted her for several minutes, until she pushed gently against him, and he released his hold.

"That's enough bein' miserable." Sarah wiped the tears away from her eyes. "I want to know about what you're up to. How's that lovely man of yours? What's 'is name? Jason?"

Billy had forgotten how the illness or the drugs sometimes affected his mother's memory. She confused the past with the present.

He patted her arm. "Jason was over a year ago, Mum," he said. "I've started seeing someone else now."

"But I thought you an' Jason was so close," Sarah replied. "'e was really ill wasn't 'e? Pneumonia? And you looked after 'im all through it."

Billy sighed. He had told her about the reasons for his breakup with Jason when it first happened. But now he could only guess at how his mother's memories were muddled in her mind.

"I did. But he's got better. Sort of."

Billy wanted to tell his mother about Daniel. How happy he felt. Maybe it was too soon. It was only a few weeks after all. Perhaps he should wait until the relationship—if it was to become a relationship—had developed a bit further. Her voice jolted him from his musings.

"You were so happy with 'im," she continued. "Australian, wasn't he? Very tall. Very good-lookin'. I would have fancied 'im meself if he wasn't interested in you." She winked at Billy, who tried to smile back. But his mother could read him too well. "Why so glum all of a sudden?" she asked. "Do you miss 'im?"

Billy shook his head.

"Not at all. It's…things didn't end well with Jason. I'd rather not talk about him. Let's talk about something else."

"Oh, right. Yes of course." Sarah looked down at her hands. She rested her palms on the bedcovers and distractedly smoothed out the creases in the white linen sheet. "You said you had a new fella. Is he as good-looking as Jason?"

Billy reached out and held her agitated hands in his. "Mum. Please don't talk about Jason. He wasn't good for me."

She looked up at him and smiled. It was a *here we go again* sort of smile. "So is this new fella good-looking? What's his name?"

"Daniel. He's a musician. Well, music director in fact. He's great. Kind. He's…nice." It seemed a lame description for the days he had already spent with Daniel. "He makes me happy." That was better. Although it was still insufficient to describe how he felt right now about Daniel.

Sarah gave her son's fingers a squeeze and smiled. It was a more contented *I'm pleased for you* kind of smile. "When can I meet him?"

Billy laughed. "It's all a bit soon," he said. "But I'll see if he'll come along one day. We're going on a picnic next week."

"Ooh, that'll be nice. Where are you going?"

"Cambridge. Well." Billy stopped. He was still waiting to hear if Chuck would agree to go to Cambridge. Or even go on the picnic. "At least, we should be going to Cambridge. We're taking one of my clients for his birthday. He's going to be seventy-nine next week."

Sarah looked surprised. "You're goin' on a date and you're takin' one of your clients with you? What on earth are they goin' to do? Play gooseberry while you two look all dewy-eyed at each other?"

"It was Daniel's idea." Billy was stung by his mother's criticism. "And I thought it was really kind of him. That's the sort of man he is."

Sarah patted his arm. "It's all well and good 'im being nice, or kind," she said. "But you're a young man, Billy. You need more than that. Is 'e—?" She paused, leaving the incomplete question hanging in the air.

Billy raised an eyebrow. "Is he what, Mother?" He sniffed, affecting the tone of a character from an Oscar Wilde play.

Sarah looked at him sternly. "You know exactly what I mean," she said, a note of irritation in her voice. "Is 'e a good shag?"

Billy laughed. At that moment his phone rang. He looked to see who was calling before he answered it.

"Hi, Daniel," he said, and winked at his mother. "Your ears must be burning. We were just talking about you. You'll never guess what Mum asked me."

Chapter 13

Daniel warmed to Chuck soon after meeting him. The cantankerous man was certainly a challenge, but an interesting one. He behaved like some of the more difficult children he worked with in music therapy. The difficult ones were often the most creative, and for that reason they interested him. He believed rules had to be broken for someone's imagination to be set free. The constraints of convention tied people to traditional, accepted ways of doing things. Adults rarely challenged what is deemed normal for fear of being alienated by the group they belonged to. As they got older, adults settled into a safe, secure, and ultimately dull existence, based on the need to feel accepted. Daniel called it *The Rut of Respectability*.

By contrast, most children were happily unconstrained by the pressures of societal norms. The more interesting ones openly challenged when they were told to "do the right thing."

Chuck was one of those interesting ones.

"What the hell are ya doin'?" he barked as Daniel pushed Chuck's wheelchair towards the top of the staircase outside his flat. The landing was lit by a single fluorescent light, which flickered on and off at random intervals. There was no natural light, but there was a definite smell of stale urine. Brown watermarks stained the bare cement walls. Faded graffiti was barely legible in the flickering light.

"We're going to carry you downstairs," replied Daniel. "Seeing as the lift's broken."

Daniel took hold of the wheelchair's detachable armrest and tried to remove it.

"Let go," Chuck said. "No need to do that. They fixed the goddam elevator two days ago." He turned to glare at Daniel. "You think I'd make you two fellas carry me down seven flights of stairs otherwise?" Chuck snorted. "Damn fool. Don't tell me you walked up all those stairs this morning? When there's a perfectly good elevator?"

Daniel smiled. He fixed the armrest back on the chair. "We can always do with the exercise." He released the brakes and spun the chair away from the stairs. Billy emerged from Chuck's apartment carrying a shopping bag.

"Forget something?" Billy asked.

"We don't need the stairs," Daniel said. "Apparently the lift's fixed."

Billy looked at Chuck. "Why didn't you tell us?"

"You never asked." Chuck shrugged. "Our luck if the damn thing breaks down again this morning."

Billy pressed the call button. "Well, if it does we can sit inside it and have a nice long chat," he said.

"I can't believe you guys were even thinkin' of carryin' me down those damn stairs." Chuck shook his head. "Do you know how heavy I am?" He turned to look over his shoulder at Daniel. "You're some guy, you know? What makes you give up your day off to come carry a two-hundred-pound lump of lard down seven flights of stairs? You must be mad."

Daniel squatted on his haunches alongside Chuck. He opened his eyes wide, in what he hoped was an approximation of Heath Ledger's character The Joker in *The Dark Knight*. His voice was breathy and agitated as he spoke.

"Maybe I am. So you'd better watch out. Especially when I've got control of your wheelchair at the top of a flight of stairs." He jerked the arm of the wheelchair. Hard.

"Yeah?" Chuck responded defiantly. But his voice had lost some of its confident tone.

Daniel laughed. "Only kidding," he said. "I'm a guy who likes to meet new people. Whoever they are. Billy's told me a lot about you."

"Oh yeah?" Chuck said again. His voice had regained its confidence. He looked up at Billy. "What you been sayin'?"

Billy warmed to Daniel's teasing. He squatted alongside Daniel, rested his hand on the arm of Chuck's wheelchair, and smiled beatifically. "That you're a nice, sweet old man who's stuck in his gloomy flat all day."

Chuck snorted. "Less of the old, sonny," he said. He turned from Billy to Daniel. "How long have you two been dating, then?"

The directness of the question took Daniel by surprise. He looked across to Billy, who stood hurriedly. Daniel opened his mouth to speak, but he was interrupted by the ping of a bell.

"Lift's here," said Billy brightly. There was the sound of relief in his voice. He stood aside to let Chuck and Daniel pass.

"Who says we're dating?" Daniel asked. He carefully steered the wheelchair into the confines of the gloomy stainless steel box in front of them. "We might be nothing more than suitable friends. You never know."

He turned to kiss Billy, who followed behind. "What do you think, Billy?"

From the depths of the chair they heard Chuck snort contemptuously.

Daniel blinked as they emerged from the entrance of the apartment block into the intense light of another bright summer's day. He unhooked his sunglasses from the neck of his T-shirt and put them on. It was not yet ten in the morning, but the heat of the day had already begun to build. Daniel paused for a moment as he felt the warm air on his face and bare arms. It was in stark contrast to the damp chill in the apartment block.

"What you waitin' for? Lost the car?"

"Feel that warmth, Chuck," Daniel said. "Isn't it glorious? Now don't you wish you'd put your shorts on?"

Both Daniel and Billy wore shorts, but Chuck had refused point blank.

"You want me to look even more ridiculous?" he asked. "As if I didn't feel bad enough already. Stuck in this damn chair."

"Cooee, Daniel," called a woman's voice. "Over here."

A woman wearing dungarees and a thin cotton blouse stood by a dilapidated Volvo. Her faded auburn hair was gathered together in an untidy ponytail. Her tanned face was lit by a beaming smile.

"And who the hell's that?" asked Chuck. "Your girlfriend?"

Daniel pushed Chuck's chair rapidly towards the car. "That's Maggie," he said. "Our chauffeur for the day."

"Hurry up," Maggie called. "I'm parked on a yellow line, and there's an army of wardens round here."

Daniel stopped the wheelchair alongside the car. Maggie leaned forward and kissed him on the cheek.

"Thanks for doing this, darling," Daniel said. "You're an angel. Let me introduce you to your passenger and co-pilot for the day. Chuck Stuart."

Maggie looked down and held out her hand. "Delighted to meet you, Chuck," she said. "It's all right to call you Chuck, is it?"

"It's my name, lady," Chuck harrumphed. He reached out, grasped Maggie's hand, and shook it firmly. "It's better than hey you."

Maggie turned to Billy. "And you must be the famous Billy I've heard so much about." She looked at Daniel and arched an eyebrow.

Billy leaned forward and kissed her on either cheek. "And you must be the famous Maggie I've heard so much about." He stepped back and turned to Daniel. "Is a raised eyebrow a good signal or a bad one?"

Maggie laughed. "Oh darling. A raised eyebrow from me is *such* a good signal." She placed an exaggerated stress on the word such. "I always told Daniel he'd strike it lucky one day. And it looks like he has."

Daniel hoped Maggie would hold back on any more comments about Billy. After all, they only met a few weeks ago. They were hardly going steady. He looked past Maggie to see a woman wearing a uniform and a peaked cap approach them.

"You might want to try to sweet-talk that traffic warden, Mags," he said. "Although I've got a feeling it's already too late."

"Oh shit." Maggie turned and walked briskly towards the warden.

"Young man," Chuck said to Billy. "If you look inside that bag you're holding, you'll find my blue badge."

Billy opened the shopping bag and rummaged inside. He pulled out a blue disabled parking permit and held it in front of Chuck. "Why didn't you say you had one of these in the first place?" he asked.

"I think I know the answer to that," Daniel said before Chuck had a chance to respond. "It's because—"

"I didn't ask," Billy finished.

Chuck sat back in his chair and folded his arms. "You two are learnin'," he said. There was a note of triumph in his voice.

Billy ran across to Maggie with the parking permit. A few minutes later they both returned. There was a broad grin on Maggie's face.

"Oh my God," she said to Chuck. "You're my knight in a shining wheelchair. You should ride with me more often. Those blue badges are gold dust. How much to hire you for a journey?"

Billy wagged his finger at Maggie and shook his head.

"I'd wait until you've spent a day in the car with him before you offer invitations like that," he said. "You don't just get the blue badge. Chuck has to travel with you as well."

"Hold on a goddam minute, fella," Chuck complained. "Are you tryin' to say I'm bad company? Because let me tell you," he looked up at Maggie, and winked, "with the right company, I can charm the birds from the goddam trees."

"Well, now's your chance to charm this particular old bird, my darling," Maggie cooed. She opened the front passenger door and held her arm out to the seat. "In you hop. We've got a long journey ahead of us. Especially with the Saturday traffic." She patted the roof of her car. "And Velma here doesn't go as fast as she used to."

"Velma?" Chuck stood up before Daniel had a chance to apply the brakes on the wheelchair. He half walked, half shuffled over to the car at a surprising pace, and settled himself into the front seat. "Why the hell did you call your car Velma?" he asked as he fumbled with the seatbelt.

Daniel folded up the wheelchair and took it round to the back of the car. "Maggie named it after Velma Dingley." He collapsed the wheelchair and swung it into the car. "Velma was the smart one in Scooby Doo. I guess you never watched the cartoon. It was a TV series."

"Sure I did," Chuck said. "We used to watch it in the afternoons sometimes."

Maggie got into the car and started the engine. She turned to look at Chuck and arched an eyebrow once more. "We?" she asked. "Who's this 'we'? Is there a significant other?"

Daniel climbed into the back seat behind Maggie and turned to Billy, who was trying to fasten his seat belt. "You didn't mention Chuck had a partner?" he whispered.

"That's 'cause I ain't got one," Chuck said. "And don't you fellas start whisperin' about me in the back there. 'Cause I can hear you loud an' clear."

Billy rested his hand on Daniel's knee, leaned over, and kissed him. "Thank you for doing this," he whispered into Daniel's ear. "It's really generous of you and Maggie. I hope Chuck behaves himself. So I'm going to say sorry in advance. In case he does anything or says anything—"

The car lurched violently as Maggie accelerated into the stream of traffic on the main road, and then braked suddenly. Daniel was thrown against Billy, and the two men crashed against the back of Chuck's seat.

"Hey, hey. What you two doin' back there?" Chuck snapped.

Daniel looked up to see Maggie's face in the rearview mirror. This time, both eyebrows were raised.

"Now, boys," she said. "No canoodling in the backseat while I'm driving. You might distract me."

"Don't worry 'bout them, young lady," Chuck said. "You an' I can have a nice chat up front here, an' leave the kids to horse aroun'."

Daniel sat back in his seat and sorted out the tangle of his seatbelt. He caught a glimpse of Chuck's face in the wing mirror. Was he mistaken, or was the man actually smiling? He grasped the headrest of Chuck's seat and leaned forward.

"Now, Chuck," he said. "You look after Maggie today. You're going to be her wingman. Make sure she doesn't stray from the straight and narrow."

Maggie laughed loudly. "Too late for that, my darling," she said. "I left the straight and narrow years ago. As well you know it, Daniel Richards."

The gearbox grumbled noisily, as Maggie appeared to select a gear at random without troubling the clutch. She regarded Daniel in the rearview mirror with a quizzical look. "Where are we going to, then?" she asked. "You've brought enough food to feed a small town. Is anyone else joining us on this picnic?" Maggie glanced away from the road to look at Chuck. "I nearly forgot. Happy birthday. Is it today?"

Chuck shook his head. "Last Wednesday. Not that it matters a damn at my age."

"Oh, nonsense and fiddlesticks," Maggie said. "I'm the wrong side of fifty and I relish every birthday I have. They're an opportunity to thank God one's still alive." She leaned over to Chuck and added in a confidential manner. "Those children in the back don't know what it's like to have survived as long as us."

Chuck nodded enthusiastically. "Too right, lady."

"Are we nearly there yet?" Billy called. He raised the pitch of his voice to that of a petulant teenager.

Daniel chuckled. "Yes, Mummy," he added, in a similar high voice. "Are we nearly there yet? Billy's going to need a weewee soon." He grabbed Billy's side and began to tickle him. Billy folded up in a fit of giggles.

"Stop it," he cried. "Stop. Please."

"Oh for God's sake, Daniel," Maggie said. The gearbox made another loud complaining sound. "Are you going to be like this the whole journey? Will you two stop for a second and answer the driver's question? Where are we heading?"

Daniel stopped tickling, grasped Billy's thigh, and gave it a squeeze. Billy turned and kissed him again on the lips.

"Cambridge," they said together.

Maggie let out a deep sigh. "Yes, my darlings. I know that already. But where in Cambridge?"

Daniel sat back in his seat and watched the construction sites of East London speed past the window. "Well," he said. "We were thinking how difficult it is to park in the middle of the city so we thought we'd stop outside Cambridge. We've arranged with Billy's friends to meet them in Grantchester. We'll have a picnic on the green."

"Stands the church clock at ten to three," Billy began.

"And is there honey still for tea?" Maggie finished the verse for him. "Yes, Billy my sweet. I have heard of Rupert Brooke's poetry. I studied the war poets for English Lit at school. Admittedly it was a few years ago. But some poets stay with you."

"No." Chuck's voice interrupted the banter. Maggie glanced away from the road to look at him.

"What's the matter?" she asked.

"Like I said. No," Chuck repeated. He stared straight in front of him at the road. "No way I'm goin' to Grantchester."

Daniel leaned forward. "What's wrong with Grantchester? It's a lot easier—"

Chuck turned his head with difficulty to glare at Daniel. "Didn't you hear me the first time, sonny? I'm not goin' to Grantchester. You can turn the car round right now."

Chapter 14

Maggie was the first to break the uneasy silence in the car. "Daniel my dear," she said, brightly. "Why don't we picnic by the river in the middle of Cambridge? There's absolutely no need to worry about parking. We've got Chuck's magic blue badge. We can drive right up to Midsummer Common and park in a disabled space there."

"Of course," Daniel said with relief. Chuck's reaction had caught him by surprise. It was partly aggressive. But it also sounded fearful. "I'd forgotten about that." He leaned over to Billy. "Will it be okay if your friends meet us there?"

"Oh sure," Billy answered. "I'll give Tom and Simon a ring now. They can easily get the bus into Cambridge. And we can sit by the Cam in Cambridge instead of Grantchester."

Maggie reached across and patted Chuck's leg. "All sorted, my lovely," she said. "Any reason why Grantchester gives you the heebie-jeebies?"

Chuck said nothing. He leaned back in the seat and closed his eyes. Maggie looked at Daniel in the rearview mirror, and mouthed *What the fuck?* Daniel shrugged. He turned to Billy, who shook his head and took out his mobile phone.

"Hey, Simon?" Billy said. "Yeah, yeah. All good. We're on our way. Traffic doesn't look too bad so far—"

"Don't jinx me," called Maggie from the front. "We haven't got to the motorway yet."

"Yeah," Billy continued. "Daniel's designer friend's driving. Maggie Ambler. She's kindly lent us her car."

Billy paused.

"No way?" He leaned forward to Maggie. "Simon says he knows you."

"I'm sure he does, if he's an actor." replied Maggie. "I've worked with pretty well everyone in the business." She caught

Daniel's eye in the mirror and winked. "Anyone who's worth knowing that is. What's his name?"

"Simon," Billy said. "Simon McDonald."

The car lurched as Maggie swerved to avoid a pedestrian who mistakenly assumed he had the right-of-way on a pedestrian crossing.

"Oh my God," she said. "Sexy Simon? God's gift to the human race? Of course I know him. You remember him, don't you, Daniel?"

Daniel wracked his brain. He had met many of Maggie's friends over the years. Usually at one of her outrageous Sunday lunch parties. The lavish events started at midday and often went on until at least midnight. Maggie invited an eclectic mix of television, stage, and film people. Somehow she managed to get the right balance of egos to guarantee an afternoon and evening of highly entertaining, competitive conversations.

"Doesn't ring a bell," he said.

"Of course you do," Maggie said dismissively. "He came to my Mayday madness lunch a few months ago. Turned up on his motorbike in the tightest fitting leathers I've ever seen. You could clearly see the outline of his—"

"Hi, Simon," said Billy loudly into his phone. "Maggie says *hi*. Look. There's a slight change of plan. Are you okay to meet on Midsummer Common instead? We thought it would be nice to come right into Cambridge." Billy listened for a moment. "Yeah. It's not a problem. Chuck, that's my client. He's got a blue badge. So we can park in a disabled bay." There was another pause. "Really? Oh, cool. Okay. See you later."

Billy ended the call and turned to Daniel. "Tom can get us into the rowing club car park," he said. "It's right on Midsummer Common. He's got a free pass. Apparently he used to row for Cambridge."

Daniel clasped Billy's thigh. "A rower, is he?" he said. "I wonder if he's got thighs as hunky as yours?"

"If Simon's anything to go by," Maggie said, "he'll be like an Adonis." She licked her lips appreciatively. "Lots to look at this afternoon." She turned to her passenger. "What do you think, Chuck? Looking forward to your birthday party now?"

The sound of snoring answered that question.

***

Cambridge was full. A small city that was completely overrun with summer students and tourists. The narrow streets and lanes were crammed with people. Velma the Volvo crawled along Chesterton Road towards the University boathouse. Maggie had insisted on taking the scenic route along the River Cam so they could admire the famous view of King's College Chapel. That meant they hit one traffic jam after another as they neared their destination.

Daniel first visited Cambridge when he was a teenager. He made the hour-long train journey from London for an interview to study at Trinity College. His music teacher had been a student there, and she had pulled a few strings to get Daniel the invitation. The interview was on a freezing February day. Cambridge was bleak, and it was snowing. The interview had gone badly, and he hated the stuffy, elitist attitude of the gown-wearing men who interviewed him. The strong sense of claustrophobia only left him when he got back on the train, and he headed back to London. A few weeks later, much to his relief, he won a scholarship to the Royal College of Music in London.

Today, as he listened to Maggie's breathless commentary about the beauty of Cambridge, he wondered if he had misjudged the city. Chesterton Road followed the course of the Cam as the river flowed past a large expanse of fields called The Backs. Beyond the fields was the graceful Gothic architecture of King's College Chapel, reproduced on a thousand tourist postcards. Daniel could see people lounging in the meadows beside the river, picnicking, or simply sunbathing. Meanwhile, handsome young men wearing straw boaters, striped T-shirts, and blue shorts propelled tourists along the river in graceful, flat-bottomed punts. It could have been a scene straight out of E. M. Forster's *Maurice*.

After Chuck's earlier outburst, Daniel had lost his initial enthusiasm for the day, even though it had been his idea. Chuck made no effort to explain why he was opposed to going to Grantchester. For much of the hour-long journey he dozed in the front seat, despite Maggie's frequent attempts to cajole him into conversation. It was only when she pointed out the signs to the Duxford aircraft museum south of Cambridge that Chuck woke up. Maggie usually found a way to win over grumpy people. It was something Daniel had long admired in her. But he wondered if she had met her match with Chuck.

"You're not planning on wheeling me across them meadows, are you?" he asked, looking out at The Backs. "The wheels on that darn wheelchair are soon gonna give out if you are."

"No, Chuck, darling," Maggie replied. She waved at the large number of people on the river. "We're going to strap you to a punt, and take bets on how long it will be before you tip into the river. Aren't we, boys?"

Billy leaned forward and rested his hands on the back of Maggie's seat. "Now, now," he said. "Chuck can walk a little way without his chair, can't you?"

There was a loud snort from the passenger seat.

"So why use a wheelchair at all if you can walk?" Maggie asked.

"Because I need it, lady."

"He's got nerve damage in his feet and legs," Billy answered quickly. "It comes and goes. But when it's bad it hurts him to walk."

Maggie stopped the car suddenly, as another group of tourists meandered out in front of them. "That's rotten luck," she said. "My sister used to have something similar with her legs. When they were bad it was excruciating. She could hardly walk at all. She wasn't one for malingering, and I'm sure you're not either, my dear."

"I hate bein' in that darn thing," he said. "I'll do my best to walk a bit today. Given how you folks have all been so kind to me."

"Oh, think nothing of it, dear man," Maggie said. "Any excuse for a bloody good party. It's your birthday. That's excuse enough for me."

The car lurched forward once more. Seeing a clear road ahead, Maggie accelerated hard. Billy was thrown back onto Daniel. After little more than a hundred yards, Maggie swung the car sharply to the left into the entrance of the University Boat Club.

"You didn't warn me about her driving," Billy whispered to Daniel as he struggled to sit up again.

"I thought you might relish the sense of unbridled adventure," Daniel whispered back. "Especially as you said the other night you were looking to do something different with your life."

"Doing something different doesn't include nearly getting killed in the back of a clapped-out Volvo." Billy kissed Daniel on the lips. "Even if it's with a cool music director."

"Now then, you two. No necking in the back of my car please. This is a respectable vehicle." Maggie swung open her door and got out. She stretched her arms above her head and twisted her neck from side to side.

Daniel and Billy unfastened their seatbelts and climbed out of the car. It was warm inside the Volvo. The air conditioning was clearly long overdue for a service. The temperature outside was even hotter. Daniel stood in the full heat of the lunchtime sun, extended his limbs, and luxuriated in the warm breeze.

It was going to be a good day. Chuck appeared to have softened, thanks to Maggie's sympathetic, yet no-nonsense approach. Billy was on good form, and the two men bantered throughout the journey. It was a welcome surprise to discover Billy had a wicked sense of fun beneath the surface of his fretful seriousness. Maybe today would give Billy the chance to leave behind the stress of his mother's illness.

"Hey, Billy." A tall man strode towards them. He was stripped to the waist, and wore pale blue shorts and espadrilles. It had to be Simon. Maggie's label of Adonis was not far from the truth. His chest and shoulders clearly benefited from frequent trips to the gym. His thighs were like tree trunks, and his sharply trimmed beard highlighted the dimple in the middle of his cleft jaw. He was irritatingly handsome.

"Good to see you. How you doing?"

Simon's accent was difficult to place, it sounded somewhere between South African and New Zealand. Daniel usually had an ear for accents, but this one had him stumped. Billy and Simon first embraced, and then kissed on either cheek.

"Where's Tom?" Billy asked.

Simon pointed to the river. "We got here early and found a great spot for a picnic. Tom's making sure no one nabs it from us."

"Daniel," Billy called. "Come and meet Simon."

Daniel stepped forward and held out his hand. Simon grabbed it firmly, pulled Daniel towards him, and they hugged tightly. Daniel held on to Simon to steady himself. There was clearly not an ounce of fat on Simon's toned body.

"Great to meet you, mate." Simon's broad grin displayed a mouth full of perfectly white teeth. "Good to know someone's keeping this guy protected and safe from the world."

Not only did Simon have an apparently perfect body, but his comment betrayed an insight to Billy that surprised Daniel. Did the man have no failings?

"Oh, you know." Daniel felt overwhelmed by Simon's confidence. "We've met recently. I'm along for the ride and to help out with Chuck."

"Oh, he's the old guy, right?" Simon asked.

"Don't you go using words like old, young man," Maggie warned. She had her hands on her hips and looked at Simon with one eyebrow firmly raised. "Especially when there's the likes of me hanging around."

"Maggie." Simon strode towards her and hugged her.

"Jesus, Simon. Are you eating steroids with every meal now?" Maggie pushed him back forcefully. She reached for her sunglasses, which were tangled in a knot of hair on the top of her head, and set them into position on her nose. She put her hands back on her hips and tilted her head to one side.

"*Theseus the musical*," she said. "You were a statue that came to life. Adonis, if I'm not mistaken. Zipped up in that fetching fig leaf catsuit every night." She tilted her head to look him up and down. "You've grown even more since we first met. I doubt you'd fit into it now."

Simon laughed. "That's right. It was such a cool set you designed for that production. Didn't you win the Olivier that year?"

Maggie sniffed. "Nominated, darling. Sadly, I was passed over. Again." She straightened up and folded her arms in front of her. "So what are you doing now? Hercules?"

Simon laughed again. "Not far off. I'm about to head back home to New Zealand for three months. Shooting a Netflix series about Troy." He turned to Billy. "You should come down while I'm there. Stay with my folks. They'd love to meet you." He turned to Daniel. "You too, mate. They'd put you up for a couple of weeks, no sweat."

Billy shook his head. "I can't really leave London at the moment. Mum's ill, and I'm visiting her nearly every day." He shrugged. "Maybe another time."

"Oh shit," said Simon. "I forgot Sarah was sick. I'm so sorry, mate."

He stepped forward and hugged Billy again. Daniel was forced to admit his initial dismissal of Simon as another vain, gym-loving actor was misjudged.

"Hey. Anyone remember me?"

Daniel turned to see Chuck struggling to get out of the car.

"I'm sorry, Chuck." Billy turned to Simon. "That's my client," he said. "He's the one whose birthday we're celebrating today." Billy started to walk back to the car. "Daniel, can you get the wheelchair out of the back, while I help Chuck?"

Daniel nodded. As he turned to walk back to the car, his mobile phone rang. He looked down at the screen.

Anthony.

Chapter 15

Chuck needed no assistance to get out of the car. Billy thought he was almost a different man to the one who slowly propelled himself about his flat in a wheelchair. He dismissed Billy's offer of help and stood unaided alongside the car.

"Don't worry about me, young man," Chuck said with a sniff. "I took a couple of those horse pills the doctor dishes out. They work a treat. No pain at all today." He leaned against the car and breathed heavily. "Just floatin' on the ceiling. Not sure what's in them, but I'm goin' to have some darn interestin' dreams tonight."

"Are you sure you're okay?" Billy asked. "Don't you want the wheelchair?"

"Of course I do," Chuck said. He blew out his cheeks and continued to breathe heavily. "Just 'cause there's no pain doesn't mean I've suddenly got strength in ma legs. The darn muscles are just wastin' away stuck in that damn contraption all day."

"I need to get some physio booked for you," Billy said. "I'll sort it out next week." He looked around for Daniel, but he had walked off, his mobile phone clutched to his ear. Billy turned back to Chuck. "Are you okay to hang on there while I get the wheelchair out?"

"I told you, boy," said Chuck. "I'm floatin'." He lifted his arms with the palms of his hands raised to the sky. Then he leaned heavily against the side of the car. "It's good to feel the sun on my face."

Billy walked around to the back of the Volvo and opened the hatch. He looked over his shoulder to see Daniel was still deeply engrossed in conversation on his mobile. He guessed it was something to do with work. The wheelchair lay folded flat in the back of the car. Billy grabbed hold of it and pulled hard. The chair bounced off the back of the car, and fell with a clatter on the ground.

"Billy?" Maggie called. "What are you doing to my car?" She walked towards him.

"Sorry." Billy bent down to unfold the wheelchair. "It was heavier than I expected."

Maggie helped him to stand the wheelchair upright, and open it out. "I thought Daniel was supposed to be doing this," she said. "Where's he gone?"

"He's over there." Billy pointed to the small clump of trees where Daniel was standing, still talking into his phone.

"Hey, Daniel," Maggie called. "Don't be an arse. Come and give us a hand. I've done all the driving. Now it's your turn."

Daniel waved and pointed to his phone. He raised the palm of his free hand as if to say, *what can I do?*

"He's always doing this to me," Maggie grumbled. She shook the wheelchair roughly, to check it was securely locked open. "Doesn't matter if we're in a restaurant. He even took a call in a cinema once. The people around us were furious. That thing's almost permanently glued to his ear."

She turned to Billy. "Doesn't it drive you mad?"

Billy shrugged. "It's his work, and it's important to him. It's okay, I understand."

Maggie tipped her sunglasses onto the end of her nose, and looked at him over the top of them. "If you say so," she said. "I think it's bloody rude."

***

Billy rested his head on Daniel's chest and put his arm across his face to shield his eyes from the sun. The heat of the afternoon was intense, even with the gentle breeze blowing from the river.

The picnic was a triumph. Simon and Tom had supplied half the food. Billy remembered Simon was a good cook, but this time he had excelled himself. There were tomatoes marinated in Worcestershire sauce and vodka, miniature Scotch eggs made with quail's eggs, and a dressed side of salmon served with Lebanese tabbouleh. Daniel had created an Eton Mess, a pudding of strawberries and cream with crushed meringue that was the perfect end to the meal.

Chuck ate enthusiastically, but he held back from joining in the conversation. He seemed content to sit in his wheelchair and watch everyone as they talked. He wore an oversized fedora Maggie had supplied that sat jauntily on his head, protecting him from the sun's heat.

Simon and Tom were always good company. Tom had set up his own production company, and he talked enthusiastically about his latest passion project, a new creative space in the heart of Cambridge. Like Simon he was stripped to the waist and attracted admiring looks from both men and women around them. He had a rower's physique, with broad shoulders and a well-developed chest.

Meanwhile Simon had clearly put in a lot of hours in the gym in preparation for his role once more as a Greek god in the Netflix series he was going to shoot. The two men sat back to back, resting against each other. Their legs stretched out in front of them, their arms extended either side with their fingers intertwined. Simon gently rubbed the back of his head against Tom's.

"Hey, Chuck," Simon called. "Billy said you were based out here as a pilot in the US Air force. How long ago was that?"

Chuck opened his eyes, and surveyed the group of young men sat around him. There seemed to be the ghost of a serene smile on his face. Whatever was in his medication had created a miraculous change in his mood. He looked across to Maggie and smiled broadly at her.

"Happy memories are what keep us alive, eh Maggie?" he said.

Maggie snorted. "I'm still making my memories thank you very much." She picked up the bottle of wine, poured herself a glass, and took a long drink from it. She set it down next to her, lay back on the grass, and pulled her sunhat over her face. "Daniel. I hope you've not had too much to drink, because I nominate you to drive back. Chuck clearly seems to think I need to drown myself in the sorrows of my days long gone by."

"Hey, Maggie," Chuck said. "I didn't mean...that is...I was jus' sayin'..."

Maggie." Daniel sighed. "You can be a bit too bloody touchy sometimes. Come on, Chuck, tell us what you got up to out here."

"Well, I—" Chuck looked at Maggie. "I'm not sure it's all that interestin'."

Billy sat up, and rested a hand on the arm of Chuck's wheelchair. "Of course it is," he said. He turned to Simon and Tom. "Chuck wasn't only a pilot. He was middleweight?" He looked across to

Chuck, who nodded. "Middleweight boxing champion three years—"

"Four years," Chuck corrected.

"Sorry. Four years in a row at RAF Alconbury. They even renamed it the Chuck Challenge."

"Alconbury?" Simon enquired, his head still nestled against Tom's. "Isn't that where that hunky oarsman of yours came from?"

"Which hunky oarsman?" Tom asked.

"There've been so many?" Simon sat up and turned to Tom. There was a quizzical look on his face. "The one with the American accent. Enormous—"

"Oh, him," Tom replied quickly. "He was from RAF Lakenheath. That's farther east."

"Lakenheath?" Chuck sniffed. "Our sworn rivals. My sworn rival was Mad Joey Walsh. He was their middleweight contender, and crazy as anythin'." Chuck sat back in his chair and jutted out his chin. "I still beat him four years in a row."

Maggie sat up and pushed back her sunhat.

"I thought you were in the US Air Force? Why were you on an RAF base?"

"Chuck explained that to me," Billy said. "Churchill lent the Americans our airfields at the end of the war. They used lots of them around the country. Especially during the Cold War with Russia."

Maggie lay back again. "I suppose I should have known that. My dad was in the RAF."

"Really?" Daniel asked. "I didn't know."

Maggie rolled onto her side, rested her head on her hands, and looked at Daniel. "Oh, darling. There's *so* much you don't know about me. He left after the war and became a pilot for British Airways. Well, British European Airways as it was known in those days. I nearly followed in his footsteps."

"You?" Daniel sounded incredulous.

Maggie lifted an eyebrow. "There's no need to be so surprised. He took me flying in a little plane he owned with a friend. He used to let me take control. I was really rather good." She sighed. "But I was mad keen on theatrical work, so I ended up being a designer instead. Just think. If I'd been a pilot, I could be retired on a big fat pension by now." She rolled onto her back and pulled her sunhat over her face again.

"The US Air Force never allowed women pilots in my day," Chuck said. "Damn fools. After all, women flew in the war. Never understood why they stopped 'em afterwards." He looked across to Maggie. "I'm sure you'd have made a mighty fine pilot, young lady."

Maggie tilted her sunhat back and squinted at him against the sun. "Were there women pilots in the war?"

"Oh, sure." Chuck smiled. "Called 'em the WASPS. The Women's Airforce Service Pilots. Then they banned 'em at the end of the war, and didn't let 'em in again until long after I'd left. Yet another damn fool mistake the so-called higher-ups made."

Maggie tilted her head to one side and looked at Chuck with renewed interest. "Not one for authority, are we, Chuck?"

Chuck snorted and winked at Maggie. "I wouldn't say that, ma'am. I was a good officer. In my own way."

"Officer? Mmm," said Maggie. "I like a man in uniform. You should tell me more."

Billy laughed. "He's got quite a few photographs of himself in uniform with the other pilots. Haven't you, Chuck?"

"Well, I—" Chuck seemed lost for words. But he continued to stare at Maggie.

Billy looked between Chuck and Maggie. Maybe it was time he and Daniel went for a bit of exercise.

"Ever been punting, Daniel?" he asked.

Daniel looked surprised. "Can't say I have. Why? Are you going to show me how?"

Billy got to his feet and stood over Daniel. "Well, you can't come to Cambridge and simply watch the punts go by on the river." He looked across to Simon and Tom.

"What about you boys? Come on, Tom. I'm sure you're an expert with your rowing skills."

Simon cut in before Tom had time to answer. "You've got to stand up to do punting," he said. "And Tom's rowing is a strictly sitting-down kind of sport. It's what you British excel at when it comes to the Olympics. Rowing, riding, cycling. You name it. They're all sitting-down sports. You're pretty crap at all the rest."

"Hey, hey." Tom spun round to face Simon. "That's not fair. Britain won sixty-seven medals at the last Olympics, second only to the U.S. And how many did New Zealand win?"

He lunged forward and grabbed Simon in a headlock. Simon wrapped his arms around Tom's waist and attempted to drive him backward towards the river. Tom fell back and released Simon's head. Simon took his chance to jump astride Tom, grab his arms, and pin them to the ground. The two men's well-developed muscles glistened with sweat in the sunlight. Simon's huge chest swelled as he breathed heavily. He sat triumphantly on top of Tom, whose thigh muscles flexed as he tried to throw Simon off.

"Boys, boys," Maggie called. She sat up, placed her hands on her hips, and looked sideways at Daniel. "Sexy Simon seems to be living up to his name. And as for Tom." She looked back at the two men writhing on the ground. All that could be seen of Tom were his legs. Simon lay prostrate across the rest of his body.

"I think I'll call him Tom the Thighs," she continued. "Billy's right, Daniel. I think it's time you all went and worked off a little surplus energy. Chuck and I can stay here and watch you fall in the river."

"All right then." Daniel took hold of Billy's outstretched hand and got to his feet.

"We may have to wait a bit for a punt." It felt good to hold Daniel's hand so publicly. "There'll be a lot of people wanting to rent one this afternoon." Billy looked back at Maggie. "Will you two be okay?"

Maggie smiled and winked at him. "Oh, Chuck and I will have lots to talk about. We might even go for a little walk." She looked across to Simon and Tom, still wrestling on the ground. "Take the two Titans with you, there's a love. They're beginning to draw a bit of a crowd."

Chapter 16

The meadows bordering the River Cam were crowded with picnickers that hot August afternoon. Simon led the way past a sea of sunbathing bodies towards the quayside where they could hire punts. Tom followed close behind, and behind him Billy and Daniel strolled, still holding hands. It had been nearly two years since Billy last visited Cambridge, but the city had hardly changed. It was timeless. As he walked alongside Daniel, following his friends Simon and Tom, Billy felt happy. Right now was a scene in his life he wanted to distil and bottle. Rarely did moments like this happen, and Billy wanted to capture every aspect of it. He allowed his senses to absorb every minutiae of detail, from the sounds of people on the river, to the saturated scents of summer in the breeze that filled his nostrils. Thoughts of his mother were still in the back of his mind, but they could not outweigh this moment of bliss.

After walking in silence for a few yards, Billy turned to Daniel. "So. What do you think?"

"About what?"

"Chuck and Maggie, of course. I'm sure something's happening there."

Daniel laughed. "Is that why you bundled us away from the picnic?"

"Was it that obvious?"

"Probably Chuck didn't notice," Daniel said. "Especially as he's so spaced out on those horse pills of his. But Maggie won't miss a trick."

After a few more minutes' walk, they arrived at a wooden jetty floating on the river. At one end was a large wooden kiosk. On its roof was the sign *Scudamore's Punting Company*. A single wooden punt was left tethered to the jetty. It bobbed up and down as the wake from a passing tourist boat lapped against it. Billy watched nervously as the long, flat-bottomed boat rolled from side to side. He had forgotten how vulnerable he had felt the last time he rented a punt. His earlier confidence ebbed away, and he hoped he could still remember how to propel the fragile craft without tipping both himself and Daniel into the water.

Simon was deep in discussions with a young student whose sun-bleached blond hair was tied in an untidy topknot. The student's T-shirt had the words *Punt Rocker* emblazoned on it.

"You know Chuck might end up disappointed, don't you?" Daniel asked.

"Sorry?" Billy was still worrying about his punting technique.

"Disappointed," Daniel repeated. "If he tries it on with Maggie. After all, she's—"

"Oh, of course," said Billy, as he guessed Daniel's meaning. "Well. She did say in the car that she left the straight and narrow many years ago. So you mean she's—"

"She's got a partner called Sarah," Daniel said. "Off and on, that is. More off than on these days. Nevertheless."

"I think you're jumping to conclusions. I'm sure Chuck's pleased to talk to someone who's not a carer. He looks so much happier than when I've been visiting him. He's a different person today." Billy turned to Daniel, and kissed him. "Thank you. You've been truly kind."

Daniel shrugged. "Oh, come on. It's not a hardship. I'm in a beautiful city, on a beautiful day, with a beautiful man who's about to show off his punting prowess."

"Ah," said Billy. "I was coming to that. The truth is, I've not done this for years."

Simon broke off from his discussions with the student with the topknot. "Bad news," he said. "There's only one punt left. All the others are booked out for at least the next hour."

"Oh, that's a shame," Billy said. He hoped his disappointment sounded genuine. "Why don't you and Tom take it? Daniel and I can go for a walk."

"No way," Tom stated. "You guys are the visitors. We live here, and we can go punting anytime."

"Exactly," Simon agreed. "We'll go back to Chuck and Maggie to make sure they're not getting up to any mischief."

"Only if you're sure," Daniel said. "It's something I've never done, and I wouldn't mind trying."

"Of course," Tom replied. "I'm sure Billy can't wait to show off his punting skills."

"Well…" Billy felt a sinking feeling in his stomach. "The last time I did this was over three years ago. Do you remember, Simon? I came up to Cambridge that summer after I'd finished my social work training."

"Oh God." Simon put his hand on his forehead. "I remember now. You were pretty crap, weren't you?" He turned to Daniel. "Have you got a change of clothing with you? There's every chance you're going to get a soaking."

Daniel laughed. "It's a hot day, so I'll guess I'll dry out quickly enough."

"I've got a better idea," Tom offered. "Simon can be your chauffeur. That way, the two of you can lie back in the punt and whisper sweet nothings to each other while the world floats by."

Simon turned to Tom and kissed him. "You old romantic, Tom North. And of course, you've nominated me to be chauffeur because you admit that a Brit like you can't do standing up sports like punting."

"Fuck off." Tom lowered his head and extended his arms to rugby tackle Simon. But the New Zealander anticipated the move and stepped out the way. Tom caught his foot in the planking of the jetty, and fell sideways into the river. As he disappeared beneath the surface, a spout of water shot up over the jetty, and rained down on the three men.

"Oh shit," Simon cried out. "I hope he hasn't got his phone on him." He knelt down at the edge of the jetty as Tom's head reappeared a short distance away.

"You bastard," Tom called. He wiped water away from his eyes and paddled back. Billy knelt beside Simon to help Tom from the murky green water. Tom reached up, and grasped Billy's arm firmly, ignoring Simon's offer of help. He levered himself back onto the jetty, stood up straight, and shook his head like a wet dog. Billy was still on his knees, and water showered down on him. His eyes were level with Tom's crotch, so he could see how Tom's wet shorts clung to his body, throwing into sharp relief the outline of his thighs, and his not-insubstantial cock.

"I'm sorry," Simon apologized. "But if you hadn't—"

"Yeah, yeah," Tom cut him off. "I should have thought better than to rugby tackle a former New Zealand rugby player." He shoved his hands into his pockets and pulled out his wallet and a set of keys. "No harm done. Thank God these shorts have got deep pockets."

He turned to Simon and gave him a wet embrace.

"Hey, you shit." Simon tried to shrug him off. "You're soaking me."

Tom released his grip. "Serves you right. Now we're almost quits. Right. I'm going back to lie in the sun, and get dry. You'd better book that punt before someone jumps ahead of you."

Tom walked off down the jetty. At the end he turned, and shouted back, "And don't let Simon try to serenade you with his rendition of '*O sole mio*.' He's a crap singer."

***

Between the rhythmic slapping of water against the wooden sides of the punt, and the warmth of the sun on his body, Billy drifted in and out of a dreamlike state of contentment. Daniel lay beside him, nestled into his arm. Plump red cushions supported their heads, and their legs intertwined in a comforting embrace. An empty bottle of wine rolled lazily back and forth beside them, as Simon propelled the punt along the river.

When they first set off from the jetty, Billy watched with admiration as Simon skillfully maneuvered the ungainly craft, using a single, sixteen-foot-long pole. Maggie's nickname of Sexy Simon was well chosen. Simon was bare-chested and barefoot. He stood on the back of the punt, shorts clinging tightly to his well-developed thighs. Water droplets from Tom's earlier damp embrace glistened on Simon's broad chest.

The punt was probably over twenty feet long, but only three feet wide. It was flat-bottomed, and rocked alarmingly from side to side when Billy first stepped into it. It felt more stable once he and Daniel lay down together in the middle of the boat. Simon stood at the back end, thrust the long pole firmly into the riverbed, and pushed them away from the jetty. He used the pole to both propel them forward and to steer the fragile craft.

"I'll take you on the classic tourist route." Simon's arm muscles flexed as he pushed hard against the pole to turn the boat away from several other punts heading towards them. "We'll go under the Mathematical Bridge, and then past our picnic spot on The Backs. Then we'll head for the Bridge of Sighs, and I can sing to you."

"I thought the Bridge of Sighs was in Venice." Daniel said.

"Yes, it is," Simon replied. "This one was built about three hundred years later. It's called the Bridge of Sighs because of the students who cross it, sighing on their way to their exams."

"Take us wherever you want," Billy said. He lay against Daniel with his eyes closed. His hand idly toyed with the belt of Daniel's shorts. "It all sounds good to me. But lay off the singing."

Simon rocked the punt violently from side to side, and Billy opened his eyes wide with alarm.

"All right, all right," he said, and tightened his grip on Daniel's belt. "I was only kidding. You know I love to hear you sing."

Simon smiled serenely and steadied the punt once more.

"So what really happened the last time you came punting?" Daniel asked.

Billy turned his head and whispered into Daniel's ear. "Let's say I didn't look as cool as Simon. On the plus side, I didn't fall in, but I came close. And I was glad I didn't have the responsibility of a passenger."

"I thought you were a bit reluctant, back there," Daniel noted. "Why did you suggest it, if you didn't really want to go punting?"

Billy kissed the side of Daniel's cheek. "I forgot. Anyway. It's all worked out for the best. Here we are, punting on the Cam with our own sexy chauffeur."

Daniel chuckled. "Never mind Sexy Simon. Did you see Tom when you pulled him out of the water? Those shorts of his."

"Did I see?" Billy rasped, his whisper getting louder. "I couldn't help but see. I was kneeling down in front of him when he stood up. I can say for a certainty he's not circumcised."

Daniel snorted with laughter.

"He's certainly a big boy," Billy continued, and began to giggle. "He and Simon are made for each other."

"What are you two laughing at?"

Billy looked up. He hoped Simon had not heard any part of their conversation.

"I was telling Daniel about my last time attempt at punting."

Simon snorted. "I thought it was your first attempt at punting?" he replied. "You had so many near misses that day. What was the problem? Couldn't you balance properly? You? The natural ballerina?"

Daniel lifted his head, and turned to Billy. "Ballerina? You never told me ballet was one of your talents."

That's because it's not," Billy said. He wished Simon would keep his mouth shut.

The punt rocked from side to side again. "Ahem," said Simon. "Clearly, Billy hasn't told you about his triumphs in the ballet class at RADA. I really don't know why he's not on stage at Sadler's Wells more often." He held the punt pole horizontally, and performed a clumsy turn on the back of the boat. The punt rocked alarmingly, but amazingly, Simon kept his balance.

"RADA?" Daniel asked with a note of admiration in his voice. "I forgot you went to RADA. Is that where you two met?"

"That's right," Simon replied. "We were both on scholarships. Me from the Commonwealth and Billy from the mother country. We even roomed together. Do you remember that shitty place in Brixton? I've never been so fuckin' cold."

Billy did remember. They shared a large, drafty room on the top floor of a crumbling Victorian building in south London. He and Simon had the room for two out of the three years of their course.

Simon had been Billy's first love.

Billy remembered the day they first met. Their tutor paired them for an Alexander technique exercise. It was a physical session. By the end of it, Simon turned to Billy and said, "Well that's the foreplay over with. Do you want to come over to mine now and fuck?"

And Billy did. Night after night. Day after day. Simon was three years older than Billy, and proved to be an excellent tutor in sexual technique. He was a passionate lover, but also a tender one. When they were not in bed together, they rarely left each other's side. Their fellow students called them "the perfect couple." After years of teenage turmoil, with his father abandoning him, and his mother struggling to make ends meet, Billy thought he had found contentment. He was sure he and Simon would spend the rest of their lives together.

Simon had left on a Tuesday. Billy had an audition with a theatrical agent, who subsequently took him on and built his career. Simon had planned his trip to Australia many weeks before. His divorced father, who lived in Melbourne, had fixed up his son with an audition for a daytime TV show. "I'm sure I won't get it," Simon said. "Even if I do, I don't think I'll take it."

But he did get the part. It was the lead role in a new Australian daytime soap. "You'd be a fool not to take it," Billy had told him when Simon called late at night with the news. He knew their relationship was over. "The perfect couple" was no more.

Billy looked up at Simon now, standing majestically on the back of the punt. He confidently plunged the punt pole vertically into the water, dropped it down to the riverbed, and pushed back to propel them along the river. His relationship with Tom seemed to be strong. They had been together for nearly three years, and Billy was pleased for his ex-lover. Simon glanced down at him, and winked.

"What are you thinking about? Student days? All those times we—"

"What the hell's going on over there?" Daniel sat up and pointed to a small group of people on the riverbank. They seemed to be involved in a heated argument, and their voices were getting louder. Billy looked in the direction Daniel was pointing.

"Oh no," he said. "It's Chuck."

Chapter 17

"I still don't understand. Why was Chuck so upset?"

At ten o'clock that evening, Billy was in Daniel's garden with Daniel and Maggie. A gentle breeze rustled the leaves of the rhododendron bushes, but the heat of the day persisted. Billy and Daniel lounged on a large iron bench, the hardness of its seat made more forgiving by half a dozen ill-matched cushions. Maggie sat opposite on a canvas director's chair. Above their heads, a string of flickering lanterns illuminated a wall of herbs alongside them. The heady scents of thyme, oregano, and curry mingled with the delicate smell of chamomile from the lawn at their feet. Instead of recorded birdsong, Daniel had opted to play the sound of crickets to mask London's traffic. If Billy closed his eyes, the garden was transported to a mythical location, somewhere in the Mediterranean.

Maggie paused, a glass of wine halfway to her lips, and raised an eyebrow at Billy. "Chuck upset? Isn't it his way, dear?" She took a sip from the glass.

"Up to a point," Billy replied. "But, from what we could see from the punt, it looked like they were ready for a fight. I grant you Chuck can be a bit argumentative—"

"A bit." Maggie almost choked on her mouthful of wine. "I've never met a more awkward, cussed, obtuse, ill-tempered, surly, cantankerous—"

"Hang on, hang on," Daniel interrupted, before Billy could say anything in defense of his client. "I think that's a bit harsh. Anyway. I thought you two were getting on like a house on fire when we left? In fact, that's why we left. It seemed as if you might want some time alone together."

"Me? With Chuck?" Maggie's laugh was loud and long, halted only by a fit of coughing. She raised her wineglass once more and drained it. She held out the glass to Daniel and looked at him with her head tilted to one side. "Is the spare room available?" she asked.

"I'm not going to be able to drive now. The events of today seem to have turned me to drink."

Daniel took the glass from her and stood. "Darling Maggie," he said. "I can't think of a time when you weren't turned to drink. All right. I'll open another bottle. But don't try to pretend you and Chuck didn't give off signals this afternoon. Because you did."

"Oh nonsense." Maggie waved her hand. "There was a bit of harmless flirting, I grant you. But you seem to forget, young Daniel, that the male of the species no longer interests me. And, if I'm not mistaken," she paused, and looked first to Daniel, and then Billy, "Chuck's not interested in the female of the species either."

"What?" Daniel sat down heavily on the bench beside Billy. "You're not serious?"

Maggie sat back and smiled triumphantly, as though she had unmasked the killer in a game of wink murder. "He might conceal it quite well, I grant you," she continued. "But, in my humble opinion, Chuck's about as camp as a row of tents."

Billy laughed and shook his head. "I'm sorry, Maggie. But I find that difficult to believe."

"Have you two boys lost your gaydar all of a sudden?" Maggie asked. She sniffed and shook her head. "Oh, I get it. It must be lurve."

Billy pretended not to understand. "What do you mean?"

"You two," she replied. "Nature's switched off your gaydar to stop you getting distracted. Even you gay boys need a bit of monogamy." This time she raised both her eyebrows. "At the start of a relationship at least."

"Ignore her." Daniel turned back to Maggie. "I think maybe you've had enough wine for one night."

Maggie snorted. "Oh my darling boy. Don't be such a puritan. And if you want to know what I think was happening between Chuck and his former lover—"

"What?" Billy was now even more confused. Maggie ignored his interruption and held out her glass to Daniel.

"…then you're simply going to have to pour me another glass." She smiled at Daniel, who sighed and stood.

"I'll go and open a bottle." Daniel walked back along the chamomile path to the kitchen.

Billy looked at Maggie, unsure what to think. How many glasses of wine had she drunk? He had not been counting. Perhaps, even though she denied it, Chuck had aroused her. Or at least, she was curious, despite her comments about her sexuality. Perhaps she was offended when Chuck rebuffed her, and she made up a story about him being gay as some sort of childish revenge. Perhaps she would deny it all in the morning, once she had sobered up. Perhaps.

"I'm not making it up." Maggie seemed to have read his thoughts. "It was something the other man said before he left. '*My door is always open if you want to come back, Chuck. It always was.*' It's obvious they lived together."

"I think you're jumping to conclusions," Billy argued. "They didn't have to be intimate to have lived together, Lots of straight guys do. All the time."

"Yes, darling, I know." Maggie's tone was that of a short-tempered schoolteacher dealing with the dunce in her class. "It wasn't only the words, my dear. There was definitely something between them. Or at least, there had been something between them."

Daniel returned, holding a newly opened bottle of wine in one hand and a jug of water in the other. Maggie picked up her glass and held it out expectantly. Daniel ignored the glass and turned to Billy. "Do you want any more wine?"

Billy shook his head. "'I'm fine, thanks." He held up his glass. "But I'll have some water."

Daniel filled Billy's glass, then he turned back to Maggie and handed her the bottle of wine. "Looks like the rest of this is yours," he said. "Billy and I are done with drinking for the night."

Maggie took the bottle and filled her glass. "It's all for the lush in the corner, I suppose."

Daniel sat and poured himself a glass of water. "So. What did he look like?" he asked.

"Who?" asked Maggie.

"The man you're alleging is Chuck's ex-lover."

Maggie waved her free hand in the air, as though dismissing a troublesome servant. "I'm merely reporting what I saw, darling." She lounged back in the garden seat, and looked thoughtful. "He was tall, and extremely handsome. Elegantly dressed. Quite the contrast to the young men around him." She looked directly at Daniel and raised an eyebrow before she continued. "A good head of hair for his age. Well spoken."

"English?"

"Oh yes, of course. I'd say more Harrow than Eton."

Daniel laughed. "How on earth could you tell which school he went to? From his accent?"

Maggie looked sideways at him. "One can tell, darling. Believe me. I know these things. I'd say he was ex-military. Definitely an officer."

"Inside leg measurement?" Daniel teased.

Maggie pouted. "If you're going to make fun of me, I'm going to bed." She took another swig of wine. "I didn't see him for more than a couple of minutes. Tom and I had gone to get ice creams from the van by the bridge. When we came back, they were already in full flow."

"What were they saying?"

"Chuck was shouting at the man to go away. The chap seemed upset by what Chuck was saying. Tom tried to calm things down, and the man was terribly polite. He introduced himself as Mr Frobisher." She paused for a moment. "Guy Frobisher, he said. He was terribly sorry for disturbing our afternoon and didn't want to cause us any further trouble. That's when he turned to Chuck and said the thing about his door always being open."

"Did you ask Chuck who he was?"

"Of course we did."

Maggie took another drink of wine. Billy and Daniel waited expectantly.

"And what did he say?"

"Well, he didn't tell us," she replied finally. "He said he'd had enough of birthdays and wanted to go home. Then he sat there sulking. That's when you two finally turned up."

Chuck had soured the happy atmosphere of the day, and forced Billy to repeatedly apologize to his friends. It had been a long car journey back to London with few words exchanged in the cramped confines of the Volvo. Chuck snored in the front seat. Maggie played a CD of Broadway musicals and sang along at the top of her voice. Daniel had been reassuring, but Billy decided it had been a bad idea to introduce Chuck to his friends that day.

"I'm sorry, Maggie," he said, not for the first time that day. "If I'd known Chuck was going to behave so badly—"

"Oh, darling boy, I've told you already, stop taking the blame for everything. He's a grumpy old man. I don't envy you having to care for him."

Billy smiled. "He's not the worst of my clients. Perhaps the sun and his medication didn't help."

Maggie drained her glass. She stood, swayed gently back and forth, and held out her arms to steady herself. "Stop making excuses for him. Right, boys. I'm going to leave you two in peace."

She bent down to kiss Daniel on either cheek. She turned to Billy and cupped her hand around his cheek. "You're so sweet. Both of you. To have wanted to do that for Chuck's birthday. Thank you for inviting me. It's been a lovely day. Truly. Now. Allow yourselves a little 'me time', as the ghastly phrase is these days."

She kissed Billy on either cheek, straightened up, and walked unsteadily along the path back to the house. Billy sighed and leaned back against Daniel's shoulder. He was growing fond of Maggie, despite her abrupt manner and insistence on dominating every conversation. She reminded him of another of his clients. A once successful film star, whose career had been cut short by multiple sclerosis: a strong woman who faced her terrible disease with fortitude and grace. Her strength was not limited to refusing to allow the setbacks in her life to take her down, but also in directly challenging people who exaggerated the simpler problems in life, such as a lost mobile phone or a late train. "First-world problems," she would say. "They should try living with a terminal disease."

"Penny for your thoughts?"

Billy shook his head slowly at the sound of Daniel's voice. "I like Maggie," Billy said. "I was thinking how she reminds me of one of my clients. Janet du Prés."

"The actress who played the dowager in that costume drama for years?"

Billy nodded. "She's got MS, sadly. But an amazingly strong woman."

Daniel laughed. "Oh, Maggie's strong all right. A bit too strong sometimes. But I'm glad you like her. She's important to me. A great friend. And, of course," he gestured around him at the garden, "a great designer."

He kissed Billy on the cheek. "So. What do you think?"

"About what?"

"Maggie's bombshell about Chuck of course. Do you think she's right?"

Billy nodded. "I'm annoyed with myself," he said. "I'm clearly not an observant person."

"Oh, nonsense." Daniel squeezed Billy's shoulder. "I've said it before. You've got a lot on your plate right now. So you believe her?"

"Oh, yes. It's beginning to make sense now."

"In what way?"

"Well, if Chuck is gay, then he's of that generation that would, by default, keep it a secret. If that man, what was his name?"

"Guy Frobisher."

"Oh, that's right. If he and Chuck were lovers, and they've split up, that would be the reason why Chuck moved to London. I wish I'd known before." Billy sat up. "That's why Chuck didn't want to go to Grantchester. It's probably where they lived."

Daniel rubbed his hand gently down Billy's spine.

"That's going to be an interesting conversation for you."

"What is?" Billy turned his head to Daniel. "Oh no. I'm not going to be the first to raise it with Chuck. If he wants to talk to me about it, he can. But I'm pretty sure he'll want to keep it to himself. And I'm not going to intrude."

"Aren't you curious?"

"Of course I am. But that doesn't justify poking my nose into his private affairs."

Daniel pulled Billy back against his chest and kissed him on the top of his head.

"You're right. Infuriating. But right."

He slid his hand between Billy's thighs. Billy relaxed his muscles and felt Daniel's hand slide up slowly towards his groin. His cock twitched with anticipation, and Billy turned his head to look up at Daniel.

"Are you poking your nose into my private affairs, Mr Richards?"

Chapter 18

They remained on the bench for several minutes more. Daniel unbuttoned Billy's shirt and slipped his hands inside it to massage his chest. His kisses progressed, sensuously, around Billy's face: first his lips, then his cheeks, then onto his nose, and, delicately, to his forehead. Billy closed his eyes as Daniel gently kissed his eyelids. He felt his cock harden as Daniel kissed him on the lips again, easing them apart with his tongue, and bringing their mouths into a close embrace. Daniel was an inventive kisser, and his tongue stimulated the inside of Billy's mouth in ways no man had ever done for him before.

"Fuck this bench," Daniel said suddenly. He pulled away from Billy and held his hand to his back. "It's about as comfortable as a marble mattress. Wait there a minute."

Daniel stood and walked away from Billy down the garden towards the large mirror at the end. Billy watched as Daniel grasped the mirror with both hands and pulled. It split in the middle and opened. It seemed to be attached to two large doors. Daniel pulled them fully open and stepped into a dark space beyond the entrance.

Billy was fascinated. He stood, repositioned his hardened cock to be slightly more comfortable, and followed the path down the garden. As he reached the mysterious dark entrance, he could see Daniel removing plastic sheeting from a large double bed. Daniel looked up as Billy approached.

"Another of Maggie's brilliant ideas," he said. "This space is so much more than a garden house, and you wouldn't know it was here, hidden behind the mirror."

Daniel removed the last of the plastic sheeting and cast it aside. "Do you like outdoor sex?" he asked and continued without waiting for a reply. "Good. So do I. But I like to do it in style. And in comfort."

He crouched down, reached under the mattress, and fiddled with a mechanism. There was the sound of a double click from beneath the bed. Daniel straightened up and began to push the bed forward. Billy stepped back as it rolled into the garden. When Daniel drew level with Billy, he paused, turned, and kissed him. "Maggie's endlessly inventive, isn't she?" He stared into Billy's eyes. "Sex indoors if it's raining. But tonight, we'll be under the stars."

Billy looked around him. "Aren't we overlooked here?"

"No. That's why I chose this house. The trees give me perfect seclusion from next door."

"What about Maggie?"

Daniel laughed. "Maggie's out for the count. She won't be coming outside again tonight. And anyway, she and I go back years. She's seen me naked on more than one occasion."

"But not me," Billy replied with a smile.

"What? Are you bashful all of a sudden?" Daniel kissed him again. "Don't be. Relax and enjoy the liberation."

Daniel pushed the bed forward a couple more feet. He reached down to lock off the wheels, leapt onto the mattress, and rolled over onto his back. He lay with his arms behind his head and stared up the stars. Billy climbed onto the bed beside him and lay on his back with his head resting on Daniel's chest. Despite the light pollution from thousands of London streetlamps, Billy could see a swathe of stars painted onto the nighttime canopy above their heads.

"It's beautiful," he said. "We could be a thousand miles away, on some Mediterranean island somewhere. Lying on a hilltop in Greece or Italy—"

"Instead of the back garden of a tumbledown Victorian house in Battersea," Daniel said.

Billy rolled over, rested his hands on Daniel's chest, and looked across to him. "It's not tumbledown at all. I think your home is magical. And every time I come here, you reveal some new piece of sorcery. Is it all Maggie's design?"

Daniel nodded. "Pretty much. She's quite clever, and super creative. She won two BAFTAs for her film set designs you know."

"How did you get her to do all this work for you? She must cost a fortune."

Daniel extended his arm and rested it across Billy's shoulders. He lay back and sighed. "Oh, Maggie and I go back a long way. She was my landlady when I moved out of Grandpa Bob's house for a time."

"Why did you move out of your grandpa's house? It was free, after all."

Daniel smiled. "When I started at college, I decided I was too grown up to live with family any longer. I must have been a real little shit. Maggie had a tiny flat in Bateman Street in Soho, right at the top of a ramshackle old building. She charged me next to nothing. There were seventy-two stairs and no lift. And a sex shop on the ground floor."

"That was handy."

"It was. That was where I worked. I can honestly say, I know everything there is to know about dildo sizing."

Billy laughed. "And you were only eighteen?"

"Nineteen. But I grew up quickly. It was probably the best education I could have had. I worked in that shop for nearly three years while I went to college."

"Where did you go?"

"RCM. The Royal College of Music. The one by the Albert Hall. I used to walk there from Soho to save money on the Tube."

"That's a long way."

Daniel sniffed. "Not really. I could run it in twenty-five minutes. I got fit fast."

Billy extended his hand and ran it along the taut muscles in Daniel's thigh. His fingers gently combed through the curls of black hair on Daniel's leg. "That explains your amazing legs, then."

Billy ran his hand up inside Daniel's shorts to his groin, and felt the stiffened bulge beneath his briefs. His fingertips followed the contour of Daniel's cock and massaged its tip. He looked up to see Daniel had closed his eyes. He breathed in short, staccato bursts as he reacted to Billy's stimulation.

"I want you inside me tonight," Billy whispered.

Daniel opened his eyes.

"I want to ride you," Billy continued. "Out here. Beneath the stars. I want to take you deep inside me."

Billy felt Daniel's cock stiffen further. He withdrew his hand and moved into a kneeling position astride him. He placed the palms of his hands on either side of Daniel's shirtfront, and used his thumbs to locate his nipples. He massaged them firmly through the fabric of the shirt and watched with pleasure as Daniel squeezed his eyes closed.

After a few moments he opened them again and reached up to Billy's shirt. He began to unfasten the buttons, one by one. When the final button released, Daniel pulled the shirt wide open, slid his hands up the sides of Billy's body, and slipped the shirt off his shoulders. Billy shrugged the shirt free and reached down to unfasten the remaining buttons on Daniel's shirt. He pulled the shirtfront apart and lowered himself flat, enjoying the warmth of Daniel's bare chest against his.

Their mouths connected, and their tongues intertwined. Saliva flooded into Billy's mouth as the two men kissed deeply, passionately. Their heads switched angles, as they each attempted to find new ways to stimulate the other, with their lips and their tongues. Then there was the simple pleasure of sharing each other's breath. Daniel wrapped one hand around the back of Billy's head. The other he massaged firmly up and down the middle of Billy's back. Waves of pleasure flooded through Billy's body.

As he lay against Daniel's chest, Billy slipped his hands down between their two bodies and found the waistband of Daniel's shorts. He lifted his pelvis slightly, to allow his fingers to grapple with the single metal stud securing the shorts, and released it. He tugged on the zip to loosen the shorts further, slipped his hands inside Daniel's briefs, and wrapped his fingers around his engorged cock.

Daniel's body tensed, and he groaned loudly into Billy's open mouth. Billy felt Daniel's cock stiffen further beneath his grasp, and he squeezed its shaft with one hand, while sliding the fingertips of his other hand down to caress Daniel's ball sac.

"Oh, fuck," Daniel moaned, his lips moving against Billy's. "Where the fuck did you learn to do that?"

Billy lifted his head and ran his tongue around the curve of Daniel's chin. The salty taste of men's stale sweat had always aroused him. He rested his own chin against Daniel's, and felt their breath mingle. It combined to form a hot, erotic mist between them.

"That's nothing." Billy squeezed the shaft of Daniel's cock again. "I'm going to bring you so close to the edge, you're going to explode like a firework when you finally get inside me."

Billy released his grasp on Daniel's cock. He withdrew his hands from the briefs, took hold of their fabric, and pulled down both

Daniel's briefs and shorts in one swift move. Daniel kicked his legs to free himself of the clothes. Billy sat back to unbutton the front of his own shorts, and twisted aside to remove them, together with his briefs. He rolled back to sit astride Daniel and rested on all fours. In this position, he could slowly bend his arms, until his mouth was above Daniel's.

As Daniel lifted his head to kiss him, Billy slid his mouth down onto Daniel's neck. He ran his tongue down the salty curve beneath Daniel's chin, past his Adam's apple, and settled it in the concave spot at the middle of his chest. He ran his tongue back and forth between Daniel's nipples, allowing it to caress each one in turn, and listened with satisfaction as groans of appreciation slipped from Daniel's lips.

Billy's tongue continued its journey down the middle of Daniel's flat abdominal muscles. When he reached Daniel's navel, he slipped it into the concave indentation. At the same time, he slid his hands up the side of Daniel's body, and reached for his nipples. He grasped them between his fingers and thumbs, and began to massage. Daniel's groans became louder. Billy could feel the tip of Daniel's penis connect with the underside of his chin. He moved his head from side to side, to rub its tip against the bristles of his beard.

"Oh fuck," Daniel moaned. His body flexed as Billy stimulated his nipples and his cock simultaneously. "That's incredible."

Billy lifted his head and looked down at Daniel's penis. It twitched and flexed as though charged with electricity. Billy filled his mouth with saliva and released it onto the tip of Daniel's cock. As the saliva dribbled down, he extended his tongue and caressed around the frenulum.

Daniel's cock twitched hard against Billy's lips. He opened his mouth and lowered it, to take the head and the shaft deep inside. He ran the tip of his tongue along the opening at the top of the glans, and tasted the sweetness of Daniel's precum. Gently, he rocked his head back and forth to massage the length of the shaft. At its deepest, he could feel the glans connect with the back of his soft palate. Above him, he could hear Daniel's rhythmic moans.

As the minutes passed, Billy's own cock became unbearably hard, and pulsed in time as he deep throated Daniel. He continued to massage Daniel's nipple with one hand, took hold of his cock with the other, and squeezed and released it, as Daniel's penis slid back and forth in his mouth.

The sheer intimacy of the shared sexual stimulation was exquisite. Billy could not only hear Daniel's groans of pleasure, he could feel the physicality of that pleasure in his mouth. For Billy, giving Daniel such intense pleasure was highly erotic, and he could feel the endorphins flood through his body in waves.

It was almost a sixth sense that caused Billy to release Daniel's cock from his mouth.

"Oh God," gasped Daniel. "I'm so on the edge of cumming. You're amazing."

"I thought you would be. But I want you to cum inside me, not in my mouth."

"Hold that thought." Daniel rolled onto his side, leaned over the edge of the bed, and opened a drawer beneath. He rolled back a moment later with condoms and lube in his hand.

Billy laughed. "I can't believe this setup," he said. "It's the ultimate garden shag bed."

Daniel threw the lube to Billy and fumbled to open a condom packet. "If you're going to do something," he said, struggling to slide the latex over his penis. "Then you should do it well. There." He lay back on the bed in triumph. "Come and get me, sexy man."

Billy finished preparing himself with the lube. He massaged his lubed fingers on the tip of Daniel's cock, gripped its shaft, and carefully aligned himself into position. He looked down at Daniel, waiting expectantly. "Ready?"

Daniel nodded. "Oh fuck, yes."

Billy lowered himself, and felt Daniel's cock enter him, making him feel complete and intimately connected with this beautiful man. Physically, it was as though they had been designed to connect in this way. There was no discomfort. Simply a oneness, and a deep pleasure.

Daniel had been right when he said he was close to cumming. But so was Billy. As Daniel exploded in orgasm inside him, Billy swiftly brought himself to climax and ejaculated across the broad sweep of Daniel's chest. As he felt the last, shuddering wave of climax subside, Billy slumped forward. He placed his hands either side of Daniel's head, and the two men stared intently, adoringly at each other. Even their deep, exhausted breathing seemed to synchronize.

Daniel smiled, turned his head to one side, and kissed Billy's hand. "There are no words," he said.

Daniel curled his body around Billy's. He placed his head against Billy's neck, and Billy could feel the bristles of Daniel's beard rub pleasantly on his skin as he moved into a comfortable position. Daniel rested his arm against Billy's chest and hugged him tight. He felt secure, cocooned in Daniel's arms. His breathing slowed to a deep, even rhythm, and his mind floated into that blissful state between waking and sleeping.

A loud crash shocked him from his doze. Billy's chest tightened, and his breathing became rapid and shallow. Daniel pulled away and sat up.

"Maggie?" called Daniel. "What the fuck?"

"Sorry, boys." Maggie's slurred voice came from somewhere down the garden. "I left my phone out here. Carry on as if I'm not here."

Chapter 19

Billy stirred, and woke from his dream. He was relieved to return to reality. The dream had started so well but developed into something sinister and threatening.

In it, he stood on the back of a large wooden punt, stripped to his waist. He navigated the boat through an immense field of lavender. The strong scent from the blue blossoms filled Billy's nose, and he felt lightheaded. Daniel lay naked in the bottom of the punt, with his head propped up on a pillow of white rose petals. His body glistened with sweat in the sunlight, and his muscles flexed as he stretched his arms lazily behind his head.

The sky was deep azure. Huge branches from the willow trees on either side waved back and forth in a warm breeze. Billy could hear the gentle sound of running water. He looked ahead, and saw they were approaching a waterfall. He tried to slow the boat with the punt pole, but it continued relentlessly towards the fast-flowing water. He looked down to Daniel to warn him about the approaching danger. But Daniel was no longer there. Lying in his place was a different man, his face indistinct, like a blurred photograph. Billy looked down at himself, and realized he was now also naked.

The roaring of the approaching waterfall was much louder now. Frantically, Billy shouted to the man to grab on to one of the overhanging willow branches to slow their progress. But the anonymous man ignored him. As the boat reached the top of the waterfall it tipped, and Billy threw himself backward to avoid plunging into the abyss.

Billy's head sank deep into the pile of pillows, and one fell across his face. He pushed the pillow aside and blinked open his eyes. For a moment he was confused. Not only was he no longer plunging down the waterfall of his dream, but he was not lying on the bed in Daniel's garden. Slowly, he recalled how they had crept into the house, giggling, at 4 a.m., expecting to bump into Maggie at any moment.

Sunlight filtered into the bedroom through the blinds, which gently swayed back and forth in the morning breeze. Billy rolled over to cuddle Daniel. But the space in the bed beside him was empty. He sat up, stretched out his arms, and breathed deeply. The images from the dream were fading rapidly, but he could still hear the distant sound of rushing water.

Billy pushed back the covers, swung his legs over the side of the bed, and stood up. Naked, he padded over to the bedroom door and pulled it open a few inches. The sound of water became louder. Daniel was in the shower. As Billy stood listening, the noise of running water stopped. He gently pushed the door closed, walked back to the bed, and threw himself prostrate on the white linen. He inhaled deeply, and Daniel's scent filled his nostrils. Billy shivered with a frisson of excitement and happiness.

The buzz of a mobile phone rattled on the wooden floor to the side of the bed. He raised himself on one arm, slid over to the edge of the bed, and reached down for the phone. As he picked it up, he realized it was Daniel's and not his. No matter. He was curious to know what time it was. He turned the phone over and saw that it was nearly ten thirty. He also saw a message on the screen:

What time are you coming this evening? I'm missing you so much. Can't wait to see you. Yours forever Anthony xx

Billy held the phone for several minutes after the message faded. There was a sick feeling, deep in his stomach, and his mouth was dry. His breathing reduced to shallow, rapid panting, and his skin prickled with the sensation of a dry sweat.

A thousand thoughts filled his head. None of them made sense of what he had just read.

The sound of the bathroom door opening interrupted his jumble of half-formed conclusions. Carefully, he placed the phone back on the floor face down. He rolled onto his side, curled up into a fetal position, and closed his eyes.

Somewhere on the landing another door opened. Daniel used one of the bedrooms as a dressing room. Billy squeezed his eyes tight shut and rehearsed a series of conversations in his head. What other possible conclusion could he draw from the message he had read on Daniel's phone? Was it fair for him to challenge Daniel about another relationship? After all, they had only been seeing each other for a little over three weeks. Surely Billy was being unreasonable to claim exclusivity, to claim monogamy even, after such a short period of time. Besides, was that what he wanted? It was not something either of them had yet discussed. It was far too early to think of.

And yet.

Daniel said he had not been in a relationship *"for a while."* How long was a while? If he was still seeing this other man Anthony, then that meant he had been lying. And if he had been lying about that, what else was a lie?

But.

Daniel did not strike Billy as being a liar. He seemed a straightforward man. Open. Someone who was consumed by his work. And it was good work. Philanthropic work. He helped children with different abilities discover their potential through theatrical performance.

Was that a lie as well? Billy rolled onto his back and stared at the ceiling. He had no idea what to do next. Two minutes ago he had felt excitement and happiness at the mere prospect of spending more time with Daniel. But one message, one private message on Daniel's phone, had changed all that.

Billy felt foolish. How could he reveal to Daniel he had read a private message on his phone? He would look like a snoop. A possessive stalker. Trust had to be the basis of any relationship. Jealousy could be the end of this one. From zero to sixty and back to zero in less than a month. Billy shook his head and screwed his eyes shut. He needed to think.

Daniel's lips touched his, and Billy opened his eyes again with a start.

"Morning, sleepyhead." Daniel smiled and sat on the edge of the bed as he draped an arm across Billy's chest. He was already dressed in a pair of khaki shorts and a T-shirt. "I'm sorry if I woke you. Do you want a coffee?"

Billy pulled himself up the bed and rested his head against the headboard.

"Are you off somewhere?"

Daniel nodded. "Didn't I tell you? I had a message from Jenny yesterday. She's the director on the youth show we're doing next week at the Lyric in Hammersmith. The sound guys have got a major issue with all the instruments we're going to be using with the kids. She wants me to go in and supervise the setup."

"On a Sunday?"

"It's the only day I can manage. I'm starting rehearsals on another show over in Clapham tomorrow and Tuesday. And we open at the Lyric tomorrow evening." Daniel leaned forward and kissed Billy. "It's crazy busy at the moment. I'm so sorry. It's another beautiful day. We could have spent it chilling here. Instead..." He shrugged and smiled. "I'm sorry."

"What time do you finish?" Billy asked.

"Today? I honestly don't know. It could be a half hour thing to sort out. But I think it's going to take a lot longer. We've never had anything as complex as this before. And it's got to be right. We've got a television crew coming in to record it on the Tuesday. They'll add a whole other layer of complexity to the sound situation, unless we fix it now."

Daniel removed his arm from Billy's chest and reached down to pick up his mobile phone. He glanced at the screen before shoving it in his pocket. "You're welcome to come along. But you could be sitting around for a long time, and that would be boring for you."

Billy reached out and rested his hand on Daniel's thigh.

"Don't worry. I should go and see Mum."

***

Billy looked through the small window in the door to his mother's room. He could see her sitting up in bed, the long tresses of her white hair lying across the pillow. She was watching a television screen fixed on the wall across the other side of the room. Her eyes flickered and her head nodded forward a couple of times, as though on the verge of falling asleep. When Billy pushed open the door, she looked away from the screen, and a beautiful smile lit up her face.

"Billy, love." She removed a pair of headphones from her ears and gently shook her head from side to side. Her hair dragged lazily across the pillow. "I wasn't expecting you this afternoon. What a lovely surprise."

Billy crossed to the side of the bed and kissed his mother on the cheek. "I brought you these," he said, and held out the bouquet of flowers he had bought in the hospital shop in the lobby. "I thought they'd brighten up your room."

"Oh, they're smashin', Billy, love. If you pop down the hall, you'll find the nurses' station. They'll give you a vase for them. Get yourself a cup of tea if you want one while you're there."

"Do you want anything?"

His mother shook her head and pointed to a glass on the table beside her.

"I've got me water, thanks. That's all I can manage right now."

A young male nurse found a vase for Billy and showed him where he could fill it with water.

"Do you want to hang on while I get you your tea?" the young man asked. "As you're here, they'd like to talk to you about hospice care for your mum. We've got the possibility of a place coming up, and we'd like to move her there next week if it works out. We haven't mentioned it to Sarah yet. We wondered if you'd—" The young man tailed off and smiled.

"Where is the hospice?" Billy asked. The conversation was not unexpected. Dr Jerome had already told him there was not much time left. But the move to a hospice made that discussion more real. More final. While she remained in a hospital ward, Billy could keep up the pretense to himself that she was receiving treatment. That somehow there was hope. The hospice would be her final resting place.

"It's a lovely place," replied the nurse. "It's across the river on Clapham Common. She won't be moved far. The senior sister is here today. I'll get her to come and talk to you. She's nearly finished talking to the husband of another patient. How do take your tea?"

***

His mother's eyes were closed when Billy returned to her room twenty minutes later. He set the vase of flowers down on the table next to her bed and stood sipping his tea, watching his mother. The bedclothes rose and fell steadily with her breathing. She was so peaceful, and it seemed she was not in any pain. Her eyelids flickered open, and she smiled.

"You were a long time, love. Come and sit down 'ere. Next to me."

Billy sat on the small plastic chair next to her bed. He held his mother's hand, and with his other hand gently massaged the thin skin covering her fingers. She closed her eyes.

"That's nice, love. Not too 'ard, now. I'm not as tough as I used to be."

"Have you got some moisturizer?"

She nodded towards the small cupboard beneath the bedside table. "That would be nice, love. You'll find some of that pH neutral stuff in there. You know I can't take any of those fancy-smellin' ones. Bring me out in a rash, they do."

Billy released her hand and bent down to open the cupboard. He remembered as a child how his mother complained bitterly about her allergies. So many different creams and perfumes irritated her skin and created a red, itchy rash. She used to complain about how unfair life was.

"A woman needs to smear stuff on 'er body to make 'er beautiful," she would say. "'ow can I be a complete woman if I can't put on a bit of makeup without flarin' up like a fireman's bloody 'elmet?"

When Billy reached puberty, he used to wonder if his mother had meant this deliberately as a sexual reference, or whether she was simply unaware that firemen wore helmets that were yellow and not red. He found the bottle of pH neutral skin moisturizer and squeezed some into his palm. He sat back, gently took his mother's hand, and massaged it with the cream. She sighed and nestled her head into the pillow.

"How's that boy you're seeing? Daniel, isn't it? Must be a few weeks now."

"Nearly a month, Mum," Billy replied. "It's been lovely. We went on a picnic to Cambridge yesterday."

"Cambridge? Don't you have a friend livin' there?"

Billy nodded. "Simon, that's right. I forgot you'd met him. Yes. We got together with Simon and his boyfriend, Tom. A friend of Daniel's drove us there. Maggie. She's lovely. A set designer for film and TV."

She nodded. "I remember now. Hunky Simon, the actor. He was at that little birthday party you 'ad when you were twenty-five. You were mourning the first 'alf of your twenties. God knows what you're going to be like in November when you're thirty." She opened her eyes and frowned at him. "It's only a number, love. Don't run away from age. Embrace it. Every year is a blessin', not a curse." She closed her eyes again. "God, don't I know it."

Billy took some more moisturizer and massaged her other hand. "Talking of old people—"

Sarah reopened her eyes and glowered at him.

"...we took one of my clients with us. It was his seventy-ninth birthday."

"Workin' on a weekend? You're gettin' a bit keen, aren't you?"

"It was Daniel's idea."

"Daniel's? He sounds lovely. Only just met you, and already gettin' involved with your work."

Billy paused. Yes, it had been kind of Daniel. After what he had read on Daniel's phone that morning, he had thought about talking things over with his mother. Asking her for advice. She had often been his confidante when it came to relationships. But he decided today was not the time.

"Chuck, that's my client, he's been a bit gloomy. Well, grumpy to be honest. So Daniel thought it would be nice to take him out for his birthday."

"Why Cambridge? It's a long way to go. Especially for a grumpy old man you don't know very well."

"Chuck used to live there. Daniel thought it might cheer him up to go back again. And anyway, we could see Simon and Tom, and have a nice day by the river. But then it all got a bit unpleasant. Have you got any tissues?"

"There's a box in the cupboard. Why unpleasant?"

Billy reached down for the tissues and wiped the surplus moisturizer from his hands. "Chuck got into an argument, well, almost a fight, with this man he met. He was shouting at him apparently and being abusive."

"Is he ill? 'e's not got that Tourette's thing has he?"

"No, nothing like that. It turns out he knew the man. Maggie thinks they were lovers."

"Blimey. That's a bit of a conclusion to jump to, isn't it? What made 'er think that?"

"She said it was the way the other man was talking. Daniel says she's perceptive about these things, and I think she's probably right."

"So she thinks your man Chuck is gay. What do you think?"

Billy sighed. What did he think? Chuck had not struck him as gay. But then, jumping to that conclusion meant he was making an awful lot of assumptions. Not all gay people fitted a stereotype.

"Chuck was in the American Air Force," Billy said. "Based near Cambridge during the sixties. The other man looked like he was about the same age. English accent. Proper-looking."

She put her hands down on the bed and, with an effort, eased herself into a more upright position.

"Shove that pillow behind me, will you, love?"

He did as he was asked.

"Sixties, eh? Cold war. Forbidden times." She shifted her back to get comfortable. "Perhaps they could 'ave been lovers. They'd 'ave kept it secret. Especially if they were in the forces." Her eyes twinkled and looked at him with an air of mischief. "'ow intriguin'. There's only one way to find out."

He shook his head. "I'm not going to ask. Daniel's already suggested that. It's not for me to poke my nose in—"

"Did you get the name of the other man?"

"Um, Guy Frobisher, I think. Yes. Guy Frobisher. Why?"

"That's not a common name. It wouldn't take you long to find 'im, I'm sure."

Billy laughed. "Who do you think I am? Miss Marple?"

She shook her head and closed her eyes. "Oh no, love. I'm Miss Marple. You're my assistant. Why don't you get onto that interweb thing of yours? I'm sure it wouldn't take you long."

Chapter 20

Billy turned the key in the lock of 149 Honeydew Lane and pushed open the front door. The accumulated heat inside the house, even though it had only been closed for a few days, hit him like the blast from a furnace. He switched on the hallway light, closed the door behind him, and bent down to pick up the collection of letters and advertising junk piled on the doormat. The warm, stale air in the house was suffocating. Billy carried the mail along the hallway to the kitchen at the back of the house, dropped it on the small wooden table, and fumbled with the security locks on the backdoor. His mother had insisted on having multiple deadlocks fitted after a television news reporter declared Wood Green to be the most dangerous suburb in London.

"They're talking about fights between gangs on the streets, Mum, not break-ins," Billy had tried to reassure his mother at the time. "This house is more than secure enough."

"I'm not takin' any chances," she had replied. "I don't want to wake up dead in me bed from bein' stabbed 'cause I didn't 'ave decent locks fitted."

Billy asked her why she only fitted the extra locks to the backdoor and not the front, to which his mother replied she had had enough money only for the backdoor, and anyway, it was a well-known fact burglars came in the back way and not the front, on account of the front door being in full view of the street.

As he struggled with the bottom bolt on the door, Billy recalled his mother's final statement of fatalistic logic. "It's like forgettin' to take your sunglasses with you when you go out. It's always sunny then. If I 'ave extra locks fitted, I'll never get broken into. Stands to reason."

Billy used his foot to put pressure on the bottom of the door, forced the key to turn in the lock, and the bolt slid back reluctantly. He pulled the door open wide, stood on the threshold, and looked out at the small patch of brown grass surrounded by patio pots filled with scorched and shriveled shrubs. The evening air was warm, and there was only a little breeze. Even so, it was more bearable than the claustrophobic atmosphere inside the house.

He went back into the hallway and opened the door of a large cupboard under the stairs. A mop, a broken ironing board, and a collection of plastic bags fell out on top of him. He left them lying on the floor while he rummaged among the motley assortment of domestic debris accumulated in the cupboard. Finally, hidden behind an empty cardboard box, saved for no reason he could remember, he found what he was looking for. He shoved the collection of objects lying on the hall floor back into the cupboard as best he could, forced the door shut, and carried the folding garden chair back through the kitchen to the outside.

Cautiously he tested his weight on the faded canvas of the small chair. He had no idea when it had last been used. When his mother became ill, he rarely found time to tidy the flower borders or mow the tiny lawn of the small garden for her. Satisfied the chair was safe, Billy returned to the kitchen once more, took a glass from the drying rack by the sink, and filled it from a half-empty bottle of Pinot Grigio he had left in the fridge over a week ago. Back outside, he settled himself in the garden chair and took a long sip from the glass. He leaned cautiously against the canvas back of the chair, looked up at the cloudless night sky, and pondered the events of the day.

He had been pleasantly surprised at his mother's curiosity about Chuck's outburst. He worried she had lost interest in the world outside her hospital room and had become introspective. But she was always quick to gather or deliver gossip, and the speculation over Chuck's relationship with Guy Frobisher had clearly intrigued her. For her to even suggest Billy use the internet to find the man's details showed she was still interested in events going on around her, despite the concoction of painkilling drugs she had to take.

Whether he would do anything about her suggestion was another matter. Billy was mildly curious about Chuck's past, but there was another, more important mystery distracting him. He wished he had asked his mother's advice about the message on Daniel's phone.

Now he had seen it, he could not stop thinking about where Daniel was tonight. Who was Anthony? Billy tried to tell himself it was no business of his, and he was certain he was a fool to feel any pangs of jealousy. Jealousy was the death of relationships. He felt confident in that. But secrets were also the death of relationships. And Billy had kept no secrets from Daniel. After all, he had told him everything about Jason.

Well, not quite everything.

Billy took another sip of wine. No, it was up to Daniel to tell him about his other sexual encounters. He was curious about Daniel's past, but had no intention of acting on that curiosity. After all, it was hardly a long-term relationship. They were still getting to know each other. He had no right to demand the information.

And yet…the twinge of jealousy was there.

Billy had several friends in long-term relationships, which were also open. Simon and Tom for example. When Simon headed off to New Zealand for his filming next month, he would probably find some temporary company while he was there—maybe more than one guy. He and Tom would doubtless discuss the encounters in their daily chats. For his part, Tom also had semi-regular playmates whenever Simon went away for extended periods. Simon had confided in Billy over a beer or two the year before. He said the open relationship worked well, and on a few occasions they had brought a guy back to their house to play together as a threesome. By this time into their third beer, Simon invited Billy to do the same one day. But Billy refused. Simon had been Billy's first love. He was now a close friend, but no longer a sexual partner. And Billy preferred to keep it that way.

In all of Billy's relationships since Simon, there was only one that had been open. That had been with Jason. And that ended badly. He had always blamed Jason for the breakup. But maybe it was a little too easy to do that. Perhaps it was his own suppressed jealousy that turned things sour and caused the relationship to end.

After all, it had started so well. When he first met Jason in the Admiral Duncan pub in Soho, there was an immediate attraction. Billy thought Jason was the sexiest man he had ever encountered. Jason was a big, hairy, loud Australian. Funny, in a down-to-earth way. And passionately sexy. During the first year of the relationship, they spent a lot of time in bed in the large room in Soho Jason rented from a rich Australian friend called Oliver. The sex was good, and frequent.

Then Billy's mother became ill. Billy wanted to be around for her when she came back from treatment sessions at the hospital. Inevitably, he spent less time in Jason's room in Soho. Jason had been understanding about it. "No worries, mate," he would say. "Your mum comes first."

Jason would occasionally stay with Billy at the house in Wood Green. The paper-thin walls and the constant presence of Billy's mother meant sex was out of the question. Despite this, Jason got on well with Billy's mother, and they used to sit playing cards together while Billy cooked supper. The two would roar with laughter and behave like a couple of naughty schoolchildren. "You've picked a good one there," Mum would say to Billy. "I'd go for 'im meself if I didn't know 'e wasn't that way inclined."

When winter arrived, Billy's work was more demanding. He found himself rushing from one client to another while his boss asked him to cover for colleagues who had gone down with flu. His mother was noticeably weaker from the aggressive treatment she received for her cancer, and she needed more help. Jason was a welcome refuge from the stresses of his life. Late on a Saturday night, when Jason had finished working, they would climb into bed. Jason would turn to Billy and say, "I've pulled up the drawbridge. The buggers can't get us now." They always had long, satisfying sex sessions, and afterwards, they lay in each other's arms, drifting in and out of sleep. The problems of Billy's life melted away on those precious Saturday nights.

In late January Jason got sick. He declined quickly. Billy was helping his mother get back home from a treatment session when he received a phone call from Westminster hospital.

"We've been given your name as the next of kin for Jason Dean. Is that correct?"

It was a shock to receive the call. All the way to the hospital, Billy felt guilty that he had not paid more attention to the decline in Jason's health. But he was more involved with his mother's ill health. He had never expected the big Australian to end up with pneumonia.

Jason was in hospital for five days. When he was discharged, he returned to his rented room in Soho and spent several weeks recovering. His Australian landlord Oliver was staying in London and helped Billy to look after him. It was fortunate Oliver was around, because Billy found himself rushing between his mother and Jason. And both patients were demanding in their own ways.

Oddly, the pneumonia brought Billy closer to Jason, and he was disappointed when the Australian returned to work at the Admiral Duncan after only five weeks. Billy said it was too soon, that he was concerned Jason needed more time to recover from the pneumonia. But Jason dismissed the advice. "I'll be fine," he had said. "I'm a fit bloke. Really."

During a weekend in spring, Jason had brought up the subject of sex with Oliver. "He's a nice bloke. Nothing special like you, mate. But he's asked me for a shag during the week. You know, when you're away at your mum's. Of course he knows you're my boyfriend, and I told him I wanted to ask you first. What do you say?"

The question made Billy feel vulnerable. He and Jason had talked about open relationships in the past. They agreed it could be a possibility, provided they were always honest with each other. Now here was Jason being honest, and Billy preferred not to hear it.

He knew his mother's illness meant he and Jason rarely got together during the week. It was unsurprising Jason was tempted by the invitation from another man. If Billy refused, he risked pushing Jason away, especially after their previous discussion about open relationships. He smiled at Jason and kissed him. "Sure," Billy said. "Why not? Perhaps he'll teach you some new techniques you can try out with me."

At the start of summer, Billy got home from work to find his mother collapsed on the living room floor. While he waited at the hospital for news of her condition, he tried to call Jason. Billy needed to hear a reassuring voice. But the call went to voicemail. There was no response to his text messages either. The next day Jason contacted him. "Sorry, mate," he said. "I was with Oliver last night. He's got a new job back in Oz, so we kinda celebrated. We had a bit of a night of it."

"What do you mean 'a bit of a night of it'?"

"Well, mate," replied Jason. "We shagged, of course."

Billy was furious. There was a row. More than one. Billy told Jason how much he felt hurt, betrayed, unsupported at a time he needed it most. Jason was equally angry. He reeled off a list of times he had supported Billy or his mother, or both, during her illness.

There was the day Jason had taken time off from work to go with her to the hospital, because Billy had to attend an important meeting. There were the times he sat with Billy and listened to him talk about how he hated to see his mother's condition get worse. Or he simply held Billy when emotion overwhelmed him. He remembered the first time it happened. "You know, mate," Jason had said, as Billy sobbed on his shoulder, "I'm not the sort of bloke to do this kind of touchy-feely shit. Blokes don't do it in Oz. If they do, they get called pansies. But for you, mate," he went on, "I'll do whatever you want to help you get through this."

They tried to patch things up. But the relationship changed. In the same way a broken porcelain ornament is never the same after it has been mended. The end came for Billy when Jason had booked a flight to Australia.

"I need to see the family," he had said. "Haven't been back there for three years. My niece was born two years ago and I haven't seen her yet. The blokes at the pub are keeping the job for me. And I'll be gone only a month. I can't afford to stay away any longer. And anyway. I wanna be back with you."

As it got closer to the day of Jason's departure, Billy's mum had collapsed again and was rushed to hospital. After Billy visited her one evening, he went to Soho to see Jason. He badly needed someone to talk to. It had been a Wednesday, and he hoped the pub would be quiet. Then Jason would have time to spare for him.

When Billy walked through the door of the Admiral Duncan that evening, he saw Jason talking to his landlord, Oliver. Billy was surprised. Oliver was supposed to have returned to Australia several months before.

"Hey, Billy," Oliver had called him over. Jason looked uncomfortable and walked away to serve a customer.

"I thought you were back in Oz?" Billy had asked as he joined Oliver at the bar.

"No, mate. Didn't Jason tell you? I decided not to take the job and stay here in London instead. But I'm going back next week to sort out my visa extension." He waved a hand in Jason's direction. "It's only three days before him and me are back in the motherland." He'd slapped an arm across Billy's shoulder. "It's great you're okay about us going. But I guess with your old mum crook, you gotta stay here."

Billy shoved Oliver's arm away and walked out of the pub. Billy ignored Jason's phone calls and messages. Deep down, he had known it was a childish reaction. But his mother's illness was enough to deal with. He wanted to avoid another emotional confrontation with Jason.

And that was how his life continued. From time to time he had thought about contacting Jason to talk about what happened. But it was always easy to find something more important to do.

Billy's phone rang. He pulled it from his pocket and looked at the screen. It was Jason calling.

He pondered for a moment, and then answered the call.

Chapter 21

Daniel sat in the dimly lit waiting room of the hospital and looked around. The hot drinks machine was broken, paint peeled from the walls, and there were dark stains on the faded carpet. Piles of well-thumbed magazines lay scattered across the surface of a low wooden table on one side of the room. Next to it was a bizarre collection of broken toys shoved carelessly into an old blue plastic crate. Daniel shifted uncomfortably on the hard plastic chair and listened to the nighttime sounds of Starlings Psychiatric Hospital. They were sounds he was familiar with since he became a regular visitor eighteen months ago.

Doors slammed, voices shouted, and feet thundered up and down the uncarpeted staircase of the rambling Victorian building. The insistent beep of an unanswered alarm sounded incessantly in the distance. Daniel knew the hospital was woefully understaffed, that psychiatric care had long been the Cinderella service of the NHS. In recent years, there was growing public awareness of the extent of mental health issues in the UK. Despite this, there was still far from enough care available. Starlings hospital was in the poorer part of the wealthy Borough of Kensington and Chelsea. The state of the waiting room reflected a long-term funding shortage. Priority was given to staff and medicines, not luxuries like hot drinks machines for visitors.

The waiting room door opened, and a man in his late forties walked in. His white tunic top was under constant pressure from his bulging waistline. His dark brown hair was close-cropped, in a futile attempt to conceal the fact he was going bald.

"Hey, Daniel," he said. "How are you doing?"

Daniel rose to greet him. "Hi, Ramesh. I'm glad you're on tonight. I had a bit of a run-in with the duty nurse who was on last time I was here."

Ramesh smiled. "Yes. I got the full report from Frank the following day." He sat down in the chair next to Daniel. "You won't be bothered by her again. She was a contract nurse. She'd had quite a few bust-ups with the visitors. Frank's let her go."

Daniel was disturbed by the news. "Oh, I didn't want to cause trouble. But she acted like she knew everything about Anthony. But what she was saying was wrong. And it sort of threw me."

Ramesh held up the medical chart in his hand and patted it. "Don't worry. We've put you on the front page of Anthony's notes now. *'If in doubt, ask the boyfriend'*."

"But I'm not his boyfriend," Daniel protested.

Ramesh smiled again. His manner was always calm, always reassuring. "But you were. And Anthony still thinks you are. It's shorthand. And it makes sure anyone who's not familiar with Anthony's case doesn't make the same mistakes that the nurse did." He stood. "Are you ready to see him?"

Daniel remained seated. "Wait a moment. Tell me how he is first. I didn't get much chance to find out last time. And the doctor wasn't around. I want to hear it from you."

Ramesh resumed his seat next to Daniel. "You know, you should really ask Dr McKenzie, not me. I'm Anthony's primary contact nurse. Dr McKenzie's in charge of his treatment plan."

Daniel shook his head. "You're more than his nurse. You seem to be the only person in this world he trusts. He confides in you. So you're the best person to tell me whether he's getting better or not."

Ramesh put the medical chart on the chair next to him and stared at it for a moment. Finally, he turned to Daniel. "It's good news and bad news. The good news is that Dr McKenzie's pleased with how he's responding to the new drug regime. Anthony's only had one psychotic episode since you last saw him. The doctor's confident they might stop altogether if we continue."

"And the bad news?"

Again, Ramesh paused and stared off into the distance before he answered. "See what you think when you see him. I don't want to prejudge, but I think you'll notice a difference. He's not the Anthony we knew. Even the Anthony of a few months ago."

"What do you mean?"

"He's much more—" Ramesh struggled to find the right word. "...withdrawn and paranoid. It's not nearly as extreme as when he expressed it previously. But now it's always there. His dominant emotion. Before, his paranoia would come and go. Even when he relapsed back to the skunk after he was discharged for that short period last year." Ramesh paused, drew breath, and exhaled slowly, as if to calm himself. "Skunk. It's such a hip name for such an evil drug. The people who take it delude themselves, thinking it's only a bit of fun." Ramesh shook his head. "If they saw the permanent mental damage it does to people like Anthony, they'd think twice about taking it."

"So is this new drug regime causing the paranoia? Is it permanent?"

Ramesh shook his head. "Doctor McKenzie thinks she can get the balance in the dosage right. But for the moment I'm finding it harder to get through to him."

"So he doesn't even trust you now?"

Ramesh picked up the medical chart from the chair next to him and stood. "I won't say any more. You should see him now."

Daniel bent down to pick up his bag. "Is he likely to change?" he asked again.

Ramesh shrugged. "It's too early to say. He's only been on this treatment for five weeks. Doctor McKenzie's still adjusting the dosage." He rested his hand on Daniel's shoulder. "I know it's hard for you, but I'm not sure the man you once loved is still there."

Daniel forced a smile.

"He hasn't been for two years."

***

Anthony sat in a shabby green armchair in the corner of the dayroom. His eyes were closed and he wore a large pair of headphones. His head nodded back and forth to an unheard beat. Daniel walked across the room and sat in the chair opposite. He waited and watched to see if Anthony would open his eyes. Anthony's burgeoning beard had grown stragglier since Daniel's last visit a week ago. His shirt was buttoned wrong, the fly of his jeans was open, and there was a hole in his left sock. A big difference from the days when Anthony would spend hours on a Friday or Saturday evening preening in front of a mirror before finally going out. Daniel closed his eyes and tried to picture Anthony in the good times.

They had met when they had been working on a low-budget children's charity show in London. Despite the small budget, the one-night-only performance involved over two hundred children on stage with an audience made up of celebrities and others who had donated generously to the charity in return for expensive tickets. Daniel was music director of the show and Anthony the stage manager. The show's main director was a highly volatile man who had clearly never directed such a large-scale production before.

Before the technical rehearsal, the director had walked out, leaving Anthony and Daniel to co-direct the remainder of the rehearsal and the performance. They were both only twenty-five years old with limited experience. Daunting, to say the least, but the performance was a great success, and at the end it received a five-minute standing ovation from the enthusiastic audience. Afterward, Anthony and Daniel had shared a bottle of champagne in a cramped dressing room to celebrate their achievement.

Anthony lived in a low-rent house that was due for demolition to make way for luxury flats. He had shared the house with four other people who were also involved with performance arts in some way or other. That Friday night, it was a short taxi ride back to the house. Daniel had stayed the weekend and spent most of the summer living with Anthony. They were together for the whole of the following year.

In the spring of their second year together, Daniel landed a six-month contract in Scotland to work with a performance arts therapy company. The hours were long, and he could only free up one or two weekends a month to see Anthony. Daniel was working so hard he failed to notice the changes. Reflecting back now, he recalled there were times when Anthony seemed confused, or got muddled during a conversation. But mostly he was the same enthusiastic, fast-talking, crazy-headed guy Daniel had first met.

In July, Daniel received a phone call from one of Anthony's housemates. "Anthony's in hospital," she had said. "It might be a good idea if you went to see him."

The police had sectioned Anthony under the Mental Health Act. They said they had found him naked in the middle of Parliament Square claiming to be the natural successor to the prime minister. He was sent to a psychiatric hospital because he was a danger to the public. During Anthony's first stay in hospital, the cause of his psychosis was quickly pinned down to his usage of super-strength cannabis, or skunk. Anthony had been taking the drug on an increasingly regular basis. Daniel was furious with Anthony and with himself. How had he failed to notice what was going on?

He resolved to nurse Anthony back to good health. By a stroke of luck, a prestigious music therapy company headhunted him to be their music director. He moved back to London and into his grandfather's empty house. It took him a long time to admit the extent to which Anthony had changed.

There were occasions when Anthony blamed Daniel for keeping him in the psychiatric hospital. Increasingly, he made it clear he no longer trusted him. But in between these periods, he was the same loving, fun, and wildly inappropriate man Daniel had first met. Daniel had felt confused as Anthony's moods swung from one extreme to another.

Then there was the day Anthony had attacked him. Fortunately, his nurse, Ramesh, had been nearby and was able to restrain him. The episode left Daniel badly shaken. Anthony was a strong man. Almost immediately after the attack, he was full of apologies. Tearful and remorseful. He had begged Daniel's forgiveness. But by then, neither man trusted the other. Even so, Anthony still sent affectionate, witty text messages to Daniel, asking him to come visit. Each time, he promised to be a better person. Whenever Daniel received them, he had flashbacks to the old relationship they once had. He would arrive at the hospital full of hope and optimism. Then he would meet Anthony and be forced to face reality.

Daniel felt tears forming. He opened his eyes and wiped them away.

"Why are you here?" Anthony had removed his headphones and was staring at him. "You've been talking to them again, haven't you?" Anthony's words were cold and emotionless. "You told them to put me on this new medication. Do you know what it feels like?" He raised the palms of his hands and pressed them hard against his cheeks. "It's shit. Like my head's trapped in a vice. I can't think. I can't feel. Anything." He looked at Daniel. His eyes were reproachful and sullen. "Why are you here?" he asked again. "Duty?

Guilt? Don't tell me it's love. I don't feel any. Not anymore. I don't believe you do either."

Daniel felt the tears again. This time they were tears of anger as well as sorrow. "I do love you, Anthony." He wiped his eyes again. He tried to choose his words carefully. "I don't love the way the skunk has screwed you up. But I know that the real Anthony is still there. Somewhere. Inside you."

Anthony sniffed. He wiped his nose with the back of his hand. "Who is the real Anthony?" he asked. There was a note of mockery in his voice. "How would you know? How would anybody know? What makes you so sure that this isn't the real Anthony?"

He stood up suddenly, swayed unsteadily, and held his arms out wide.

"Take a good look, Daniel," he said. "This is the real Anthony. This is what you've made me. You and those poisoners out there." His mouth shaped a mirthless smile. "Pleased with yourself, aren't you?"

Daniel suppressed the anger that arose in him. He felt like he was dealing with a belligerent teenager. Anthony had never been so direct in his accusations before. Ramesh was right. The new drug regime was having a profound effect on his mood. Daniel only hoped they could adjust the dosage, but right now, Anthony's words stung him.

"Anthony," Daniel began, "I think this new medication is distorting your view of the world. Let me have a word with—"

"No." Anthony raised his fist at Daniel. "If you talk to anyone, I'll kill you." He sat down heavily in the chair and lowered his head into his hands. The noisy silence of the hospital continued. In the distance, Daniel heard a patient shouting, the unanswered alarm continued to beep, and feet thundered on the carpetless staircase. Inside his head, Daniel could feel his pulse beating loudly. He could not think what to say or what to do next.

Finally, Anthony looked up at him.

"Just go," he said.

Chapter 22

"Priceless artwork has entered the premises," Maggie bellowed from the hallway down below. "Where d'you want it, love?"

Daniel lifted his head from the pillow. He was taking a catnap after a grueling week of rehearsals followed by two performances. Friday evening, and he was exhausted. Maggie had a key to his house. Useful if he wanted her to look after something when he was away, or he was working late, but unnerving when she burst in unannounced. He rubbed his eyes, sat up, and ran his fingers through the tangles in his hair.

"Daniel? Are you at home?" There was the sound of a crash from downstairs. "Bugger. That was clumsy."

Daniel reached for a sweatshirt lying on the floor and pulled it over his head. "Maggie?" He stood and headed for the top of the stairs. "What are you doing here?"

"I've got a nice surprise for you. Well. Two surprises now. And I'm afraid the second one isn't so nice. Sorry about that."

Daniel hurried down the stairs. He found Maggie on all fours in the drawing room, picking up the remains of a once attractive flower vase. Until a few moments ago it had stood on a table by the door. Propped up against the wall was a large flat parcel wrapped in brown paper. Maggie looked up when Daniel arrived in the doorway.

"Where's your dustpan and brush, sweetheart? I'm afraid I've been a bit clumsy. I hope you weren't too fond of it."

Daniel leaned against the doorjamb and folded his arms. "If I remember rightly, you stole that from the set of *Downton Abbey* for me. So, go on. You tell me. Was it valuable?"

Maggie got to her feet. She stepped forward and kissed Daniel on the cheek. "Not a brass farthing, darling. The props buyer got it from a charity shop the day before the shoot when he panicked about the lack of background dressing on the set. Bloody thing was never even seen in the final show." She raised an eyebrow. "And I didn't steal it, darling. Jimmy very kindly donated it to me when I expressed an interest in its future well-being. And after he gave it to me, out of the goodness of my heart, I gave it to you."

Daniel laughed. "Touché." He looked over to the brown paper parcel leaning against the wall. "So what's the priceless artwork you're going to replace that priceless vase with?"

Maggie sniffed, walked across to the package, and began to unwrap it. "I'm far too generous to you, Daniel Richards. It took me a good bit of persuasion to get Jonathan Weller—"

"Not *the* Jonathan Weller?"

"If you mean Jonathan Weller, artist to the stars, specialist in re-creating famous canvases authentically on demand, then yes. I was working with him on that awful movie about David Hockney last year." Maggie undid a final knot on the string binding the parcel, and pulled apart the two edges of its brown paper wrapping as though drawing the curtains on a window. She revealed a five-foot square canvas showing the rear view of a naked man climbing out of a swimming pool. Daniel stepped forward, one hand outstretched before him, as though sleepwalking.

"It's beautiful." He knelt down beside Maggie in front of the canvas, and reverently touched the acrylic surface of the paint. "It's an incredible reproduction. It could be the actual painting." He turned to Maggie. "Are you sure you didn't break into the Moores Gallery in Liverpool at dead of night and steal it?"

Maggie laughed. "That would have probably been easier. Jonathan's a *très* difficult man to negotiate with. He re-created several Hockneys for the movie. I argued that he really didn't need to keep them all, and he could generously give me this one in return for the hours I spent looking after his bloody dog." She laughed contemptuously. "Dog. I've seen better trained wolves."

"But why did you go to so much trouble to get it for me? It's not as though it's my birthday. Although, of course, I'm supremely grateful, my darling Maggie." Daniel kissed her on the cheek. He leaned back and continued to gaze at the painting. It was called *Peter Getting Out of Nick's Pool.* The original was painted by David Hockney in 1966. Daniel remembered talking about it with Billy the day they went to Cambridge. And then he realized. He turned back to Maggie and smiled.

"Now I understand. You heard Billy and me talking about it on the way back from Cambridge. I've never found anyone else as obsessed with this painting as I am. Until I met Billy. I thought I was unique."

"Darling Daniel, you are unique, thank God," she replied. "It was lovely listening to you two talk so passionately. I wanted to join in. But I had old grumpy face sitting next to me, telling me to concentrate on the road and not be distracted by the kids in the backseat. I nearly brained him towards the end of the journey."

Maggie got to her feet and cleared the brown paper and string away from the canvas. "So. Where is the gorgeous Billy this evening? I didn't expect to find you in on a Friday night. I thought you two would be on the town somewhere."

Daniel ignored the question. "Where do you think I should hang it? I'd love to put it in here. But I'm going to have to rearrange things a bit."

Maggie stopped in the middle of folding the brown paper and turned to him. "Don't change the subject. That makes me think something's happened." She leaned forward and stared intently at him. "Has something happened, Daniel? Have you two fallen out?"

Daniel looked at Maggie and sighed. "I don't know, to be honest. I haven't heard from Billy all week."

"Have you called him?"

"Of course I have. It's been manic for me in the last four days, what with the show yesterday. But he hasn't replied to any of my calls or messages."

"No missed calls?"

Daniel shook his head. "I don't think it's a problem. Really. We're both busy people, and it's not as though we've been—"

Maggie held up her hand to silence Daniel. "This calls for emergency gin," she said. "Go and fix the drinks, while I find the dustpan and brush and clear up my mess."

"I'll get them," said Daniel. "They're in the cupboard under the stairs."

"Good idea," replied Maggie. "I'll do the drinks. I'm more generous with the gin than you."

Before Daniel could protest, she strode off into the kitchen.

"When did you last speak to Billy?" Maggie asked. They sat together in the drawing room on the chaise longue. A gentle breeze blew in through the open sash of the bay window behind them. There were two large drinks and a bowl of olives on the oval teak coffee table in front of them.

"Last Sunday. I had this last-minute sound tech at the Lyric for the youth show. Then I went to see Anthony."

"Does Billy know about Anthony?"

Daniel shook his head. "I've been meaning to tell him. But I haven't really found the right moment. We've not talked about exes much. Although I did sort of meet his, the first evening we were in a restaurant together."

Maggie reached for her glass and took a drink. "What do you mean 'sort of meet his'?"

"We were sat in the window of Bento in Brewer when this big Australian guy suddenly pops up outside shouting and making obscene gestures. He was pretty obnoxious."

"Delightful." Maggie wrinkled her nose. "Billy seems such a nice young man. What was he doing with a prick like that?"

Daniel shrugged. "Anthony could be pretty obnoxious on occasions. Especially after a few drinks."

"Does Billy know about New York?"

Again, Daniel shook his head. "It's all up in the air at the moment. So it seemed a bit premature."

"Isn't Billy interested in your work?"

"Yes, but—"

"But you've avoided telling him about New York because you don't want to put him off."

"That's not fair."

Maggie took a sip from her glass. "So you saw Anthony on Sunday. How is he?"

Daniel reached for an olive. "Pretty bad. They've put him on this new medication. It's making him even more paranoid." He bit into the olive and spat the stone out into his hand. "He was really shitty, if I'm honest. He threatened to kill me at one point."

Maggie laid a hand Daniel's his arm. "That must have been tough. You're good to go to see him so regularly."

"Of course I should go to see him."

"But it was finished between you two a long time ago."

Daniel shook his head. He sighed. "That's the problem. I still feel something for him."

"Surely not, my darling? You've said before that he's not the man you met anymore. The skunk screwed him up permanently. And now you've met Billy."

"It's not as simple as that. You know, every now and then, I get glimpses of the old Anthony. It's as though he's trapped inside this nasty, vicious old queen's body."

Maggie snorted. "I've met a few of those doing wardrobe on the productions I've worked on over the years."

Daniel laughed, and laid his hand on top of hers. "Thanks, Maggie. I'm so glad you're here. Do you think," he paused for a moment, "do you think it's possible to fall in love with more than one person?"

"Of course it is." Maggie took another drink from her glass. "Are you in love with Billy?"

Daniel shrugged. "It's a bit early to say. It's not even two months yet."

"But you're still in love with Anthony? Aren't you? In some way at least." Maggie set her glass down on the table. She took Daniel's hands in hers and clasped them together. "All I can say is, you and Billy are good for each other. At least, it looks that way from here. But you're going to have to talk to him about Anthony."

"I would if he answered my calls."

Daniel's phone rang. Maggie leaned forward to look at the screen.

"Talk of the devil," she said. "It's Billy. I'll go and powder my nose."

***

"You're a bloody fool, Billy Walsh." Sarah looked at her son in disbelief.

He sat in the chair beside her bed, his face crestfallen, showing the same signs of guilt he had as a child when he denied having licked the icing off the chocolate cake.

"There could be all sorts of simple explanations," she went on. "And why was you readin' 'is messages? Don't you trust 'im already? You know what I always says? *Better to be sometimes cheated than never to trust.*"

"Dr Johnson," Billy said. "Back in the eighteenth century. That's who actually said it. I looked it up once. You've said it so often to me. I know it by heart. Anyway. I didn't mean to read Daniel's message."

"Oh, come off it." She was irritated by Billy's childlike defensiveness. "If you didn't want to read it, why pick up 'is phone?" She lay back on her pillow and ruminated for a minute. It was only yesterday they moved her to this new room in the hospital. She knew where she was. The hospice. That meant there was no more treatment. The end. Before the move she had felt helpless and despondent. Now she was here, she felt a new sense of rebellion rise within her. Modern medicine may have given up on her, but she was not prepared to go without a fight. And today that meant giving her son the benefit of her wisdom. Sometimes the painkillers muddled her mind, but right now, she was absolutely clear.

"Just because, what's 'is name, the Australian?"

"Jason."

"Yes, 'im. Just because 'e cheated on you, doesn't mean every other bloke's goin' to as well. An' from what you've been tellin' me, Jason asked your bleedin' permission before shaggin' the other bloke. So it's 'ardly cheatin'."

Billy smiled. "Well, it wasn't quite as simple as that."

"It never is with you." Sarah pointed to the cabinet by the bed. "Hand me that glass of water, will you?" Billy did as she asked, and she took a sip.

Her lips felt dry, and the action helped her take a moment to think what to say to Billy without biting his head off. She knew she had a tendency to do that. But he was really being dense. It was all so clear to her. Jason had asked Billy's permission to have a bit on the side. So why, when Jason took him up on the offer, had Billy got all uptight and refused to speak to him for a year? In her experience, bad communication was the quickest way to end a relationship. And her Billy was making the same mistake again now. Jumping to conclusions about something that could have a simple explanation, although it was difficult to see how at the moment.

"So you finally spoke to Jason. What did you talk about?"

Billy sighed. "It was good to talk to him. He apologized for how he acted in Soho the other week when I was with Daniel. Said he had wanted to talk to me, and when I gave him the brush-off he got angry. He's a nice guy really. I should have spoken to him a long time ago."

"Exactly." Sarah reached forward and ran her fingers through Billy's hair, the way she did when he was eight years old and his hair was long and wavy. "Why do you do this, son? Why do you bottle it all up?"

She looked at him as he smiled back at her. He seemed so lost, so vulnerable. But he was also a bloody fool.

"I hate confrontation," he said. "I do anything to avoid an argument. I used to spend night after night hearing you and Dad fighting. I used to turn my headphones up loud to drown it out."

Sarah slid her hand away from Billy's hair and rested it on her lap. The comment had stung her. "That was a while ago, Billy love." She looked at him with a feeling of sadness. "How much longer are you goin' to keep blamin' me for what goes wrong in your life?"

"I didn't mean it like that."

"But that's how it sounded, love. So your dad and I weren't good role models for you? Well, I'm sorry. I tried to do my best after 'e left."

"And you did, Mum." Billy looked genuinely upset. "I'm not blaming you. Not at all." He slumped back in his chair and turned his head to stare at the wall. "I don't want to fight like that."

Sarah reached out to rest her hand on his shoulder. "You don't have to, love. Me and your dad did it wrong. Don't you think I know that? But you don't have to have a blazin' row like we did every time you disagree with someone. You need to talk. Didn't they teach you anythin' useful at that fancy drama school you went to?"

Billy turned his head and smiled at her. He could melt an iceberg when he smiled like that.

"In a way, they did, Mum. You're right. I'm a bloody fool."

Chapter 23

Maggie opened the door to Billy when he arrived at Daniel's that evening. Before he had a chance to speak, she stepped out of the house and stood on the top step beside him. "Don't mind me, darling, I'm just going." She put her hand on his shoulder and reached up to kiss him. "Now you two boys have a good talk. It'll do you both the world of good, my dear." Maggie walked off down the street to her car, waving a hand in the air as she went.

"Hey, Billy." Daniel stood in the hallway. He held a hammer in his hand.

Billy looked down at the hammer and raised his arms in mock surrender. "Don't hit me," he said. "I'm unarmed and come in peace."

Daniel laughed, bent down, and placed the hammer on the floor outside the drawing room. "It's okay. I'm not in attack mode. I'm trying to hang a painting Maggie's given me. You can give me a hand if you like."

Billy stepped into the hallway and closed the front door. Daniel walked down the hallway and stood in front of him. "I've missed you this week," he said. "I tried to call, but you didn't get back to me."

"I know. I've bought a gift to say sorry." Billy held up a brown paper bag. "Chocolate chip cookies. I know you like them. You got them for me at the hospital the first time we met."

Daniel smiled and took the bag from Billy. "Thanks. Come on in. I'll make some tea, unless you want something stronger."

"If we're going to eat cookies, I'll have one of those fresh mint teas you do so well."

Billy followed Daniel down the hallway to the kitchen. In truth, he wanted to avoid alcohol to keep his head clear, in case they ended up in an argument. Was that calculated of him? Possibly. But at least he was prepared to face the discussion he needed to have head on, instead of shying away from it as he had done all week, and as he had done at so many difficult moments in his life in the past.

Daniel filled the kettle and got mugs down from a cupboard. "How have you been?"

Billy crossed to the open backdoor and looked out. Evening sunlight dappled the topiary hedges on either side of the garden, and the air was heavy with the scent of chamomile. The unmistakable song of a nightingale cut through the rustle of the wind through the trees.

"I've not had a great week." Billy turned from the view of the garden and watched Daniel preparing the tea. "I've got a confession to make."

Daniel paused, a pair of scissors in his hand. He looked at them, and back to Billy. "Don't worry, I'm not arming myself again. I need to get some mint from the garden." He crossed to the backdoor and stopped to face Billy. "Confession? What sins have you committed, my son?"

Billy smiled and prepared himself to ask Daniel the question that had dogged him all week. "Last Sunday morning, I saw a text message on your phone. I'm sorry. I picked it up by accident. It was while you were in the shower. The message was from someone called Anthony."

"Oh."

Daniel walked into the garden and down the path to the herb wall. He cut a handful of mint and carried it back with him to the kitchen. He smiled at Billy as he passed in the doorway and crossed to the worktop. "I should have told you sooner. But it's complicated."

"Can you tell me now?"

"Of course I can." Daniel dropped the mint and scissors on the worktop and walked back to Billy. "It's me who should say sorry. I'll tell you everything. No secrets." He kissed Billy slowly on the lips. "I don't need to forgive you for seeing the message on my phone. I know you weren't spying. We've not known each other long, but I'm confident you wouldn't do that."

Daniel walked back to the worktop and continued making the tea. "Anthony was my boyfriend. We're not together any longer. He's in a psychiatric hospital. He's been in and out of the place since he reacted badly to taking cannabis. Skunk. He gets psychotic episodes, but they're trying to control them."

Billy was shocked. He had not expected to hear this. "I'm so sorry. How long ago did it happen?"

"Nearly two years now. I was working in Scotland, and Anthony was living in a shared house in London with a lot of drugs around. It could have been worse, I suppose." Daniel picked up the two mugs of tea and crossed the kitchen to Billy. "Let's go and sit in the garden."

He led the way outside to the bench by the herb wall. They sat next to each other, and Billy placed his mug on the ground by his feet. He was confused by Daniel's use of the past tense to describe the relationship. It conflicted with the affectionate tone of the message he had read on the phone. He picked his words carefully as he phrased the next question. "You say he *was* your boyfriend? But you're still going to visit him. And in the text he seemed—"

"Yes, I know." Daniel took a drink from his mug and cradled it in his hands. "The Anthony I know now is different from the person I first met. The skunk made sure of that. There are times when he hates me. The psychotic episodes make him believe many things. Sometimes he says I'm the one who's caused all his suffering. But in between…" Daniel's voice faded and he looked down at his mug. "In between, for brief moments, he's like the old Anthony. No paranoia. No hatred. No fear. I get these emotional texts from him, full of love and fondness. Then I go to see him…" Daniel looked up at Billy. His eyes were blurred with tears. "Then I go to see him and I have to face the reality."

"Oh Daniel." Billy leaned across and put his arms around Daniel's shoulders. It was instinctive. He hated to see him suffer like this. Daniel leant against Billy's shoulder.

"I've been trying to find the right moment to tell you." Daniel sighed, and lifted his head to look at Billy. "No. In truth, I could have told you any time. Like the way you told me about Jason. But ever since that first night when we were in Soho together, when I dashed off because Anthony called, I've felt, guilty I suppose. And the longer I've left it, the harder it's been to tell you."

Billy leaned his forehead against Daniel's. "You love him still, don't you?"

Daniel leaned away and sat back against the bench. He rested a hand on Billy's thigh, turned his head to look at him, and smiled. "I feel a lot of things for Anthony. He makes me mad as hell. But also, we had some great times together. And I was deeply in love with him. I can't dismiss that. But I also can't go back to the past. Too much has changed. There's too much hurt that can't be undone. I need to face that."

He leaned across and kissed Billy. "I'm sorry. I should have told you. You've been far more open about Jason."

"Ah, Jason." Billy reached down for his tea. He took a sip from the mug and rested it on his thigh. It had been an interesting week, he reflected. "He called me last Sunday," he began. "Actually, he's been trying to call me several times since that night when we were in Soho and he banged on the window at the restaurant. But last Sunday I decided to answer his call."

Daniel leant his arms on the back of the bench and rested a hand on Billy's shoulder. "How was it?"

"We met up." Billy took another sip of tea.

"And?"

Billy reached forward and put his mug back on the ground. He leaned back against the bench and turned to Daniel. "Things are never straightforward, are they? In my head, Jason was always the one who cheated on me. The one who went off with Oliver to Australia when Mum was really ill."

"Oliver?"

"He was Jason's Australian landlord. The thing is, Jason actually asked me if it was all right if they got together occasionally. And I'd agreed to it."

"You had an open relationship with Jason? I didn't know that."

Billy nodded. "It was open on his side."

"But not on yours?"

Billy shook his head. "It could have been, but I wasn't interested."

"Were you happy with that arrangement?"

Billy sighed. Was he happy? Obviously not, judging by the way he had reacted when Jason and Oliver left for Australia together. But last Thursday, when he went for a drink with Jason, he realized how contradictory his reaction had looked at the time.

Jason reminded Billy how he had agreed to the request for an open relationship. He also reminded him the Australia trip had only been for a month, and that Oliver had stayed in Australia after Jason returned to London. Jason asked Billy why he had agreed to an open relationship, only to end everything when Jason took him at his word. Billy found it hard to answer.

Why had he agreed? He could only conclude he feared losing Jason at a time he needed emotional support. He would have agreed to almost anything. Billy sighed again.

"It wasn't great. But I didn't think much about how I was actually going to feel when I said yes." He looked at Daniel. "Do you want us to have an open relationship?"

Daniel looked surprised. "The thought hadn't crossed my mind. Do you?"

"I don't know. I haven't thought about it either. Only, with what you've said about Anthony…"

"Oh, I see." Daniel placed his hand on Billy's thigh and turned his head to look at him. "Can you understand if I say I still love Anthony, but it's no longer the relationship we once had? And it won't ever be again?"

"You mean it's over?"

Daniel shook his head. "I think we use the wrong words when we talk about relationships." He stood and began to pull small weeds out of one of the herb pots on the wall behind them. Billy turned around to watch Daniel.

"We say a relationship is over," Daniel continued, "that it's broken, or it's finished. But I think those words are far too strong. They're too final. Most of the time, I think relationships simply change. My relationship with Anthony changed after the skunk made him psychotic. But the love doesn't switch off. I can't dismiss what I felt for him. He was a big part of my life."

"You mean you're not over him yet?"

Daniel paused in his weeding and turned to Billy. "Wouldn't that be terrible if I was? I don't think it would be particularly human of me. I've known so many people in my life. But I'm not *over* any of them. They're still around. Somewhere. It's our relationships with each other that change over time." He walked back to the bench and sat next to Billy.

"I can't imagine you're over Jason." Daniel leaned back and rested his arms on the back of the bench again. "You saw him this week, which proves my point. But I'm guessing your relationship with him has changed."

"Aren't you using different words to say the same thing?"

Daniel shook his head. "I don't like the way our society tries to make everything over-simple. Either one thing or the other. Married, divorced. On, off. Love, hate. It's much more complicated than that. And I'm bloody pleased it is." He turned, placed his hands on Billy's knees, and turned his beautiful face to look at him. "I think you and I have something special happening here. I don't think either of us knows quite what it is yet. But it's special. At the same time, it's not like we've stepped onto this earth yesterday. We've had relationships before. Of course we have. Some people call that baggage. I disagree. I think it's what makes us human."

Billy placed his hands on top of Daniel's, and leaned his head forward until their foreheads touched. "I suppose I'm not really over Jason. But the relationship we once had is gone. He told me this week he was really hurt when I ended everything." Billy smiled as he recalled part of their conversation. "Apart from anything else, he's really fond of Mum. We talked about her quite a lot."

"He sounds like a lovely man. Even if he did give me the fright of my life when he banged on the restaurant window." The corners of Daniel's eyes crinkled into a smile.

Billy placed his hands on either side of Daniel's face and kissed him on the lips.

"Are you staying the night?"

Chapter 24

Somewhere in the distance there was a buzzing noise. Billy screwed his eyes tight shut and rolled over in the bed. After a few moments the buzzing stopped, only to start again a few seconds later. He blinked his eyes open. Chinks of sunlight found their way through gaps in the venetian blinds and created contrasting patterns of dark and light lines on the floor of the bedroom. Billy turned to Daniel, but the space beside him in the bed was empty.

The buzzing persisted. Billy shuffled across the bed and leaned over the side. Daniel's phone was vibrating on the floor. Billy resisted the temptation to pick it up. He had learned his lesson on that one. Instead, he picked up his own phone lying beside it, and checked the time. It was nearly ten. He lay back on the pillows and thought back to the night before.

Making love with Daniel had, once again, proved sensuous and inventive. It was well after three in the morning before they had gone to sleep. Daniel's ability to bring him right to the edge of climax, only to frustrate him by pulling away, created an explosion of pleasure when Billy finally came.

He was gratified to discover Daniel was more than happy to be versatile. It added a richness and sensuality to their lovemaking. Billy had rarely experienced it before. Jason had refused to be anything but a top. Adrian, his big love at the Royal College of Music, was predominantly a top. He flipped occasionally, and had done so reluctantly when Billy asked him to experiment.

Daniel was a much more thoughtful and caring lover. He made it clear he wanted to give pleasure as much as to receive it. Billy put his arms behind his head, closed his eyes, and smiled broadly. There was still so much more to explore with Daniel, and that beautiful body of his.

"You look happy."

Billy opened his eyes. Daniel stood naked at the foot of the bed. He grinned broadly. "Did my phone wake you? Sorry. But now you're up, I've got something really exciting to show you."

Billy looked down at Daniel's cock. "Don't worry. I can see it from here."

Daniel laughed. He launched himself onto the bed and landed beside Billy. "Good morning, sleepyhead." He placed a hand behind Billy's head, pulled him close, and kissed him. "Thank you for last night. You're one of the sexiest men I've ever met."

"Only one of?" Billy raised an eyebrow. "Who were the others?"

Daniel laughed. "My mistake. How English of me. To add a qualifier to the superlative."

Billy smiled and kissed Daniel again. "You're surprisingly grammatical for a musician."

This time it was Daniel's turn to raise an eyebrow. "Why are you so surprised? I don't only write the music. I write the lyrics as well. You've not experienced the sheer poetry what I wrote yet, have you?"

"'What I wrote'? Is that an example of your command of the English language?"

Daniel reached down and began to tickle Billy's thighs.

"Get off." Billy fought the attack, but his susceptibility to being ticklish overcame him. He pleaded with Daniel to stop. Billy lay back on the pillows. Daniel sat astride him and massaged his shoulders.

"There," said Daniel. "Lie still and admit you're a simple actor, whose only ability is to read the words, not write them, like what I can."

Billy feigned horror at this. "I was never a simple actor. I'll have you know my performance as Hamlet in my final year at drama school won me a prize and lavish praise in *The Stage*."

"Then why don't you start again?"

Daniel slid his hands across Billy's chest and massaged with his fingertips. Billy sighed and closed his eyes. "That's wonderful," he said. "I return your compliment. You are the sexiest man I've ever met. With the sexiest hands." He opened his eyes to look at Daniel. "No qualifier needed to those superlatives."

"Well?"

"Well what?"

Daniel stopped massaging Billy's chest and rolled over to lie beside him. "I asked you a question. Why don't you go back to acting?"

Billy sighed. "You know as well as I do it's not as easy as that."

Daniel shook his head. "Yes it is. You're not married. You're free to do whatever you want. You've got no dependents."

"I've got Mum."

"Yes, but she's—" Daniel stopped. "I'm sorry. That would have been completely inappropriate."

Billy sat up. He turned to Daniel and laid a hand on his shoulder. "No, you're right. She's dying. She won't be around much longer. You're absolutely right. I've lost my confidence, and I'm making excuses." He kissed Daniel on the lips. "Thank you. I think you need to kick me into action more often."

Daniel laughed. He jumped off the bed and walked to the bedroom door. "Talking of action, come and see what I've found."

"Not more porn?" Billy swung his legs over the side of the bed and stood. "Somehow I don't think either of us need that." He followed Daniel out of the bedroom and into the study next door. Daniel's laptop was open on the desk. "Have you been working? On a Saturday?"

Daniel pulled out a swivel chair tucked under the desk and gestured to it. "I've been working for you, darling. Here, take a seat."

Billy sat and peered at the screen. He saw a cutting from an old newspaper report, with the image of a good-looking RAF pilot next to the report. Billy turned to Daniel. "What have you been up to?"

There was a look of triumph on Daniel's face. "That, my dear, is Captain Guy Frobisher. I found this old newspaper report from 1967. It turns out he was a bit of a hero." He leaned over Billy's shoulder to read from the screen. "*RAF Captain Guy Frobisher was hailed as a hero today when he steered his stricken aircraft away from the city of Cambridge and averted a potential disaster.*"

Billy waited for Daniel to explain further. Why was he so interested in a fifty-year-old story about an RAF pilot? He rubbed sleep from his eyes and tried to concentrate. "And?"

Daniel slapped his forehead with the palm of his hand. "Guy Frobisher is that same man your lovely Chuck had a massive argument with in Cambridge the other week."

Billy looked back at the screen. "Are you sure it's the same man?"

Daniel made a sound like steam escaping from a pressure cooker. "No. It's probably his mother." He leaned over Billy's shoulder and pointed to the screen. "Look. He was based at RAF Wyton in Cambridgeshire."

"Okay, I get that." Billy peered at the black-and-white photograph of the RAF captain again. "I mean, there could be other Guy Frobishers. And I seem to remember Chuck was based at somewhere called Alconbury, not Wyton."

Daniel reached for the keyboard and brought up a map of the east of England. After a few clicks of the mouse, he turned to Billy with a triumphant look on his face.

"RAF Wyton is only six miles from Alconbury. These guys were round the corner from each other. Plus, Guy Frobisher is not exactly a common name. The man in this news report was in Cambridgeshire around the same time Chuck was there. He's either the same guy, or it's a bloody impressive coincidence."

Billy turned back to the screen, and read the article dated November 10th 1967.

Hero RAF pilot avoids disaster

RAF Captain Guy Frobisher was hailed as a hero today when he steered his stricken aircraft away from the city of Cambridge and averted a potential disaster. The English Electric Canberra crashed into fields south of the city only seconds after Captain Frobisher and his navigator bailed out and parachuted to safety. A spokesman for RAF Wyton near Huntingdon said the twenty-five-year-old captain took off from the airbase shortly before six in the morning on a routine reconnaissance mission. He headed his plane south over Cambridge city when it developed engine trouble. With a full payload of fuel onboard, quick-thinking Captain Frobisher knew a crash would cause devastating damage and the potential deaths of thousands of people. He managed to keep his stricken aircraft in the air long enough to divert it over open countryside west of Grantchester, where he and his navigator ejected. Shortly after, the Canberra plunged into the ground and exploded in a fireball.

"Wow." Billy looked up at Daniel. "He is a hero. And only twenty-five when it happened. Four years younger than me. Impressive."

"He's stunningly good-looking as well," Daniel added. "Even in that grainy photograph you can see how handsome he was." He took hold of the computer mouse once more. "And I have more." After a couple of clicks, the address and telephone number for Guy Frobisher appeared on the screen.

"Good grief." Billy stared at the information. "I didn't know I was dating a stalker."

"So, what do you think?"

"I'm impressed," Billy said. "If you ever get bored with writing music, you can always get a job as a private eye."

Daniel took hold of Billy's chair and spun it round so they faced each other. He placed his hands on Billy's bare thighs, and leaned forward to kiss him. "Sometimes, my dear Billy, I wonder if you do this deliberately to wind me up."

Billy was confused. "Do what?"

Daniel gripped Billy's thighs even tighter and rubbed his thumbs on the inside of them: completely distracting, but not at all unpleasant. "Don't you see? We can play matchmaker and agony aunts, all in one. If Maggie's right, Chuck and heroic Captain Guy were lovers. Something happened between them, which has made Chuck all grumpy. But, judging from the other weekend, Captain Guy wants to patch it up."

"Oh no." Billy shook his head. "Chuck's a client of mine. It would be highly unprofessional of me to get involved in his personal life in that way."

"But why not? Chuck's unhappy and grumpy. There's usually an underlying reason why people are like that. Perhaps this is the reason. He was once in love with this gorgeous, handsome RAF captain. Whatever happened between them has made Chuck sad and unhappy."

Billy laughed. He leaned forward and kissed Daniel. The man was really attractive, as he squatted before him with no clothes on, massaging Billy's thighs at early-o'clock on a Saturday morning. "You're really an incurable romantic, aren't you? What are you planning to do? Walk into Chuck's apartment, tell him you know all about his former lover, wave your magic wand, and heal their broken relationship?" He rested his hands on Daniel's shoulders. "Can't you see how that might reflect badly on me as one of his carers?"

Daniel stopped massaging Billy's thighs. He looked like someone told him his puppy had died. "I was only trying to help." Even his pout was attractive. "I thought you might want to make Chuck feel happier."

"The chances are it would make Chuck much grumpier, and result in a formal complaint to my boss." Billy shook his head. "Do you know what we call her when she's not listening? Man Cock ASS."

Daniel roared with laughter. "How on earth did she get a name like that?"

"It's her job title. Well, sort of. She loves acronyms so we gave her an unofficial one. Very unofficial. She'd take a dim view of me interfering in a client's life as you're suggesting."

"It's hardly interfering," protested Daniel. "I looked up a few details on the internet. So if Chuck ever shows interest in getting in touch with his former lover—"

"Possible former lover."

"Whatever. If he shows interest, then you'll have the information to hand to give to him, and help him out. It's compassion. It's caring. It's—"

"It's Dear Daniel, the Musical Agony Uncle's weekly column."

Daniel laughed again. "Not bad. I think I might steal that and set it up as a sideline business." He stood, and walked to the door. "Are you hungry? I've got some croissants and *pain au chocolat*. Or I can do bacon and eggs if you want a big fry-up."

Billy stood and walked across to him. He placed his arms around Daniel's waist and pulled him close. Daniel's cock nestled comfortingly against his. "Did I tell you what a lovely man you are? Thank you for doing that. I'm sorry if I sound ungrateful. I don't mean to be. I'm not sure what the professional guidelines are, and I don't want to get into trouble for involving myself in a client's personal life."

Daniel placed his arms on Billy's shoulders and kissed him. "Don't worry. Whatever you say to me, your cock usually tells a different story. Come on." He dropped his arms and took hold of Billy's hands. "It's another beautiful day outside, and we're in danger of missing it." He led the way to the top of the stairs and began to descend.

"What were you planning to do today?" Billy asked.

"Oh, I don't know," Daniel replied from halfway down. "It's so nice, I thought we could have a picnic. Do you fancy a trip out to Cambridge?"

Chapter 25

The lone sheep lifted its head from the grass and looked up. Its unblinking eyes stared directly at Daniel. The rest of the flock was some distance behind. It was the only sheep adventurous enough to break away from the flock and approach the picnicking humans. Daniel held his breath. He watched through the long grass swaying in front of him in the afternoon breeze as the animal stared at him. A few yards to their right, the river Cam lapped against the grassy bank, its flowing waters chilled the summer air. Ducks called plaintively for food. The sheep cocked its head to one side, raised and then lowered its ears. All the while, its mouth chewed rhythmically.

"Do you want another sandwich?" Billy's voice cut through the quiet.

The sheep turned and bounded towards the rest of the flock. Daniel exhaled, rolled over onto his back, and propped himself up on his elbows. Billy stood at Daniel's feet with his hands on his hips. The sun behind him cast a halo around his bare chest. Daniel pulled his sunglasses over his eyes and peered up at him.

"I couldn't eat another thing." Daniel patted the rug beside him. "Where've you been? Come and lie down and enjoy the sun. You got us enough food to feed an army."

"I went to put some things back in the cool box in the car. Otherwise they'll go off in the heat." Billy lay on his stomach alongside Daniel and propped himself up on his elbows. "Thanks for driving. It was really kind of Maggie to lend us Velma. Even if she did overheat on the motorway."

Billy looked from the flock of sheep in the distance to the river flowing alongside them to their left. Ducks darted back and forth on its surface, racing in between the slower, graceful swans. "It's beautiful, isn't it? Simon used to tell me about Grantchester Meadows, but it's the first time I've come here. I think I prefer it to being in Cambridge. There's the river, and punting, but there are fewer people, and it's so much more peaceful."

Daniel turned to raise an eyebrow at him. "Are you planning on taking me punting this afternoon?"

Billy shook his head. "You really don't want me to inflict that on you." He gestured to a group of students sprawled out by the riverbank. "We can hire one of those cute undergrads over there to chauffeur us if you like."

Daniel slipped his sunglasses onto the end of his nose and peered over them at Billy. "So now you've decided to make it an open relationship?"

Billy laughed. "Not quite yet." He rolled over onto his back and stretched his arms out behind him. "This summer's the best we've ever had. It feels like it could go on forever."

"Well, don't get too comfortable. We came up here for a purpose, remember?"

"You don't really mean that?" Billy rolled onto his side to look at Daniel. "Let's stay here and enjoy the day. Look, I'm serious about getting a chauffeur if you want to go on the river. I saw one of those students take that couple punting earlier. I can ask him if he's up for it again."

Daniel shook his head. "I'd rather stay here with you." He leaned forward and kissed Billy on the lips. "But later, we can walk into the village and look for our mysterious Captain Frobisher."

"You can look for him if you like." Billy rolled onto his back. "I'm keeping out of this barmy idea. I don't understand why you won't call him if you're so keen to play Agony Uncle. You've got his phone number, Mister Stalker."

"I'm not going to call him because I'm certain he'd put the phone down on me." Daniel stroked his fingers over Billy's shoulder. Billy rolled his neck in appreciation.

"And what if he's not in?"

"Then I'm going to write a little note with my business card attached, and drop it through his letterbox. That way it looks like a genuine, reputable approach, and not some nutter on the phone."

"It will look like some nutter was standing on his doorstep, posting business cards through his letterbox." Billy rested his hand on Daniel's shorts and slipped his fingers between the waistband and Daniel's exposed flesh. "Are you seriously going to say 'I know who you are, Mr Frobisher? You're the ex-lover of Senior Airman Chuck Stuart and I claim my ten pounds reward'?" He slipped his hand farther inside the shorts and massaged the top of Daniel's thigh. He rolled onto his back and groaned in appreciation.

"Not if you continue to do that." Daniel sighed. "To be honest, I don't have a script in my head. But I'm sure I'll think of something."

***

The Dower House was set back from a quiet country lane, behind a low stone wall. Its tall, tiled roof was covered in moss, and its windows were glazed with diamond-shaped glass held together by black leading. Between the boundary wall and the house was a lawn bordered by rose bushes and fruit trees. A tall, slim man stood by a sundial in the middle of the lawn. His shoulders were slightly stooped, and his snow-white hair perfectly groomed. Despite the warmth of the evening, he was dressed smartly in a shirt and tie. He had shed his suit jacket but wore a maroon waistcoat. A watch chain hung from the waistcoat pocket. The man held a pipe in one hand, which he brought up to his mouth and inhaled. Daniel recognized his face immediately. Despite the passage of more than fifty years, Captain Guy Frobisher looked strikingly like his image in the news report from 1967.

Daniel turned to look farther up the road. Billy leaned against the side of Maggie's car and gave him a thumbs-up. Daniel turned back to the house to see the distinguished-looking man walk towards him.

"Good afternoon." The man looked at his watch. "Or should I say, good evening? Hasn't it been a beautiful day? Can I help you?" His voice was precise, with a quiet authority. Each word enunciated clearly, in the manner of an English film actor of the 1940s or '50s. He stopped before the stone wall, extended a hand in greeting, and smiled warmly. "Guy Frobisher."

Daniel reached across the wall and shook hands. "Daniel Richards." Guy Frobisher's cornflower blue eyes stared intently at Daniel. His handshake was firm.

"I was admiring your beautiful house," said Daniel. "I came up for the day from London with my boyfriend, and we've spent the afternoon over on the meadows."

Guy Frobisher raised his pipe to his lips and puffed on it for a moment. "Boyfriend, eh? How refreshingly modern." He turned and waved his pipe at the house behind him. "I'm lucky. It's been in my family for several generations. Seventeenth century, although it's had quite a few alterations made to it over the years." He turned back to Daniel. "You're welcome to come and look around the gardens if you like. I used to open them to the public, but I've lost my appetite for hospitality in the last few years." He looked past Daniel up the road, and waved at Billy, leaning against the parked Volvo. "Bring your boyfriend as well. I could do with the company."

Daniel turned and beckoned Billy to come join them. Billy extended his arms in a shrug, pushed himself away from the side of the car, and walked down the road.

"It's a beautiful house," Daniel said. "And the garden. It must be a lot to look after, Mr Frobisher."

"Call me Guy. Please." He looked back at the house and puffed on his pipe. "It is a lot. But I have a gardener and a housekeeper. As I say, I'm fortunate." He turned around as Billy joined them, and extended his hand in greeting. "Guy Frobisher. I understand you're this young man's boyfriend."

Billy shook Guy's hand and glanced briefly at Daniel. There was a look of surprise on his face. "Billy Walsh. Yes. Daniel and I came up from London for the day."

"Any particular reason?" Guy asked. He led them across the lawns to a gate alongside the house. "Or simply escaping the city?"

"Well," Daniel said. He looked at Billy as they followed Guy through the gate, and down the side of the house. "It's the second time we've come to Cambridge in as many weeks."

Guy stopped and turned. He pointed his pipe at Daniel, and his face crinkled in a wry smile. "Grantchester is not Cambridge, young man. That's why I choose to live here. Cambridge is ten miles away, but it may as well be a million miles away for all I care. It's too noisy and too full of people. I try to go there as little as possible."

He turned back and continued to lead them down the side of the house. The path opened out onto a veranda, beyond which was a wide lawn flanked by well-stocked and well-maintained flower borders.

"We were in Cambridge the other weekend in fact," Daniel said as he and Billy followed behind. "We brought a friend from London to have his birthday picnic on The Backs. He's seventy-nine."

Guy walked to the edge of the veranda and stopped. He put a hand on his hips and there was a pause while he breathed deeply. "A relative of yours?"

Daniel shook his head. "His name's Chuck Stuart."

Guy turned his head sharply. "Chuck?" He lifted his pipe and pointed the stem at Daniel. "How do you know Chuck? Has something happened to him?"

Billy looked angrily at Daniel, and then took a step towards Guy. "I should explain. I'm a social worker in London. Chuck's my client. We brought him up to Cambridge for his birthday party."

"Why Cambridge?"

"I've got friends who live here. There. And it's a nice place to visit, and we thought it would be nice to get Chuck out of London for the day."

Guy turned away. He lifted his pipe and puffed on it for a few moments in silence. There was the sound of a distant lawnmower. Finally, Guy took his pipe from his mouth and turned back to them. He gestured to the open French windows.

"I think you both should come in for some tea."

***

Daniel sat next to Billy on a large, floral patterned settee in Guy's comfortable sitting room. The settee was flanked by two wing armchairs, and was upholstered in the same fabric. They faced a stone fireplace, above which was a gilt-framed mirror. A grandfather clock sat in the corner, its ticking broke the awkward silence in the room. On the low table in front of them was a large photo album. Daniel resisted the temptation to pick it up and leaf through the pages in case Guy returned to the room suddenly. Instead, he leaned across to Billy.

"Are you cross with me?" he whispered.

Billy shook his head. "No," he whispered back. "He seems a nice old gentleman. I think we've rather taken him by surprise. I hope he's not offended."

"No, I'm not offended."

Billy turned to look over the back of the settee. Behind them, Guy had entered the room holding a tray. Billy jumped to his feet.

"I'm sorry. Let me help you with that."

"Thank you, young man. This is the advanced guard of cups and saucers." Guy placed the tray on a sideboard beside him. "If you go into the kitchen, you'll find the rearguard of teapot, milk, and sugar. I'd rather you carried them for me, if you don't mind."

"Of course." Billy stood and walked out of the room to find the rest of the tea things. Guy seated himself in one of the wing armchairs, picked up a tobacco pouch, and started to repack his pipe. "What's Chuck said about me?" he asked, without looking at Daniel.

"Well, Chuck is Billy's client, not mine," Daniel said. "But as far as I know, he's never mentioned you."

Guy paused, and looked up from his pipe maintenance. "Then how did you know how to find me?"

Before Daniel could answer, Billy returned to the room with the tea. Guy looked up and gestured to the sideboard. "Thank you, young man," he said. "There's a mat on there for the teapot. Would you mind being Mother? It saves me getting up again." He turned his attention back to the pipe. "Daniel tells me that Chuck never mentions me. Is this true?"

Billy looked quizzically at Daniel, who shrugged. "Yes, that's right," Billy answered. He picked up the teapot. "We only knew your name because our friends said you introduced yourself when you talked to Chuck last week when we were in Cambridge for his birthday."

Guy put down his pipe and looked up. "Oh, I see. That's why Chuck was there. He wasn't pleased to see me. I wish he wouldn't get so angry. Sometimes, I think it's because of all those drugs they put him on." He picked up his pipe and resumed fiddling with it. "But then again, I can't blame it on the medication. He's always found something to be angry about. Milk and no sugar for me please."

Billy finished pouring the tea, picked up one of the cups, and took it across to Guy. "I've been one of Chuck's carers for only a few weeks, so I don't know him that well." He handed the cup of tea to Guy, who motioned Billy to put it on a table beside him. "But he does seem quite an angry person."

Guy chuckled. "Yes, 'quite an angry person.' You could say that."

Billy returned to the sideboard, picked up the remaining two teacups, and carried them over to the settee. He handed a cup to Daniel and sat down. "How long have you known Chuck?"

Guy smiled. He picked up the teacup from the small table beside him and took a drink from it. "So Chuck was seventy-nine two weeks ago. I first met him on his twenty-fourth birthday. That's fifty-five years ago." He took another sip of tea and placed the cup carefully back in its saucer.

"And I've been in love with him ever since."

Chapter 26

"The sixties were not a good time if you were…like us. We were illegal of course. And in the armed forces? Well, we were doubly illegal, I suppose. Not that I really knew what I was, back then. Not to start with.

"I was born in the middle of the war. There were three of us altogether. I'm the youngest. My oldest sister moved to America with her husband. California. The other one, well, that's another story. My father was a pilot in the RAF. He was killed in a bombing raid over Germany in forty-four."

Guy stood, and reached for a framed, faded black-and-white photograph on the mantelpiece. He turned and handed it to Daniel and Billy. "That's him. I can't really say I knew him. I was only two or three years old when he died." He sat back in his armchair. "I suppose it was inevitable I became a pilot.

"I went to a weekly boarding school in Cambridge. Boys only. I was good at rugger. And athletics. I was a hurdler. Captain of the county team. Always out practicing, whatever the weather. I loved it.

"I joined the school air cadets as soon as I could. Mother was quite proud of me when she came to the school on Founders Day and I was in my uniform. She shed a tear or two. Wonderful woman, my mother. Bringing up three children on her own."

Guy stopped. He reached to hold on to the mantelpiece, and turned his head away from Daniel and Billy. He inhaled deeply, moved back to his armchair with faltering steps, and sat down heavily. He looked back and smiled.

"Forgive me. So many memories." Guy inspected his pipe and prodded at the tobacco with his thumb.

"Although Mother had inherited this beautiful house, we weren't well off. She had to work. Especially after Father was killed. A practical woman, my mother. During the war she worked at Marshall's in Cambridge, the aircraft factory, until she fell pregnant with me. She was the first woman mechanic they had. After Father was killed, she got a small pension from the War Office. But as soon as she could, she went back to Marshall's. Loved it there."

Guy struck a match against the brick of the fireplace and carefully lit his pipe. He inhaled the smoke and inspected the glowing embers of tobacco before shaking the match and throwing it in the grate.

"Inevitably, I became a pilot. I left school in sixty-one and joined the RAF. They moved me about a bit. Then I ended up not far from here at RAF Wyton, flying reconnaissance planes."

"How did you meet Chuck?" Billy asked.

Guy smiled. "Oh, I'll get to that. In my own good time." He picked up his teacup, drained it, and held it out to Billy. "Would you mind? Storytelling is thirsty work."

Billy stood, collected Guy's cup, and walked over to the sideboard. Guy leaned back in his armchair and puffed on his pipe. "Do you know," he said, "I can't really say I've told this to anyone before. And yet two complete strangers walk into my house and, here I am." He turned to Daniel. "Why am I telling you all this?"

Daniel coughed nervously. "Would you prefer not to? We can go now and leave you in peace."

Guy waved his hand dismissively. "Nonsense." His face crinkled into a smile. "My ego is not averse to being massaged occasionally. I'm old enough to know that. And I'm old enough to have a few stories to tell."

Billy walked back to the fireplace and handed Guy his tea.

"Thank you, young man. Now where was I?" Billy resumed his seat on the settee next to Daniel. Guy took a drink of his tea and set the cup on the table next to him. "Oh, yes." He turned to Billy. "Did you know I was engaged to be married to a woman at twenty years old?" Guy paused, as if waiting for Daniel or Billy to comment. "No, I suppose you don't. Surprised, are you? I discovered much later that lots of men like me got married in those days to hide their true selves. Her name was Margaret. Beautiful girl. Her father owned farmland north of here. We met at a dance. Mother was so happy when I brought her home for the first time. But, of course, it was nonsense. It would have been so unfair to Margaret. Quite absurd. Deep in my heart, I already knew."

He stopped, and stared ahead of him for a few moments. Billy leaned forward. "What did you know?"

There was a pause before Guy shook his head, as though reawakening from a dream. He turned to Billy. "Oh, that I wasn't right. I don't mean not right for Margaret. But actually, not…right. I thought there was something wrong with me. I had no one to talk to about it. Not like nowadays." He picked up his pipe and puffed on it. "How times have changed."

Daniel stood and crossed to the sideboard. Guy looked up. "You're not going to help yourself to tea, are you?" Daniel looked up with a guilty look on his face. His hand hovered above the handle of the teapot. "We can't have two people pouring from the same teapot. It's bad luck. Your young man should've poured one for you."

Billy laughed and stood up. "That's exactly what my mum says." He carried his cup to the sideboard, took Daniel's, and refilled them both. "Sorry, Daniel," he whispered. He walked back to the settee. "What happened when you called off the engagement?"

"Oh Lord, there was hell to pay. Her father was furious. Margaret was distraught."

"What reason did you give them?"

Guy sighed. "It was the start of many lies. I told them that as a pilot I didn't want to risk making Margaret another widow like my mother. I was actually heartbroken. But I couldn't possibly tell them the real reason." He turned to Daniel and Billy, and smiled. "Oh, what a tangled web we weave, when first we practise to deceive."

"Shakespeare." Daniel nodded.

Guy jabbed his pipe at him. "Wrong, my boy. Walter Scott." He clenched his pipe between his teeth. "Bloody good writer."

Daniel turned to Billy and smiled. "I should stick to music, shouldn't I?"

"You're a musician?" Guy asked.

"I'm a music director in London," Daniel replied. "I use music as therapy with children."

"Wonderful, wonderful," Guy said. "Chuck and I love music. Loved music. You know he was a good dancer?"

"Really?" Billy asked. "He told me he was a boxer. He said nothing about dancing."

Guy stood and crossed the room to a large oak bookcase. He looked along the shelves until he pulled out a photo album and opened it. "Come here." He thumbed through the pages of the album. Daniel and Billy crossed the room to stand either side of him. Guy jabbed his finger at a large black-and-white photograph on one of the pages. It showed a man and woman dancing together, as others looked on.

"That's Chuck. We were at this nightclub in London where they played American big band music. That photograph ended up in the *Illustrated London News*. People came from all over to go to that club. Even though big band music was beginning to go out of fashion by the start of the sixties. Pop music was the new thing. Chuck was such a good dancer. We used to go there together. Of course, he could only dance with ladies. It didn't matter. I loved to watch him. I'd grown up with big band music. Mother used to play it on the gramophone at home, or listen to it on the wireless."

Guy flipped over another couple of pages. He pointed to a professional-looking photograph of a younger version of Chuck and Guy. They stood next to each other, dressed in their uniforms, and shaking hands. "Sixty-four. The *Wings Across the Atlantic Summer Gala* in London. That's where Chuck and I met."

He laid his hand on the page and gently caressed the photograph. "By some quirk of fate, I was chosen to represent the RAF, and Chuck was chosen to represent the US Air Force. Imagine. Of all the people they could choose from. They put us up in the Dorchester for the night. We were supposed to have our own bedrooms, but something went wrong with Chuck's booking. So I said he could share with me." He looked up at Billy. There was a bright, mischievous twinkle in his eyes. "I learned a lot from Chuck that night."

"Had you never—" Billy hesitated to complete his sentence.

Guy chuckled. "I was twenty-one. I knew nothing. I thought men only kissed women. And couples only went to bed with each other after they got married. Men shook hands and drank beer together. But that night..." His voice trailed off, and he looked down at the photograph again. "Oh, Chuck. You're a very bad man." He closed the album, placed it back in its space on the bookshelf, and walked across to the sideboard.

"It's gone six o'clock. I think it's time for something a bit stronger. What are you boys drinking?"

Billy looked at Daniel and back to Guy. "Well, we've got to drive back to London in a while. You've been so generous with your time—"

"Boys, boys." Guy bent down, opened a cupboard in the sideboard, and took out a bottle. "Have a sherry with me. Just a glass." He smiled as he pulled the cork from the bottle. "It would be rude of you to refuse. After all, I haven't finished my story yet."

"Thank you," Daniel said before Billy could reply. "That would be perfect. I'll take the tea things out to the kitchen for you."

"Thank you, young man. And while you're out there, there's a box of cheese straws on the side. The lady next door brought them for me this morning. Good cook she is."

Daniel gathered up the teacups and the rest of the tea things, and walked out to the kitchen. Guy placed three glasses on a small silver tray on the sideboard and filled them from the sherry bottle. He handed one to Billy.

"How long have you two been together?"

"Not long at all. Certainly by comparison with you and Chuck. Less than two months."

Guy picked up a sherry glass and carried it back to his armchair by the fireplace. "Oh, to be young again." He sat in his seat as Daniel returned to the room. "There's a glass of sherry for you over there." Guy raised his glass. "Your good health, young men. May you be as happy as I was with Chuck."

Daniel and Billy resumed their seats on the settee.

"So what happened between you and Chuck?" asked Daniel.

"Don't worry, I'll get to that," Guy replied. "But not quite yet. I haven't told you how I got kicked out of the air force. Pass me a cheese straw, will you?"

Daniel handed him the box of cheese straws. "Kicked out? But you were a hero, weren't you? You stopped your plane crashing into Cambridge."

Chuck's hand stopped, as he was about to collect a handful of cheese straws from the box Daniel offered him. "My, my. You have done your homework, haven't you? I presume Chuck didn't tell you that." He plunged his hand into the box and withdrew several cheese straws.

"No," Billy said. "We, that is, Daniel found the news report online. If you were a hero, why did they kick you—" He stopped when he saw the expression on Guy's face. "Oh, I see. Because of you and Chuck?"

Guy smiled. "We'd always been discreet. But after a while, we got careless. And there was someone at Alconbury who had it in for us. That was where Chuck was based with the US Air Force." Guy took a sip of his sherry. "It was a few months after I'd ejected from the Canberra. I'd been put on R and R, so I had plenty of time to go over to Alconbury to meet Chuck. It was a hot summer and we'd found this lake not far from the base where we'd go swimming. It was private, secluded. Not many people knew about it. We'd skinny dip there."

He put his sherry glass down carefully on the table next to him. "What we didn't know was that one of the Military Police at Alconbury was spying on us. He had it in for Chuck. We didn't know the reason. Or, if Chuck knew, he wasn't saying. This MP took photographs of us. And it was enough to lose us both our military careers."

"Chuck was court-martialed as well?"

"Neither of us were court-martialed. Chuck was asked to resign. It meant he at least kept his pension rights. After all, Chuck had his medals for bravery. At least they respected that."

Billy leaned forward. "Chuck? Medals? He's never mentioned that. And I've not seen them in his flat."

"You wouldn't," Guy replied. "I've still got them here. If Chuck had had his way, he'd have had thrown them out. But if you want to talk about heroes, Chuck was certainly one."

"What did he do?" Billy asked.

Guy shook his head. "Maybe you'll be able to get him to tell you one day. I don't think I should."

"What happened to you?" Daniel asked.

Guy sighed. "My lot were different. They were mealy-mouthed. They didn't want me to leave. I was a bit of a celebrity after I'd been in the newspapers, so I was good PR for them. They wanted me to say Chuck had coerced me. In effect, to say he'd raped me."

"Oh my God." Daniel leaned forward. "They'd do something like that?"

Guy smiled. "This was nineteen sixty-eight. They'd only partially decriminalized homosexuality in Britain. But it was still very much banned in the military. Which was nonsense of course. Because I'd say at least three of the chaps on my tribunal board were on our side of the fence."

"Why didn't they stick up for you then?"

"They did. In their own peculiar way. That's why they asked me to say I'd been coerced."

"And you didn't?"

"Of course not." Guy bit into his last cheese straw. "I was furious with them. I refused point blank. So they asked me to resign. Which I did. And I moved back here."

"Where did Chuck go?"

"He came to live with me. By that time both my sisters were married and moved away. Mother was ill. Dying it turned out. So Chuck and I cared for her."

"Did she know about you and Chuck?"

Guy smiled. "I'll never know. We never discussed it the whole time she remained alive. Both Chuck and I got jobs at Marshall's in Cambridge. Following in my mother's footsteps. It was wonderful."

Daniel sat back and looked from Billy to Guy. "If it was so wonderful, what happened between you and Chuck?"

Chapter 27

A bell sounded from somewhere beyond the room where they sat. It was the high, tinkling sound of a small handbell. Guy looked up. He was startled, like a rabbit in sight of the farmer's gun. The ringing stopped, but Guy remained tensed, perched on the edge of his seat. A moment later, the ringing started again, this time more insistent. It was accompanied by a woman's loud resonant voice.

"Guy. Guy. I need you."

Guy rose unsteadily to his feet. It was as though the quiet confidence he exhibited when they first arrived had vanished.

"I'm sorry, boys. I have to go. Please excuse me while—"

"Guy. Where are you?"

The ringing handbell sounded as though its clapper would fall off. Guy crossed to the door and left the room. There was the sound of another door opening somewhere down the corridor. The ringing stopped, and Daniel and Billy could hear the low mumble of voices.

"Who do you think that is?" asked Daniel. "He didn't say anyone else lived here with him."

"Perhaps it's one of his sisters," replied Billy. "She sounds terrifying."

As if to illustrate his point, the woman's voice got louder and more aggressive. Daniel stood and walked over to the half open door.

"Be careful," Billy called in a loud whisper. "He might come back at any minute."

Daniel raised a finger to his lips to silence him. Guy's voice was an indistinct murmur, and Daniel could not make out the words. But the louder, harsher interjections of the woman were clear enough.

"Send them away."

Guy's indistinct voice.

"You've no right to invite that man's friends into our house."

Again, Guy's indistinct voice.

"It's as much mine as yours. Mummy might have left it to you, but I was born here. I've every right to live here."

Guy's murmur was followed by the squeak of a door opening, and footfall in the corridor. Daniel darted back to the settee and sat beside Billy. A moment later Guy stood at the open doorway.

"I'm sorry, boys." His voice was subdued and his cheeks had reddened. "I'm going to have to ask you to go. It's getting quite late, and my sister will be needing her supper." He crossed to the French windows and stepped outside. "I'll see you back to your car."

Billy and Daniel stood and followed Guy into the garden.

"Could we speak to you again?" asked Daniel. "After all, you had got to the climax of your story."

Guy waved a hand in the air as he led them down the side path to the front of the house. "It's difficult, as you've seen. My sister doesn't like visitors, I'm afraid, and it's best not to upset her."

"Could we call you, then?"

Guy stopped and turned. Despite his age, he looked like a little boy, lost in the world. "You'll be seeing Chuck again, won't you?"

Billy nodded. "This Tuesday."

Guy sighed. "It was such a surprise seeing him in Cambridge that day. I'd long given up trying to contact him. I tried to tell him I was sorry. But then tempers frayed and we started saying things. Things we shouldn't have said." He shook his head. "We're both rather stubborn men, you see."

"What happened between you?" Billy asked.

Guy gestured back to the house. "My sister happened. She's a widow now and quite frail. I had no choice but to invite her back to live here." He shrugged his shoulders. "I pleaded with Chuck to stay. But he was having none of it. He told me it was either him or her. I said I didn't want to make that choice."

Billy fumbled in his pockets and turned to Daniel. "Have you got a business card to give to Guy? I can't find mine."

"They're in my wallet in the car. I'll go and get them."

Billy turned back to Guy. "I'll see if I can talk to Chuck on Tuesday if you like. I must be careful, otherwise he'll think I'm sticking my nose in, and—"

Guy held up his hand. "I know, I know. Don't get yourself into any trouble, young man. Not on my account."

He turned and looked back at the house. "I made a wrong decision. But I couldn't bar Elspeth from her own home. Now I'm paying for it." He turned back to Billy. "Tell him I'm sorry, will you?"

***

Daniel brought Velma to a halt outside his house in Battersea and switched off the engine. As the headlights faded to darkness, the inside of the car was plunged into a moonlit gloom. There were no streetlamps on Daniel's street. The local council's efficiency drive had long ago turned them off.

"I'll help you unload, and then we can drop the car back at Maggie's," Billy said.

Daniel unfastened his seatbelt and opened the door. "No need. Maggie's been really sweet. She offered to spend the afternoon sorting out some planting in the garden. She's waiting for us here." He checked his watch. "Although we're a bit later than I said we'd be."

As if to confirm his statement, Maggie's voice called from an upstairs window. "Where the hell have you been? I'm due on set at some ungodly hour tomorrow morning."

"Sorry." Daniel opened the backdoor of the car and pulled out the picnic hamper. "We'll be as quick as we can. Then you can get away."

Billy helped Daniel gather the rest of the day's clutter from the back of the car, and they walked to the front door. Maggie watched from the upstairs window.

"No rush," she replied. "I'm not leaving until you tell me how you got on. And anyway, you need to admire my handiwork. Although I say it in all modesty, I've excelled myself this time."

***

Maggie stood in the garden alongside what appeared to be a six-foot piece of granite. Water flowed over its semi-vertical uneven surface, as though emanating from a spring higher up the stone. Delicate alpine plants bordered the granite, while below the water plunged onto stones and disappeared into a mossy bed. The moss was surrounded on all sides by clumps of blue flowers.

"My God, Maggie." Daniel stood in the kitchen doorway. "You're right. You have excelled yourself this time. How the hell did you move that lump of rock? It must weigh a ton."

Maggie lifted her gin and tonic and smiled triumphantly.

"It's fake, of course, darling." She took a drink from her gin and tonic, and tapped the side of the fake rock. It made the hollow sound of reinforced plastic. "They built this Swiss mountain scene on the soundstage next to where I'm working. It was decommissioned last week. Nobody wanted it, so I borrowed a couple of the lovely workshop boys to help me hump it over here today." She swept her arm out in a grand gesture at the garden. "It's the final piece in the jigsaw. We can get *Hello!*.magazine to come here and do a feature on West End stars and their gardens. It'll make you even more famous."

Daniel laughed. He stepped out of the house and joined her alongside the new addition to his garden. He leaned forward and they air kissed extravagantly. "I couldn't possibly expose my private life to the hoi polloi who read that rag," he said. "And more to the point, I don't think they'd give a damn about me."

Maggie walked across to the bench by the herb wall and sat. She draped her arm languidly along its back, and rested the gin and tonic glass on the edge of the bench.

"Oh, but if you take that directorship in New York, they'll all be lining up to write features about you."

"New York?" Billy appeared at Daniel's side and kissed him. "Are you going to New York?"

Daniel glanced across to Maggie and shook his head reprovingly. She shrugged and lifted the glass to her lips. Daniel sighed. This was not the time he would have chosen to tell Billy about the directorship.

"It's not signed and sealed by any means," Daniel began. "But I've been asked if I'd be interested in setting up a version of *Therapy on Stage* in New York. This American philanthropist approached me three months ago. He's offered to fund it for two years, and wants me to be the creative director."

"Oh," Billy said. He smiled and squatted down to examine the Alpine water feature. "That would be great for you."

Daniel felt certain there was a lack of conviction in Billy's response. He squatted down alongside him. "Look. I'm sorry I haven't told you before. I was trying to pick the right moment. It's not at all certain yet, and I haven't heard from the guy for a while now. So it might not happen at all."

Billy shook his head and smiled. "Come on. It would be a fantastic opportunity. I'd be genuinely happy for you." He leaned forward and kissed Daniel. "You didn't have to 'pick the right moment.' What did you think I was going to do?"

Daniel shrugged. "I don't know. It's early days, but things seem to be, well, you know…between us. They seem to be good. After not telling you about Anthony…now the New York thing. You must be thinking—"

"That you're a serial liar and you're actually straight?" Billy kissed him again. "You're right. It's a bit early in, well, whatever's happening between us. It is good. But I'm not about to start choosing curtain material. Come on. You don't have to hold back on great news like that."

Daniel rested his hand on Billy's shoulders and gently massaged his neck. "Thank you," he said. "You're right. I was inventing nonexistent problems. Anyway, you probably wouldn't give me a second thought if I disappeared off to the States." He pulled Billy closer and kissed him slowly on the lips.

"Are you two going to spend the whole evening necking over there?" Maggie's voice cut through the moment. "Because I'm buggering off home if you are."

Daniel opened his eyes and smiled at Billy. "Curtain material? You know I hate curtains in a room. It's so chintzy." He stood and looked across to Maggie. "Have you eaten? I'd hate to think of you drinking on an empty stomach."

Maggie laughed. "I can't imagine you spend your hours fretting about that. Don't worry. I've the constitution of an ox. But if you're offering food…" She left the end of the sentence hanging in the evening air.

Billy stood and set off for the kitchen. "I'll bring the remains of the picnic out here. We can finish it before it goes off."

"Don't give me food poisoning, darling," Maggie called after him.

Daniel crossed to the bench and sat next to her. He nestled against her arm draped across the back of the seat, and she dropped her hand on his shoulder.

"Sorry I opened my big mouth about New York, love," Maggie said. "Is everything okay?"

"It's fine." Daniel shrugged. "I think you did the right thing for me. I was going to have to tell Billy some time."

"And you were chickening out." Maggie rested her head on Daniel's. "Why do you always do that? As long as I've known you, you have this habit of avoiding difficult conversations."

"I know."

"Which only makes it harder when you finally have the conversation."

"I know."

She lifted her head from his shoulder. "It's no bloody good saying that all the time. Next time, grow some balls."

Daniel instinctively placed his hands on his crotch. He turned to look at Maggie. "Do you know, sometimes you really terrify me, Maggie Ambler."

"Oh, bollocks." She leaned back against the bench and closed her eyes. "So tell me what happened this afternoon. Did you find Chuck's lover? Is he actually Chuck's lover?"

Daniel nodded. "You were right. As ever. Poor man. He seems awfully sad. A really lovely man, too. Hero of the RAF. Saved thousands of people from being killed. And then they kicked him out for being in love with another man."

Maggie sat up. "They got discovered? Oh, that would have been bad in those days. When was it exactly?"

"Guy said it was sixty-eight. A year after they partially decriminalized homosexuality in Britain. But it was still illegal in the armed forces."

Maggie nodded. "It was only at the start of this century they allowed dodgy people like you to serve their country."

Daniel laughed. "And in America it's even later. That reminds me. Chuck was apparently a hero as well. He won medals."

Maggie coughed, her gin and tonic halfway to her lips. "Grumpy Chuck? What did he do that was so heroic?"

Daniel shook his head. "We don't know. Guy wouldn't tell us. He said we'd have to ask Chuck. Poor Guy. He seemed so pleased to unburden to us. That's why we're late."

Maggie squeezed his shoulder. "Don't worry, darling. You did a wonderful thing today. Despite being a chicken, you're actually quite a saint, on occasions."

Daniel laughed again and nuzzled his head against her neck. "And you're a wonderfully generous woman. Thank you so much for what you've done to this garden."

Billy emerged from the kitchen door holding the picnic hamper. He stopped and stared at Daniel and Maggie as they nestled together on the bench. "Well, Daniel. I was joking earlier about you being a serial liar and not actually gay. But now I'm not so sure."

Daniel jumped to his feet and started to make room on the table in front of them. "Damn." He glanced at Maggie and spoke in a stage whisper. "He's discovered our special secret. Try to act normal and maybe he'll forget."

Maggie sniffed. "Billy, my darling. Daniel's about as straight as a dog's hind leg." She remained in her recumbent position. "Thank God you brought some food. I'm ravenous. Thirsty as well." She waved her glass in the air to show it needed refreshing. "Daniel tells me Chuck and this Guy fellow were in love for over fifty years. And they were heroes. Yet they were still kicked out of the careers they both loved. It's so unfair."

Billy set the picnic hamper down next to the table and began to unpack. "I think Guy's still in love. And in his own strange way, perhaps Chuck is as well."

"Heroes in love," Maggie mused. "How romantic." She leaned forward and picked up a chicken wing from a plate Billy had set down on the table. "I'm sure this is stuffed with salmonella. But maybe the gin will kill it." She bit into the chicken and continued speaking. "If they're still in love, why's Chuck so angry with the love of his life? And why did he leave Cambridge and move down to London?"

"Guy's older sister moved back into the family home," Billy explained. "We heard her shouting at Guy while we were there. She sounds pretty terrifying."

"And she obviously hates Chuck," Daniel added. He sat down next to Maggie. "It's pretty clear she insisted Chuck move out, and Guy went along with it."

"Oh, that's not nice," Maggie said. She tossed the remains of her chicken wing on an empty plate, picked up a sandwich, and inspected it. "This is a bit curled." Despite her observation, she bit into it. "No wonder Chuck's grumpy. Kicked out of his home after fifty years? He must be livid. I think Guy's going to have a tough time sweet-talking him back again. Sounds like that bird has flown."

"Not if I've got anything to do with it, Maggie." Billy pulled a half-full bottle of wine from the picnic hamper and waved it at Daniel. "Fancy some warm white wine? It's French."

Daniel wrinkled his nose. "You make it sound so tempting. Go on then."

Billy took two plastic glasses from the hamper, set them on the table, and uncorked the bottle.

"You've changed your tune all of a sudden," Maggie said. "I thought you were terrified of losing your job if you got involved? What's brought this about?"

"I saw how sad Guy was today." Billy handed a glass of wine to Daniel. "He knows he's done the wrong thing, putting his sister before Chuck. And I'm certain Chuck's unhappy because he's missing Guy."

"They say blood's thicker than water." Maggie took another bite from her sandwich and began to chew. "But we all know that's a load of old balls. Certainly young Daniel here knows it. The way his parents treated him." She looked across at Billy. "And I hear your dad was a bit of a shit as well."

"Yes, thank you for that, Maggie." Daniel looked across to Billy and tried to signal his apology for her choice of words. "But I think Guy's from the generation that puts family first. And his sister sounded awfully formidable."

Maggie shoved the rest of the sandwich in her mouth and waved her hand in the air dismissively. "Bollocks. Making an assumption that one generation thinks a particular way and remains stuck like that forever is complete tosh. Guy might carry the baggage of his upbringing, but he's old enough and bold enough to choose to think his own way. If he's got the strength of character, that is."

"Maggie's right," Billy said. "And I think Guy does have the strength of character. Unfortunately, it temporarily left him when his sister came back on the scene."

"So, what are you going to do?" Daniel asked.

Billy smiled. "I have no idea," he replied. "But I'll start by talking to Chuck about it."

"And what if you lose your job?" Maggie looked at him. "Does that no longer strike fear in your heart?"

Billy looked at Daniel and smiled. "Perhaps I've allowed fear to rule my heart for a bit too long."

Chapter 28

The rain pounded on the roof of the bus and lashed against its windows. Billy's fervent hope the storm would pass by the time he got off the bus seemed a forlorn one. He was only a few minutes away from his stop. But it was a ten-minute walk, maybe a five-minute run, to get to Chuck's apartment building. He was going to get wet. No, he was going to get soaked.

What on earth was he going to say to Chuck? How was he going to broach the subject of Guy? Billy had spent a bad night, unable to get little more than a few hours' sleep at a time, before waking from nightmares of either frightening or bizarre encounters. In one instance, he dreamed he walked naked onto the stage of the Royal Opera House, about to sing the song "Barcelona" with Freddie Mercury. Billy was definitely no Montserrat Caballé. And he needed no psychiatrist to tell him the dreams showed how unprepared and insecure he felt.

Guy's question as they left his pretty house in Grantchester came back to him.

You'll be seeing Chuck again, won't you?

The poor man looked so sad. So plaintive. His relationship with Chuck had lasted for over fifty years. Nearly sixty. Billy could not imagine how it must feel to be that close to someone for so long. It was nearly twice as long as he had been alive. He imagined the shared experiences Chuck and Guy must have had. The love that held them together for so long, surely Chuck regretted throwing all that away?

Perhaps not. Maybe the relationship had simply run its course, and Chuck was looking for an opportunity to end it. With the return of Guy's sister, he had the ideal excuse. But if that was the case, the move had not made Chuck a happier person. Perhaps he regretted his decision now and welcomed the chance to talk about it with Billy. Or—perhaps not.

Billy was not confident Chuck was a man who expressed regret easily. Even so, he was determined to fulfill his promise and talk to Chuck. Guy wanted to say sorry for putting his sister first. He made it plain he believed he had done the wrong thing. Perhaps his contrition would be enough to start Chuck talking to him again. Billy had cleared his diary for that morning, incurring the wrath of Man Cock. He no longer cared what she thought. For some reason, he found new energy to follow his own agenda, instead of the department's.

He peered through the windows at the street ahead. The rain seemed to be easing. Billy pulled up the hood of his jacket and gathered his rucksack, ready to get off the bus.

New York.

That also featured in his dreams the night before. His response to Daniel had been genuine when he told him he would be happy for him. Billy had only visited New York twice. The first time was with Simon during his student days at RADA. They had slept on the floor of a tiny studio apartment in Greenwich Village belonging to one of Simon's Australian friends. The second visit was a four-day shoot for a clothing commercial. Billy spent long days in a disused factory in Queens looking moodily into the camera. A limousine returned him, late each night, exhausted, to a boutique hotel in uptown Manhattan. On the second day of shooting there was a camera problem, and he was released early. He caught the subway to Greenwich Village and found himself back at Marie's Crisis piano bar. On his first trip, he and Simon had spent several happy evenings together singing along with the pianist and getting to know the regulars who frequented the famous bar.

No, he would not begrudge Daniel the experience of New York at all. Daniel was right. Things between them were good. Exceptionally good. But it was early days. And if he were in Daniel's position, he too would seize an opportunity to advance his career. Maybe Billy could go visit him at some point. It would be good to know someone in New York he could stay with. A cheap holiday.

Except he would miss Daniel.

Miss him terribly.

It had taken only a few weeks for him to realize Daniel was the man Billy wanted to get to know better and share his life experiences with. He remembered something Simon had once said to him. *"Wouldn't it be wonderful to find someone you could spend your whole life with, and yet still discover new things about them? A relationship that never got tired, that was constantly being renewed and reinvigorated. You'd be more than boyfriends or husbands. You'd be compatible strangers."*

Compatible strangers. He and Daniel seemed to be compatible. But it looked like they were destined to be distant strangers.

The bus lurched to a halt, and the doors hissed open. Billy woke from the daydream, picked up his rucksack, and squeezed past the passengers standing in the aisle, hurrying before the driver closed the doors again. He stepped out into an enormous puddle. The rainwater came over the top of his trainer and soaked his sock. At the same time, he felt water soak through the cotton of his hood and seep down the back of his neck.

Bugger.

***

The coffeemaker hissed and sputtered as it delivered its rich black nectar into the two cups below the spout. Billy had finally mastered the vagaries of the machine and was proud of the barista-style coffee he now produced. He topped off both cups with steamed milk, added a spoonful of sugar to Chuck's, and carried the tray back to the small sitting room. Chuck sat in front of the television watching a documentary about the Berlin Wall.

"I wasn't even born when that happened," Billy said. He set the two cups on a table beside Chuck's wheelchair and sat in the chair opposite. "Did you ever fly over Germany during the Cold War?"

Chuck looked up from the television. "The free zone was called West Germany in those days," he replied. "Sure. We had a shitload of air bases there as well as in Britain. We'd do joint missions with the guys."

"Is that how you got your medals?" Billy asked, thinking back to Guy's comments the previous day.

Chuck eyed him suspiciously. "Medals? Who've you been talking to?"

Billy took a deep breath. Fasten your seatbelt, he thought, and sit back for a bumpy ride. "Daniel and I were out at Grantchester

Meadows for a picnic yesterday. And we met Guy Frobisher." He paused, and waited to see how Chuck would react.

Chuck continued to stare at him. The documentary about the Berlin Wall was interrupted by a commercial break. An elderly actor, whom Billy had once filmed with, extolled the virtues of making funeral plans. Chuck picked up the remote control from his lap and aimed it at the television.

"Jeez," he said. "If he shows his face on the screen one more time, I'm going to throw that darn thing out the window." The TV sound cut abruptly, but the actor's mouth continued to move silently on the screen. Chuck turned back to look at Billy, his face crumpled into a frown of confusion.

"You went to Grantchester?" he began. "To see Guy?" He leaned back in his wheelchair and scratched the three-day-old stubble on his face. "What are you trying to do?"

"Nothing," Billy replied. "Well, I guess we were curious about—"

"How d'you even know about Guy? Or where he lives?" Chuck leaned forward. His hands gripped the arms of his wheelchair tightly. "What did he tell you? Some crap about being sorry? 'Cause I tell you somethin'." Chuck paused. His breathing was shallow. He was almost panting, and he pressed his hand against his chest. "I tell you, Guy doesn't mean squat when he says he's sorry. So don't go fallin' for that shit."

Billy paused. For him to pass on Guy's apology seemed redundant, even provocative.

"Come on," he said, and smiled. "Tell me about the medals, Chuck."

"No, sonny." Chuck slipped his hand slowly away from his chest and back to the arm of the wheelchair. He took a deep breath and exhaled slowly. "You tell me what the hell you're doin'. I thought you were here to sort out practical stuff." He jerked his thumb in the direction of the corridor. "You know that darn bath hoist is broke again? Why don't you do somethin' about that, instead of stickin' your nose in where it's not wanted?"

"I am trying to help," Billy replied. "Our concern at the agency is not only for your physical well-being, but your emotional health as well."

"My 'emotional health'? Whatever the hell that is, it's fine, thank you."

Billy sighed. "Okay. I'll get onto the bath hoist people in a minute. I won't say any more about Guy. But tell me about the medals. Why didn't you mention them before?"

Chuck sniffed. "I'm not one to go braggin' about shit like that."

"But you've got photos of you and the other pilots from the time you were in the Air Force. If they awarded you medals as well, then I thought you'd have—"

"What the hell did Guy say?" Chuck looked puzzled. "It's nothin' to do with the Air Force."

"But I assumed—"

"You assumed?" Chuck leaned towards him again. "You think you know everything, don't you, sonny?" He picked up his cup and took a drink of coffee. "You've got a helluva lot to learn." He placed the cup on the table, and leaned back in his wheelchair. "Thanks to me, you at least know how to make a decent cup of coffee." Chuck looked at Billy, as a doctor might assess their patient before recommending a course of treatment. "You really got time for this?"

Billy nodded. "I booked the morning off so I could spend time here."

"And what if I had guests invited for a drinkin' session? Or a sex god comin' to see me, right?" Chuck smiled. He looked like a different person when he smiled. "I guess Guy told you everything you need to know about him and me? You know I'm—" The words stalled on his lips.

"Yes," Billy said. "You know, the first time I came here, I wondered how you might react to me saying Daniel was my boyfriend. Some of my clients get a bit fazed. You didn't seem bothered at all."

"No, I wasn't," Chuck stated. "Envious, I guess. Wish I could have been that relaxed about it at your age. But then, shit was different back in those days."

"I'm sure it was," Billy said. He leaned forward and cocked his head on one side. "Come on. The medals?"

"There were only two," Chuck said dismissively. "I'd been in Britain no more than a few months. It was my first trip into Cambridge. I wanted to see what the place was like. I hitched a ride with this pilot who'd shipped his motorbike over from the States.

Like a dumbass I forgot to change my dollars for British pounds while I was still on the base, so I headed to the bank. Of all days, I pick the day these guys tried to rob it."

Billy's jaw dropped open. It was not what he expected to hear. "What happened?" he asked.

"Darn fools. They had no idea what they were doin'." Chuck smiled as he realized he had an audience. "It was late mornin', and I was standin' by the door fillin' out this damn form. All I wanted to do was change some cash. But I had to fill out a form. Anyway. Apart from me, there were three old guys waitin' in line to be served. And there was only one teller on the other side of the counter. No bulletproof glass or shit like they have nowadays."

He paused to take a drink of coffee. Billy waited expectantly.

"These two guys kinda crash through the doors into the bank lobby. Only one of them is wearing a mask. He walks up to the counter, pushes in front of the guy gettin' served, and shoves this bag at the teller. He pulls out a gun and tells him to fill the bag with cash from the drawer. His accomplice is stood right next to me. He's got no mask at all. Real baby-face. Looked shit scared. He pulls out his gun an' points it up at the ceilin'. He glances at me, an' then shouts, 'This is a robbery. Everyone get down on the ground, and you don' get hurt.'"

"What did you do?"

"Well, the three old guys standin' in line are really not up to gettin' on the ground. An' they're complainin' about their knees, and one of them asks if he can't put his hands on his head. The robber at the counter turns and shouts at his buddy to put his mask on. He had this weird, high-pitched voice and sounded real terrified. Meanwhile, the guy with the gun was gettin' upset 'cause he couldn't pull this scarf thing up from around his neck. Then I sees this big metal trash can next to me."

Billy's jaw fell open again. "You didn't?"

"Ha." Chuck laughed. It was a rare sound to hear from him. "You bet I did. The guy was messin' around so much with his scarf he never saw it comin'. I picks it up and brings it down hard on his head. He crashes to the floor. Out cold. I gets the gun from his hand and points it at his accomplice. 'Drop your gun and get on the floor,' I says. 'Or I'll blow your brains out.'"

"Sounds like a Clint Eastwood film." This time it was Billy's turn to laugh. "And did he?"

"Oh, sure," Chuck replied. There was a look of smug satisfaction on his face. "An' he didn't move until the cops showed up."

"I'm not surprised you got medals for that," said Billy. "Were the guns loaded?"

"Sure they were," Chuck stated. "An' those kids would have made a real mess of someone. They were so darn nervous."

"What were the medals?"

"The city gave me an award for bravery, and the freedom of the city. I couldn't believe it. Here I was, this American kid, bein' given the freedom of this ancient British city. I felt like a million dollars."

"And the second?"

Chuck sighed, and shook his head. "That was the most amazin'. The followin' year I gets a letter from Buckingham Palace. Asks me to graciously accept a Queen's Commendation for Brave Conduct. I went up to London, an' got to meet the Queen, an'—." He shook his head again.

"Bloody hell, Chuck," Billy said. "Why didn't you tell me about this before? That's an incredible achievement."

"Nah." Chuck waved his hand dismissively. "It's all in the past. Means nothin' now." He shook his head. "There's a lot of things that mean nothin' now."

"Like Guy?"

"Yeah." The usual grimace returned to Chuck's face. "Like Guy. The man who decides that his racist, homophobic shit of a sister is more important than me."

"But he didn't want you to leave."

"What choice did I have?" Once more Chuck gripped the arms of his wheelchair tightly. "I'd lived in that house for nearly fifty years with Guy. Then she turns up, and tells Guy he's disgustin' for livin' with me. That it's her house. Even though his mother left it to Guy." He shook his head. "She made me feel like I was back in the sixties or seventies again. Havin' to hide who I was." His breathing became shallow once more, and he panted as he held the palm of his hand to chest. "I couldn't stay there. Guy gave me no choice."

"But you've got a choice now, Chuck," Billy said. "Guy told me to tell you he's sorry. He thinks he made the wrong decision, allowing his sister back—"

"Damn right he did." Chuck's shoulders were shaking. Billy had never seen him so upset. "We had years together. Good years. Yet he does a thing like that, and makes it seem as if it was all worth squat. Like I'm worth squat. How dare he."

He paused, and struggled to catch his breath. Billy stood, and crossed to the wheelchair. "Chuck, are you okay? Do you want me to get you a glass of water?"

Chuck shook his head. Billy's phone rang. He took it from his pocket and looked at the screen.

"And if that's Guy sayin' he's sorry," Chuck was shouting now. "Tell him to go fuck himself."

Billy shook his head, and held up his hand to signal Chuck to be quiet.

"Yes. This is Billy Walsh. Yes. I'm her son." Billy waited as the voice at the end of the phone spoke. "Of course," he said finally. "I'll come right away. Thank you for letting me know. Good-bye."

He put the phone back in his pocket, took a deep breath, and stared at Chuck in silence for a few moments. "That was the hospital," he said finally. "My mother has just died. And I wasn't there with her."

"Jeez, Billy. I'm real sorry."

Billy shook his head, turned his back on Chuck, and headed for the door. "Don't say anything, Chuck. I don't want to hear your moaning right now." He stopped and turned at the doorway. "I wasn't with her. Instead, I was here, trying to persuade an old fool to stop behaving like an old fool."

Chuck opened his mouth to speak but closed it again when Billy raised his hand to silence him. "You know, Chuck, the people we love, and the people who love us, can be taken away in an instant. I wish I'd spent more time with my mother. She was a wonderful person, and I wish I'd been there at the end. I hope you never regret leaving Guy."

Billy could see his words had affected Chuck. The American closed his eyes, and his shoulders heaved as he appeared to nod his head. But Billy no longer cared what Chuck thought. He needed to get away from the suffocation he felt enveloping him. He left the room and headed for the front door.

As he walked along the corridor, he reached into his pocket and pulled out his phone.

He needed to call Daniel.

Chapter 29

Daniel wiped away the tears with the back of his hand. He knew he needed to at least appear in control at a time like this. But it was too difficult. The emotion had been welling up inside him for the past ten minutes, and it caught him by surprise when it finally boiled over. He took a deep breath, paused, and exhaled slowly. Then he got to his feet.

"Great job, guys." Daniel clapped his hands. "I think we're ready for next week. Catriona, that was outstanding. You had me completely carried away with that performance. The audience will be weeping by the end of the scene."

The cast of eighteen teenagers smiled broadly to him from the stage. They had three rehearsals left before their show the following Thursday. Daniel knew his words meant a great deal to them.

And he was truly proud of all of them: eighteen children with different abilities, some in wheelchairs, others with hearing impairments or visual impairments.

And then there was Catriona, who was autistic. When she joined *Therapy on Stage* less than six months ago, she could scarcely bear to stand with the other members of the teenage drama group, let alone perform in front of them. What a change Daniel had witnessed in the thirteen-year-old. She had delivered the key lines in a scene with a poignancy that brought Daniel to tears.

Her mother walked towards him from the far side of the rehearsal studio. "Thank you so much for what you've done." She also had tears in her eyes, but there was a big smile on her face. "Catriona's so happy now. You know, before she came here, there were days when I felt so sad for her. She was so—" She paused to find the word she wanted. "Miserable, I suppose. All I wanted was for her to be happy. Now she is, thanks to you." She stepped forward and hugged Daniel tightly.

He was taken aback by the outburst of emotion. His relationship with Catriona's mother had not started well. In the first few months after Catriona's arrival, the mother was quick to tell him her daughter was incapable of doing what he asked during a performance session. Daniel was polite and patient with each interruption, but he ignored her comments. He knew Catriona was capable of more, and gently, he coaxed her to try new tasks when they met for each weekly session. After three months, her mother finally recognized the improvements in her daughter. How she socialized more with the other children. How she had gained confidence.

And now today, Catriona stood alone on the stage and delivered her knockout performance. Daniel lived for moments like these. He called them his moments of joy. He loved working with children with different abilities. In the early days of his music career, his ambition had been to compose for West End musicals. After five years working with *Therapy on Stage*, he knew he had chosen the career he loved.

His phone vibrated in his pocket. It had been doing that for most of the rehearsal. Gently, he extricated himself from Catriona's mother's bearlike hug.

"She's done remarkably well," he said, taking a step backward. "And she's popular with the rest of the group. I'm so pleased to have her with us."

He turned back to the stage. "Okay, everyone. We'll finish there for today. Well done. You've worked really hard, and it shows. I'll see you all next Monday for rehearsal."

A small group of parents and support workers moved towards the stage to help the teenagers pack up while Daniel walked to the rear door of the rehearsal studio. He pulled out his phone and looked at the screen. Two missed calls from Anthony plus several messages from him, full of the usual apologies. In addition, there were five missed calls from Max Jablonski, and a message saying:

Where are you? Call me ASAP. Exciting news. Max

Daniel's breathing quickened. It was clear from Max's number he had called from New York.

"Hey, Daniel." Max sounded like he was in the next room instead of over three thousand miles away. "So you finally call. Do you want the good news, or do you want the really good news?"

"Hi, Max. I've been in rehearsal all morning. Tell me everything. Is it happening?"

"As soon as you can, get your ass over here. The funding's in place as of yesterday. Now here's the really good news. It's for three years. Solid. NYU is in. They want to get a research project going as well. My guys have found a great studio space down near NYU. Should get that nailed next week. It's going to happen, Daniel. When can you start?"

Daniel took a deep breath. He paused, as he thought about what he wanted to say.

"You still wanna do it, don't you?" Max's voice sounded worried. "I know it's been a while. But these things are tricky to fix. Especially in this economic climate."

"No, of course." Daniel's head was full of a million thoughts. "I really want to do it. And it's creative director, isn't it?"

"Creative director. VP creative. Whatever you wanna call yourself. You're in charge. I'm the president of Therapy Theater, of course, but you're the guy to make the magic happen."

"That's great." Daniel shook his head, and punched the air with his free hand in celebration. He could scarcely believe this was happening. "I can't start immediately, of course."

"Sure, sure. You gotta wrap things up there first. I know."

"I'm committed until September," Daniel continued. "So it won't really be until October before I can be available. Then I need to find somewhere to live."

"Oh, don't worry about that. NYU is sorting it. I can cut a deal with them." Daniel pictured Max waving his vape pipe in the air like a bald, masculine version of Bette Davis. "Look, can't you make it any sooner?"

Daniel shook his head. "I said I'd do summer school. And I've got a big music therapy workshop we're staging in September."

Max sighed. "Okay, I hear you. It's probably going to take at least that long to get your visa sorted. My guys will get contracts and shit like that together. I'm over in London in two weeks so we can get our heads down then. Great news, eh?"

"Yes," Daniel said. "Great news. Thanks so much, Max. I'm really grateful you considered me."

"*You're* grateful?" There was a pause as Max presumably puffed on his vape pipe. "*I'm* the one who's grateful. As long as you replicate the success of *Therapy on Stage* over here in New York, I'll be a happy bunny. So long, Daniel."

And Max was gone. Daniel did a small victory dance to himself. At that moment, his phone vibrated with another call. Daniel looked at the screen. Billy.

***

The Admiral Duncan pub was exceptionally quiet, even for a Tuesday night. Billy sat in the corner, an unfinished pint of lager on the countertop in front of him. He watched Jason clear away the remaining glasses from a group of men who were leaving. The Australian looked happy and relaxed, joking with the customers as they stood in the doorway.

It was three days since Billy's mother had died. When he called Jason to tell him the news two nights ago, Billy was unprepared for the wave of emotion that Jason unleashed over the phone. Billy found himself offering words of comfort to his former lover. For several minutes, Jason was incoherent with grief. All Billy could hear was sobbing. As he listened, he felt envious. Jason was crying the tears Billy had been unable to express. He had tried to cry, but he simply felt numb. Devoid of emotion. It was not what he expected, and he felt a sense of guilt in his lack of feeling for his mother, as well as a growing sense of anger.

He knew about the five stages of grief. They had talked about it at drama school, even attempted to improvise how a group of people would feel when faced with the death of a friend. But it was no preparation for what he was experiencing now. It was as though he had become misplaced, detached from both himself and the world. Time was an abstract concept. He found difficulty in making the simplest of decisions. He made a list of the jobs he needed to do to tell people about his mother's death, and to organise her funeral.

Both Daniel and Maggie helped a great deal on the first day. Billy stayed at the house in Battersea, and they talked into the night. Maggie made food that lay uneaten, and made endless cups of tea. They even sat around the piano at one point, and Daniel played some of the songs Billy remembered his mother used to enjoy. They talked until the dawn broke. Billy felt no desire to sleep. It was around four in the morning when Daniel told him about New York.

So that was another pillar supporting Billy's world knocked away. It felt like life was having a laugh at his expense. It was not Daniel's fault. Billy knew how important the chance to work in New York was to him. And it would be several months before Daniel would leave London. It was bad timing, though.

Exceptionally bad timing.

"You okay, mate?"

Jason sat down opposite him at the small, high-topped table. Billy nodded. "I should go," he said. "It's getting late, and I should get back to Wood Green."

"Don't go on my account. I'm pretty well done now, so we can sit and talk. Why Wood Green? Aren't you staying at Daniel's?"

Billy shook his head. "Not for the moment. I need some time on my own."

Jason reached across the table and laid a hand on Billy's shoulder. "Look, mate. You don't have to go all the way to Wood Green tonight if you don't want to. Come upstairs and stay at mine."

Billy smiled and shook his head. "Thanks, Jason. But I don't think it's a good idea. Anyway, three of Mum's close friends are coming over tomorrow morning, and I need to get the house ready."

Jason gave Billy's shoulder a reassuring squeeze and sat back. "Sure. I understand. Look. If there's any help you need with organising stuff, you know I'd love to help. Your mum was good to me. A great lady." He sniffed and blinked several times. "Shit. There I go again. Sorry, mate. This isn't helping you."

This time it was Billy's turn to reach forward and rest his hand on Jason's shoulder. "Don't apologize. I only wish I could do the same. I don't understand why I can't feel anything."

Jason rested his hand on Billy's. "You will, mate. Give it time. I was the same when my brother died. It was only the day of the funeral when it hit me. Christ did it hit me. I was like you. I thought I was an unfeeling bastard up until then. Shit, was I wrong about that." He blinked several times and wiped his eyes with the back of his hand. "How are you and Daniel?"

Billy sat back and shrugged. "Oh, you know. He's been great, and so has his friend Maggie. Everyone's been great."

"Yes, but you said he's going off to New York. That's a bit shitty of him, isn't it?"

Billy shook his head. "It's been on the cards for months. It's a great opportunity."

"Yes, but it's a pretty shitty time for him to up sticks and go. Leaving you back here."

Billy laughed. "We're not married, Jason. For fuck's sake, we've only just met."

Jason looked offended. "You seemed pretty serious about him. Is that it then?"

"I've no idea. I can't even think about it at the moment." Billy sighed. "Who knows what's going to happen next? I can't think beyond the funeral, let alone in three months' time." He leaned his head against the wall next to him, and stared without seeing at what was happening in the street outside.

What was he going to do next?

Life had suddenly become empty.

Chapter 30

The earliest booking for a funeral Billy could get was over two weeks away. According to one undertaker, "There's a rush on this summer. The crematoria are rammed solid." After several days of indecision, Billy found the business of organising his mother's farewell to be cathartic, and a welcome distraction from his sense of numbness. Man Cock showed a rare moment of compassion and told him to take as much leave from work as he needed. Liberated from the tyranny of his daily deadlines, Billy threw himself into planning the funeral, supported by a lot of help from Maggie.

His mother had been clear she was against a religious funeral, having discarded the remnants of her Catholic background many years ago. "Bury me in the garden, son," she used to say. "It'll be cheaper that way, and far less for you to organize."

Billy decided the best way to satisfy his mother's wish was with a humanist funeral. He visited two funeral directors, but he was uncomfortable with the almost factory-like efficiency they offered. By contrast, the third funeral director who offered a humanist funeral came to visit him. Mrs Mahabir was a kind, compassionate woman, who seemed to have the right balance of lightness and gravitas, and he felt confident she would lead the appreciation of his mother's life in the way he wanted it to be. Simon would read a WH Auden poem, and Billy would speak about his mother's life.

He contacted all the friends he could find in his mother's address book. Her two sisters still lived in Ireland. They would travel over to represent the rest of the family. He wrote to his father, but had no expectation he would turn up.

As well as organising the funeral, Billy kept himself busy with sorting out the little house in Wood Green. He decided to invite everyone back to the house after the service. It would give his aunts the chance to look through his mother's things, and take anything they liked. He preferred a small gathering at home to a party in a pub. Maggie offered to do the catering, and she spent several days in the house, helping to tidy and clean.

"You really don't have to do this," Billy told her one afternoon as she donned rubber gloves and got on her knees to clean a kitchen cupboard. "You must have far more important things to do."

"Nonsense, darling," she replied, scrubbing away vigorously with a soap-filled sponge. "We can't have your aunties coming in here and running their fingers through the dust. We must do the memory of your mother proud. And now that Daniel's done the dirty on you, I feel morally obligated."

"But he hasn't done the dirty on me," Billy protested. "This directorship in New York is a fantastic opportunity. I'd have done the same in his position."

Maggie stopped scrubbing and turned her head. "I've not known you long, young man, but I'm pretty sure you wouldn't. You'd stay with him if someone close to him had died." She turned back to the cupboard and attacked it with renewed energy. "Daniel's an ambitious man. He's quite good at getting what he wants. And he's also good at persuading other people to do things for him. Usually for free."

"You mean, like all the work you've done on his house and garden?"

Maggie's cleaning paused for a moment. "Yes, my darling. I suppose I do."

"If you resent being persuaded, why do you do the work?"

Maggie turned to look at Billy. "Because we love him, of course." She raised an eyebrow. "Don't we?"

Billy smiled. "It's a bit early for me to say that."

"Bollocks." It seemed like Maggie was about to rub away the surface of the cupboard as she resumed scrubbing. "You two are perfect together. I don't know about you, but I've never seen Daniel happier than when he's with you. And I've known him through several redundant relationships." She shook her head. "Leaving you for New York? He's a bloody fool."

***

On the night before the funeral, Daniel hired a small truck and filled it with tables and chairs borrowed from *Therapy on Stage*. He arrived late at Billy's house in Wood Green, and the two men carried the furniture through the house into the back garden. The TV weather forecaster said it would be hot and sunny, and Billy was relieved the guests would be able to spill out into the garden, to avoid a crush in the house. After they finished arranging the furniture in the garden, Daniel uncorked the bottle of wine he had brought with him, and filled two glasses.

"Here you are." He handed a glass to Billy. "Let's make a toast to your mother. I never got to meet her, but she sounded like a good person."

"She was." Billy took the glass from Daniel and looked up at the stars. "If Mum or I ever believed in such a thing, she'd be raising a bottle of Guinness in heaven right now."

"Who knows?" Daniel shrugged. "If she's drinking Guinness, at least she'll have a harp to keep her company."

Billy laughed. "She wouldn't know what to do with it if she has. Not musical, my mother." He turned to Daniel. "Sorry I had to drag you over here so late tonight. Were you working late?"

Daniel shook his head. "I went to see Anthony."

Billy looked up at the sky again. "No moon tonight," he said. "Much darker. Especially now they've turned the streetlamps off round here. It's all these council economies." He took a drink from his glass. "How is Anthony?"

Daniel shook his head. "The psychotic episodes have stopped. But the drugs aren't helping his mood swings. I think he's going to be in the hospital for a long time."

"How do you feel?"

"I don't." Daniel took a sip from his glass. "These last two visits have been...different. I sat with him for a long time this evening. And we didn't say a word. Eventually he got up and walked out."

"Will you go again?"

"I feel like I ought to. He's only got his sister to visit him otherwise. And she doesn't go that often. All the rest of his friends seem to have given up."

"Why do you think he's your responsibility?"

Daniel sighed. "Do you think I shouldn't?"

Billy set his glass down on the ground next to him. "That's up to you. What are you going to do when you go to New York? You won't be able to visit him then."

"I know." Daniel sat back in his chair and looked up at the sky. "I don't think I love him anymore. The person I loved is gone. I sort of feel sorry for him. Except he's so angry at me much of the time I even find it hard to feel that."

"You're not responsible for what Anthony did to himself." Billy reached for his glass. "People make their own choices in life. And sometimes that changes everything for everybody. At least Anthony's getting the right psychiatric help now. You can't do that for him. Stop beating yourself up."

Daniel looked at Billy. "You're not only talking about Anthony, are you?"

"What do you mean?"

"When you talk about people making their own choices and affecting everybody?"

Billy shook his head. "I didn't mean—" He smiled. "Oh really. It's not all about you, Daniel Richards. Do you really think I'm speaking in code about your decision to go to New York?"

"It sounded like you were."

"Well, I'm not." Billy reached for his glass and raised it to Daniel. "I told you before. I'm happy for you. But when I think about it, yes, your choice has affected everyone. Of course it has. It affects me, and Maggie, and all the children at *Therapy on Stage*." He took a drink. "And you won't be eating at Bento in Brewer any longer, so Akio will be upset."

Daniel laughed. "When you put it like that, I should turn down Max's offer immediately. It's not too late, you know."

"Well, don't," replied Billy. "Not for Akio. Not for Maggie. Not for me." Billy smiled. "And not for Anthony."

Daniel sighed. "I won't. I think I'm going to talk to Anthony's sister. I need to tell her I'm leaving London. Perhaps she can visit him more often. You're right. I can't carry on feeling responsible. I don't think I love him anymore. But I do feel compassion." He looked across to Billy. "I'm sorry. We should be talking about you, not me. Thanks for listening to me boring on. Are you okay?"

"Oh, sure." Billy shrugged. "I can't wait to get tomorrow over with."

Daniel put down his glass next to him. He stood and held out his hand to Billy. "Come here."

Billy took hold of Daniel's hand and also stood. Daniel pulled him closer and put his arm around Billy's waist. "No really," Daniel asked again. "Are you okay?"

It may have been the wine, or because he was tired, or simply the look in Daniel's eyes, but Billy felt enveloped by a sense of desperation and loneliness. His shoulders heaved, his chest tightened, and he gasped for air. Daniel pulled him close and wrapped his arms around him. Billy was powerless to control the wave of despair that engulfed him, and he clung to Daniel for support.

"Do you want me to stay tonight?"

Billy could not speak. His body shook, his legs felt like they would buckle beneath his weight, as he held on to Daniel even more tightly.

***

As forecast, the morning of the funeral dawned bright and sunny. Billy instructed that no one should wear black. It was the one specific demand his mother had made. He hoped everyone who attended would respect her wish. Billy wore an off-white linen suit with a pale blue T-shirt and deck shoes. He had worn it the day his mother was diagnosed, and she commented how sunny he looked, and how happy it made her feel.

Daniel stood beside him at the entrance to the crematorium. He wore his dark blue linen suit with a white T-shirt and tan loafers. Billy remembered it was the same outfit he had been wearing when they first met at the hospital.

Mrs Mahabir, the funeral director, walked across to them. She wore a bright orange and yellow dress, a white blouse with a wide, red ribbon tied around her waist. Her hair was wrapped in a large red and gold scarf.

"You look lovely," Billy said as they shook hands. "Thank you so much for dressing up brightly. My mother would have loved it."

"Of course," Mrs Mahabir replied. "This was my mother's dress. From Jamaica. I love wearing it, so it's no problem at all. Are you ready?"

Billy nodded. "As ready as I can be. I've not had much practise at funerals."

Mrs Mahabir smiled. "Practise is not what you want. Be spontaneous, and show your feelings. Forget about the British stiff upper lip."

Billy laughed. "I'm certain there won't be any of that."

"Oh my God." Daniel tugged on Billy's sleeve.

"What is it?" asked Billy. "I told you this is a non-religious ceremony, so there'll be no mention of—" He stopped as he saw who Daniel was pointing to.

Walking up the road together, leaning on each other slightly for support, were Chuck Stuart and Guy Frobisher.

Chapter 31

Over forty people came to the funeral, many more than Billy expected, and most of them also came back to the house afterwards. Even with the extra space in the garden, it was a tight squeeze. Fortunately the weather stayed warm and dry, and what could have been a sad occasion turned into a joyous celebration of his mother's life. Apart from her two sisters, the family was also represented by one of Billy's cousins called Patrick. Billy had only met him twice before, and had forgotten how witty and fun he was. They spent a long time talking and laughing together, and arranged to meet the following week while Patrick stayed over in London.

There were several people from his office, including his best friend Vikki. "Man Cock says she can't make it, but I'm to represent her here today," Vikki said as she rolled her eyes. "As if I'd do a fuckin' stupid thing like that."

Two nurses from the hospital came to the funeral and stayed on for the party. "Your mum was a shocker," one of them said conspiratorially. "A lovely lady, but a shocker." Billy never found out exactly what the nurse meant, because at that moment Chuck grabbed his arm.

"I need to speak to you, young man."

Billy turned and bent down to Chuck's wheelchair. "And I need to speak to you. Do you want me to push you into the front room? It's quieter in there."

"No need," Chuck said. He grasped the arms of his wheelchair and hoisted himself to his feet. "You can walk me there."

"You're making a miraculous recovery," Billy noted as Chuck held on to his arm. "Are the drugs that good?"

Chuck winked at him. "It's a combination of things. The main one bein' a bit of a confession. Back when I was lookin' for a place in London, it was suddenly real important if I wasn't mobile."

Billy was shocked. "You mean you lied at your physical assessment for sheltered housing?"

"Not exactly lied." Chuck staggered slightly as they walked through the house to the front room. "My legs are gettin' worse, for sure. But it was kinda helpful to maybe exaggerate the condition when I moved to London and needed somewhere to stay in a hurry."

Billy shook his head. "What am I going to do with you? Now you've told me that, I really ought to report it to my boss."

Chuck stopped. He leaned against the wall of the hall corridor, closed his eyes, and breathed heavily. "But you won't." Chuck re-opened his eyes. "An' I know you won't for two reasons. One, you're a nice guy, and you don't do shitty things like that." Chuck held up his hand as Billy opened his mouth to protest. "And two, I'm movin' out, so someone more deservin' can have that dump of a place."

Chuck let go of Billy's arm and navigated himself carefully through the open door of the front room. He shuffled across to a high-backed wing armchair, and sat down heavily. Billy followed and perched on the arm of the chair.

"You're going back to Grantchester, aren't you?"

Chuck nodded.

"What happened?"

There was a pause while Chuck caught his breath. "Although it pains me to say it, and I know this'll sound mighty strange comin' from me, I owe you an apology, young man."

Billy laughed. "It's good to hear, but yes, it must be a first from you."

Chuck narrowed his eyes at Billy. "Don't make it any easier for me, will you?" He leaned back in the armchair. "After you left, that day your mom died, I did a lot of thinking. You were right. I'd been a bit hasty with Guy. That's not to say I wasn't angry with him letting that goddam sister of his back into the house. 'Cause I was. Still am in some ways. She's a first-class bitch, you know? But Guy's spent his life tryin' to do the right thing by people. That's what he does. He's a good man. A straightforward man. That darn sister took advantage of him, makin' him feel guilty about family. Blood bein' thicker than water an' all that crap."

Billy smiled. "You've got more in common with Maggie than you might think. She was saying the same thing the other day."

Chuck nodded. "Smart lady, that Maggie. I've got a lotta time for her. Anyway. I calls Guy, an' he says he'll come down to London. But before he comes, he makes me promise not to shout, or get angry, or he'll go straight back home."

"Wow," Billy said. "Was that difficult?"

"You know what?" Chuck asked. "By the time he arrived, I was so pleased to see him, there was no way I wanted to scare him off." He closed his eyes. "Ever again."

Billy laid his hand on Chuck's arm. "I'm so glad," he said. "What about Guy's sister? How will you manage with her there?"

Chuck smiled and closed his eyes. "Oh, that's all taken care of."

***

Daniel was talking to Maggie when he felt a hand rest on his shoulder.

"Have you got a minute?"

He moved aside to see Guy smiling back at him. "I need to talk to you about a few things."

"Of course." Daniel turned back to Maggie. She shrugged her shoulders.

"Don't worry about me, love. I've got a ton of glasses to deal with in the kitchen." She held up her hands and stroked the backs of them despairingly. "Devastated. These were never cut out for washing up. I will simply have to wear silk gloves. Permanently."

Daniel kissed her on the cheek. "Pink rubber gloves are under the sink, my angel. Far more fetching."

She fluttered her eyelashes at him. "You kinky boy, Daniel Richards." She looked at Guy. "I'd watch him if I were you, my dear. You don't know where he's been." She turned and walked back into the house.

Guy laughed. "Is she a friend of Billy's? She's been nonstop with the food and drink this afternoon."

"No," Daniel answered. "Well, yes. I suppose she is now. She's a friend of mine. I've known her for years. And she's got to know Billy since we started seeing each other."

"You two make a wonderful couple," Guy said. "How many years have you been together?"

Daniel laughed. "It's only a few months. Why? Do we seem like an old married couple?" He saw Guy's expression change, and realized too late it was the wrong thing to say. "I'm sorry," Daniel said. "I didn't mean there was anything wrong—"

Guy smiled and shook his head. "Don't worry. I think I know what you meant. You seem so suited. And so happy."

"What about you and Chuck?" Daniel hoped to deflect the conversation away from him and Billy. "Are you back together?"

"He's still living in that awful flat in London." Guy shook his head. "But not for much longer. He's coming back to Grantchester. I don't know what Billy said to him, but he's a changed man. I've got a lot to thank you two for."

Daniel waved his hand dismissively. "No, really. We did nothing. It was down to you two in the end. Did Chuck change his mind about your sister?"

"No," Guy said. "I did. After seventy-six years, I finally stood up to her. Not much of a hero, am I?" He smiled at Daniel. "She doesn't approve, you see. Of us. She thinks I'm the way I am because Father died when I was young. So I didn't have a 'proper male role model,' as she so quaintly puts it. And she thinks Mother indulged me, which is probably true. But that didn't make me—" He paused. "—gay? A much nicer word than homosexual, don't you think? Of course, I've been called far worse by Elspeth over the years."

"Is she moving out?"

Guy shook his head. "Not exactly. It's going to cost me most of my savings. But I'm having the end wing of the house adapted for her. It will be a self-contained flat, with access to the garden. I'm renting a cottage for her in the village while the building work goes on, so that Guy can move back in." He sighed. "I tell you, it's costing me a fortune."

"But it's worth it, isn't it?"

Guy nodded. "Oh yes. Every penny."

"Hey, Daniel. I want a word with you."

They looked back to the house. Chuck was holding on to the doorframe, waving his arm in their direction. Billy stood behind him. Daniel noticed the resigned expression of surrender Billy reserved for Chuck's outbursts had returned.

Chuck stepped into the garden. Billy attempted to help as Chuck headed towards them at a rapid shuffle. Daniel walked forward and met him halfway.

What's the matter?" Daniel asked.

"Billy tells me you're being a darn fool."

"I didn't say that," Billy protested. He turned to Daniel and shook his head.

Chuck jabbed his finger in Daniel's chest. "He says you're jettin' off to New York, an' leavin' him behind, just when you two are settlin' down. Guy an' me were kinda hopin' we'd be goin' to our first gay wedding."

Guy shook his head. "He's exaggerating again." He turned back to Daniel. "Are you going to New York?"

"Yes, he is," Billy answered before Daniel could reply. "It's a great opportunity. Creative director of a start-up doing the same music therapy work he does in London."

"That does sound interesting," Guy said. "How long is it for?"

"The funding is for three years," Daniel replied.

Chuck jabbed his finger at Daniel again. "An' you're leavin' Billy behind. Jus' after his mom's died an' everythin'."

"I'm perfectly capable of looking after myself," Billy protested. Daniel thought he was either angry or embarrassed. Maybe a bit of both.

"Chuck," Guy interjected. "I think it's best you don't say any more. It's between these two to sort out. We mustn't interfere."

"I don't see why not," replied Chuck. "They poked their noses into our business quickly enough." He slipped his arm around Guy's waist. "And I'm darn glad they did. Sometimes you need someone to show you jus' how big a fool you are."

***

The last of the guests had gone. Only Maggie remained, collecting up the few remaining sandwiches and sausage rolls and packing them into a large plastic container she found in the kitchen. "That will do for my lunch tomorrow," she said to Daniel, who was drying up crockery. She looked out the window. "Leave those. Go and sit with Billy outside. I'll come out in a minute."

Billy was thumbing through a photo album he had found earlier. Daniel sat on the chair next to him and looked over his shoulder.

"You were stunning in those early headshots," Daniel said, pointing to a black-and-white photograph.

"Were?" asked Billy. He flicked over the page. "I see what you mean. I'm an ancient wreck now."

"I didn't mean that." Daniel leaned forward and kissed him on the cheek. "You know you still turn heads. You turned mine."

"Oh yes." Billy laughed. "I crashed into you and nearly sent you flying that day in the hospital."

"And who's to say I didn't sidestep into your path so that we might meet?" Daniel asked. "I saw you the moment you came flying through the doors. I like a man who's in a hurry. He's usually exciting."

"Are you saying it wasn't an accident when I bumped into you?" Billy stared at him. "That you actually deliberately got in my way?"

Daniel tilted his head and pursed his lips. "That would be telling. But I think you know now. All I can say is, since the offer of work in New York, I can't stop thinking I'm going to miss you like hell."

"And I'm going to miss you too." Billy leaned forward and kissed Daniel on the lips.

"Stop it, you two. You'll have that woman next door complaining." Maggie stepped into the garden. She carried three full glasses in her hand. "Last of the prosecco. I saved this bottle from the marauding hoards." She handed a glass each to Billy and Daniel, and held hers out towards them. "Cheers, my dears. I have to say, that was the nicest funeral I've ever been to."

"Thank you," Billy said. "Cheers. I can't thank you enough for what you've done today. You've been amazing. Come and sit down."

"For five minutes," she said, and sat in the chair opposite them. "I must go after that." She took a drink from her glass. "I've been thinking."

"Oh dear." Daniel looked at Billy. "This spells trouble."

"You shut up and listen." Maggie leaned back in her chair and took a deep breath. "I've been thinking about this house. You can't live here on your own. Now you'll both probably think I'm sticking my oar in here. But it strikes me I've got nothing to lose. Why don't you move into Daniel's place and rent this one out? I'm sure the rent would more than cover the mortgage here."

"That's a great idea," Daniel said. "And when I go to New York, it would be so much better if you stayed at mine." He kissed Billy again. "I don't want to stop seeing you because of this contract. We can video call every day, and you can come and visit me in New York. And I'll be back from time to time. When I can get away."

"I've not finished," said Maggie. "While you're at it, why don't you quit that job of yours you hate so much, and have another go at acting?"

Billy looked first at Maggie, and then at Daniel. "Did you put her up to this?"

Daniel held up his hands in surrender. "I never said a word." He looked down at the headshots of Billy in the album on his lap. "But I think she's right. You know I do."

"Thanks, Maggie." Billy set his glass down on the ground next to him. "But I've got other plans."

"You can't carry on in that job," Maggie protested. "I spoke to your friend Vikki from work this afternoon. Your boss sounds a positively frightful woman."

Billy shook his head. "No, I don't mean about work. I've already decided I'm not staying there."

"Have you?" Daniel sounded shocked. "You didn't say anything."

"Taking these past few weeks off from work was the best thing I've done in a long time," Billy said. "I'm going back next Monday to resign. I've got nothing to lose now. With Mum gone, I can be irresponsible again."

Daniel laughed. "Irresponsible? Is that what you call following your dream? I call it living."

Billy smiled. "You're right. That's what I'm going to do. Follow my dream." He turned to Maggie. "I'm not going to rent out the house, because I'm going to sell it. To my cousin Patrick."

"Was he the cute-looking guy you spent so much time with this afternoon?" Daniel asked.

"That's right. Only I'm afraid you're not his type. He's recently married, and his wife's got a job in London. They were going to move over here from Ireland and rent. But I pointed out how much rents are in London these days. It's cheaper overall if they buy a place. And if they buy from me directly, they won't have to pay any fees."

Daniel kissed him on the cheek again. "That's great. So you can stay in my place while I'm away."

Billy shook his head. "Once I've sorted everything out, I want to travel. Maybe I will go back to acting. Maybe I'll do something else. I've not decided yet. I've got the freedom now to think about it. So I'm going to make good use of it."

"Oh." Daniel looked disappointed. "That's a great idea. Where are you planning to go on your travels?"

Billy smiled. "I thought I'd start with New York," he replied. "I've only been there twice, but I really liked the place. And I'd like to spend some time in the city, getting to know it. Maybe a year or two, but I need to find somewhere to stay."

Daniel laughed. "Oh, don't worry about that. I know this really cute music director who'd love to have you."

ABOUT THE AUTHOR

David C Dawson writes contemporary novels featuring gay men in love. He's an award winning author, journalist, and documentary filmmaker. His debut novel won the Bronze for Best Mystery and Suspense in the FAPA awards. He has written three other novels since.

David lives in London with his boyfriend and two cats. In his spare time, he tours Europe and sings with the London Gay Men's Chorus.

CONNECT WITH DAVID:
website: davidcdawson.co.uk
blog: blog.davidcdawson.co.uk
instagram: instagram.com/davidcdawsonwriter
facebook: facebook.com/david.c.dawson.5
twitter: twitter.com/david_c_dawson
linkedin: linkedin.com/in/DavidCDawson
pinterest: pinterest.co.uk/mrdcdawson/heroes-in-love-influences

www.BOROUGHSPUBLISHINGGROUP.com

If you enjoyed this book, please write a review. Our authors appreciate the feedback, and it helps future readers find books they love. We welcome your comments and invite you to send them to info@boroughspublishinggroup.com. Follow us on Facebook, Twitter and Instagram, and be sure to sign up for our newsletter for surprises and new releases from your favorite authors.

Are you an aspiring writer? Check out www.boroughspublishinggroup.com/submit and see if we can help you make your dreams come true.

Printed in Great Britain
by Amazon

36492152R00128